THE RELUCTANT ASSASSIN

A Selection of Recent Titles by Fiona Buckley.

The Ursula Blanchard Mysteries

THE ROBSART MYSTERY
THE DOUBLET AFFAIR
QUEEN'S RANSOM
TO RUIN A QUEEN
QUEEN OF AMBITION
A PAWN FOR THE QUEEN
THE FUGITIVE QUEEN
THE SIREN QUEEN
QUEEN WITHOUT A CROWN *
QUEEN'S BOUNTY *
A RESCUE FOR A QUEEN *
A TRAITOR'S TEARS *
A PERILOUS ALLIANCE *
THE HERETIC'S CREED *
A DEADLY BETROTHAL *
THE RELUCTANT ASSASSIN *

* *available from Severn House*

THE RELUCTANT ASSASSIN

An Ursula Blanchard Mystery

Fiona Buckley

CRÈME de la CRIME

This first world edition published 2018
in Great Britain and the USA by
Crème de la Crime, an imprint of
SEVERN HOUSE PUBLISHERS LTD of
Eardley House, 4 Uxbridge Street, London W8 7SY
Trade paperback edition first published
in Great Britain and the USA 2018 by
SEVERN HOUSE PUBLISHERS LTD

British Library Cataloguing in Publication Data
A CIP catalogue record for this title is available from the British Library.

ISBN-13: 978-1-78029-103-1 (cased)
ISBN-13: 978-1-78029-585-5 (trade paper)
ISBN-13: 978-1-78010-953-4 (e-book)

All Severn House titles are printed on acid-free paper.

Severn House Publishers support the Forest Stewardship Council™ [FSC™],
the leading international forest certification organisation.
All our titles that are printed on FSC certified paper carry the FSC logo.

Typeset by Palimpsest Book Production Ltd.,
Falkirk, Stirlingshire, Scotland.
Printed and bound in Great Britain by
TJ International, Padstow, Cornwall.

ONE

Outlook Grey

'**N**o, Master Woodley, no, please . . . for pity's sake, this is a public anteroom in Richmond Palace, there are people passing us every moment, and *smiling* at your antics . . . yes, I did say *antics*. I implore you . . .'

'Dear Mistress Stannard, I am not making improper advances! I am most honourably offering you my hand and heart and my wedding ring. I would be a good husband, I promise. I am less wealthy than you but I am no beggar. My elder brother will inherit my father's drapery business and my father's modest estate, but Father decreed that the two farms that my dear mother brought with her into the marriage should come to me. I am healthy and capable; respectably employed as an assistant secretary in the household of Sir George Talbot, Earl of Shrewsbury. I can help you. You have two big houses, a stud of trotting horses to look after, and a young son to rear. It's heavy burden for a lone widow . . .'

'And it amounts to a very nice marriage portion,' I said, resorting to sarcasm. He had accosted me in a long gallery. Along one side, it had deep bays, almost amounting to small rooms, with windows overlooking the gardens, and window seats. Master Woodley had pulled me into one of these bays and in trying to retreat from his octopus-like embrace I had backed into a window seat, which had an edge that was now grinding unpleasantly into my spine.

'Listen,' I said, turning my head so that he couldn't kiss me. 'In this world marriage for the sake of wealth and good connections is commonplace, and believe me, it's no easy thing to be a well-off widow! One is regarded as a catch, which is all right for people who want to be caught, but I do not!'

'Dear Mistress Stannard, has no one ever told you that

you are beautiful? You are even young enough to have more children!'

'In this year of Our Lord 1581, I will turn forty-seven years old, and any good looks I may still possess are likely soon to fade. So will my ability to have any more children and I don't want any more anyway. I have a small son and a married daughter and that's enough. But you're right, of course, about my material advantages! Yes, I do have two good houses with land attached, and a lucrative stud of trotters. In addition, though not in wedlock, I am a half-sister to Queen Elizabeth. But there is one thing I am not, and that is prey.'

'Pray? What has prayer to do with it? I don't understand.'

No, of course he didn't. He really did see himself as an ardent lover. He couldn't conceive of himself as a pack of hounds on the trail of a tired and exasperated quarry.

'I don't mean praying to God. I mean prey in the sense of something hunted, chased, to be captured,' I said. 'And I am *not* that – though I often find it difficult to make anyone believe it. You are not the only suitor I have refused. Over the Christmas lately passed, two Surrey gentlemen honoured me with offers of marriage. They were both well-off widowers, both with much to offer, neither exactly unattractive, but I did not want them and was glad to get away to Richmond Palace. Only,' I said bitterly, 'to find myself pursued again, by you!'

'Mistress Stannard . . . Ursula darling . . .'

'I am not your darling and please don't call me Ursula. I don't wish to be rude but almost since the day I came to do my regular attendance on the queen, you have dogged my steps. It must stop! *You* must stop!'

'Am I repulsive to you?'

'You're not repulsive at all, of course not.' He was actually quite a handsome fellow, about my own age, with a head of thick red-brown hair, and bright blue eyes in a shapely face. I still didn't want him. 'It isn't that,' I said. 'It is simply that I don't wish to remarry. I have already had three husbands!'

'But I *don't* wish to marry you for material gain,' said Woodley pleadingly. 'Why won't you understand? I have fallen in love with you.'

'I said, I have had three husbands. I know all about love and its complications. I have had enough of it. I . . .'

'Madam,' said the welcome voice of my excellent manservant, Roger Brockley. 'Is this man annoying you?'

'*Brockley!*' I said thankfully. But no lady should be too insulting towards a gentleman who has offered her marriage, whether she wants him or not. 'Master Woodley has been proposing to me. But . . . well, I was just explaining that a new marriage was not among my plans for the future.'

'A proposal shouldn't be too forceful,' said Brockley, eyeing Master Woodley in no very friendly fashion. He added smoothly: 'I was looking for you, madam. The queen desires your presence.'

Woodley had stepped back. I eased myself away from the window seat. 'It seems that I must let you go, dear Mistress Stannard,' Woodley said reluctantly. 'But I shall not give up hope.'

'I wish you would!' I said, and lost no time in hurrying away with Brockley.

I had been glad to escape from my suitors in Surrey in order to make my regular obligatory visit to my royal half-sister. But because of Woodley, I wasn't enjoying myself as much as I had hoped, which was a pity for I really had looked forward to it. Richmond Palace was so beautiful.

Richmond in fact was one of Queen Elizabeth's favourite residences. She had once said to me that she called it her Faery Palace. Admittedly, on that day in mid-March, it wasn't looking its best, for its slender towers were lost in low, misty cloud and the air was so still that its musical wind chimes were silent. The Thames too was flowing past in silence, its surface leaden. No birds sang and the air was cold.

For this reason, when I rose that morning, I had asked my maid, Fran Dale, to fetch out a mustard-coloured gown, with a fashionable open ruff, edged in gold silk. 'It's a cheerful colour,' I said. 'And it isn't a cheerful day.'

'The style suits you, ma'am, and it shows off your topaz pendant very well. You'll brighten the day in that dress!' Dale looked at me with understanding. 'You are wearied, ma'am. I know the signs.'

'I'm wearied,' I said, 'because even in middle age I can't get free of nuisances wanting to relieve me of my widowed state. Two unwanted proposals over Christmas, and when I get here, instead of a respite, I find myself faced with Master Woodley. He keeps on turning up. I find him beside me when I go to watch a game of bowls, when I am out hawking, any chance he can find! I am very tired of him indeed!'

All the same, I hadn't expected him to corner me in such a blatant fashion, and babble proposals in public. That was going too far! Perhaps, I thought glumly, my attempt to brighten the world with mustard-coloured silk and a fashionable ruff had been a mistake. It had done nothing but draw Woodley's undesirable attention.

'What does the queen want, Brockley?' I asked him as we hastened through the palace. 'Is it dancing practice? I was caught by Master Woodley as soon as I had breakfasted.'

'No, I think her majesty simply wishes to speak with you.'

'You came to my rescue at just the right moment.'

'Fran followed you from the dining hall and saw what was happening. She wanted to intervene but didn't know how, so she made haste to find me – and learned that I was already seeking you. She told me where you were.'

'Dear Dale,' I said.

I called Dale by her maiden name out of habit but she was in fact married to Roger Brockley. Roger was middle-aged, a calm man with steady blue-grey eyes, and a high forehead with a scattering of pale gold freckles on it. He had been my trusted companion, my most valuable aide, through many troubled times. Dale, poor soul, was devoted but sometimes gave the impression that I was wilfully dragging her through hedge and ditch. Dale had slightly protuberant blue eyes and a few pockmarks, left from a childhood attack of smallpox. When she was upset, they became more noticeable. I sometimes felt contrite, thinking of all the times when I had brought them into prominence.

I was one of Elizabeth's ladies, but not all the time. During the last few years, she and I had agreed that I should attend court twice a year, for a month or six weeks at a time. I had other commitments, after all. Woodley had been right about that. My principal house, Hawkswood, was in Surrey, but in Sussex I had a second home, Withysham. It was also true that I had a stud to watch over and a son to rear.

Elizabeth knew all that but she liked me to be near her sometimes, partly because we were sisters, but also because I was at times one of her secret agents, often entrusted with tasks concerning the safety of the state. These assignments had frequently endangered my own safety (not to mention Dale's and Brockley's) and now that I was well into my forties, I had asked not to be given any more. For nearly two years, I had been free of them. The last one had involved an alarming number of deaths. I had felt, then, as though death were dogging my footsteps, and with all my heart, I now wished to remain at home, in peace, and leave the safety of the realm and its painful demands, to others.

All the same, notwithstanding the promises that had been made to me, I was never sure that I wouldn't be called back to duty. There was a ruthlessness in Elizabeth, and an answering ruthlessness in her main counsellors, her Treasurer, Lord Burghley, Sir William Cecil, and her Secretary of State, Sir Francis Walsingham. If people were useful to any of them, then used they would be. And if I were summoned again, I knew I wouldn't refuse. How could I? Elizabeth was at once my sister and my queen. Her royal father, King Henry the Eighth, had not been faithful to his unhappy wife Anne Boleyn. My relationship to the queen was not widely known, but nor was it exactly a secret. Walsingham and Cecil knew very well that between Elizabeth and me there was a bond of blood and understanding. When asked, I served her as best I might.

I was wondering now if, once more, I was to be called into service.

Elizabeth's private rooms were a series. They opened from an anteroom where people wishing to see or speak to her could gather, and send in their names by way of an attendant. Thereafter, beyond the big double doors guarded by armed gentlemen pensioners in red tunics, there was a small private audience chamber, and then a room which could also be used for audiences, but had in addition a spinet and a well-swept floor; this was where dancing practices were usually held.

At this point, we found a page hovering and Brockley handed me over to him. He took me through two private rooms, with no door between them but only a wide archway. These were her parlour and her bedchamber. There was another spinet in the parlour section; Elizabeth played very well but did so only when alone or with a few chosen ladies.

Beyond these again was the little room she called her study, where her collection of books was kept, and where she pursued such interests as reading in Latin and Greek and other, more modern tongues, and sometimes amused herself by doing a little translation. It was to this room that the page led me. He withdrew, closing the door behind him, and as I moved forward I saw that Elizabeth was not alone. Two of her ladies were in attendance and standing by the window was a still-faced man in a well-tailored but quiet suit of dark blue, with a modest ruff. Elizabeth nodded to the ladies, who at once followed the page out of the room.

'Good morning, Ursula,' Elizabeth said as I sank into my curtsey. 'Here is Jean de Simier. You have met before, of course.'

Yes, we had. Some time before, there had been diplomatic moves to arrange a marriage between Elizabeth and a French prince, Francis, Duke of Alençon and Anjou. Jean de Simier, the duke's servant and closest friend, had visited England to prepare the way for a visit from his master. He had been a messenger between the duke and Elizabeth ever since. Elizabeth had been at once nervous of marriage (for which she had good reasons) and attracted by the duke. She usually called him Alençon, having got into the habit when the marriage negotiations were first suggested, before he acquired the title of Anjou.

He had made a short visit to England so that he and Elizabeth could meet, but then he had gone home again and after that, the negotiations had faltered. But Elizabeth often declared that she missed him and longed for his return. So, here was his emissary once more. Bringing news of him, presumably. I waited to hear what it was.

I rose from my curtsey. 'You asked to see me, majesty?' Elizabeth indicated that we should all be seated. There was a couch in the study, and two damask-covered chairs. De Simier and I took the chairs. Elizabeth stayed where she was, on the ornately carved oak chair that went with her desk. She was informally clad, in a loose peach-coloured gown with no farthingale, though she was wearing a ruff, open at the throat like my own. She turned the seat round so that she could face us.

'Next month,' she said to me, 'I expect a formal embassy from France to discuss, once more, the possibility that I might marry Duke Francis of Alençon and Anjou. Jean de Simier, however, is here in advance of the embassy and privately, on behalf of his master. Duke Francis, my dear Alençon as I like to call him, it seems has certain doubts. Well, I have people in my pay whose business it is to report on events and currents of feeling out in the world, but I have a particular trust in you. You are very much in touch with what goes on in my realm, among the folk who till the fields and drink in the alehouses and buy and sell and keep shops. Jean de Simier and I would like to ask your opinion on something. If you will be kind enough to give it.'

'Of course,' I said. 'If I can.'

Elizabeth looked at de Simier. He said: 'Mistress Stannard, if my master, Duke Francis, were to come to England and marry the queen, would he be in danger? Even in France, we are aware that it is being said that many of the English don't like the idea of a Catholic marriage for their sovereign. Also, there is Mary Stuart, the dispossessed Queen of Scotland, who suffers from the delusion that the throne is rightly hers. Mary would certainly not welcome the kind of treaty which marriage with my master would bring. It is an alliance that would make it much harder for her to bring supporters from, say, Spain, to install her on the throne. Is she likely to be a threat? What is your opinion?'

Mary Stuart. Formerly Queen of Scotland. A Catholic who did not believe that Elizabeth was legitimate and as Elizabeth's cousin claimed that she had a better right to the throne of England. She had haunted the queen for close on twenty years, in fact ever since she had been cast out by the Scots after her first husband, Lord Darnley, had been murdered and she had unwisely married the chief suspect.

She had been accused of being a party to the murder and had never cleared herself.

So she had fled for her life, taken refuge in England and here she still was, half a guest and half a prisoner, in Elizabeth's hands. She had sought Elizabeth's protection but had never ceased to maintain that she should be Queen of England instead. Plots had gathered round her. She was willing to reward anyone, any foreign prince, who would either restore her to the Scottish throne or oust Elizabeth in her favour.

I could well understand Alençon's doubts. Elizabeth herself was nervous of Mary and had good cause. But as for the feeling in the countryside . . .

Both questions were difficult. I said: 'I can't read Mary's mind. To that question, I just don't know the answer, though I know she is closely guarded and watched, so that even if she has evil intentions, she would find them hard to carry out. As to the feeling in the countryside, well, I have very rarely heard anyone mention the matter. Mostly, people just don't. They have their own lives to live.'

'Yes. That is what all reports say,' Elizabeth said snappishly. 'But they must still be thinking. I want to know *what* they are thinking.'

I tried to marshal my thoughts. 'Majesty, to you, affairs of state are normal, everyday life. But to the people of the fields and shops, the fields and shops and household affairs *are* everyday life. They think about ploughing and sowing and harvesting; they think about buying provisions, and getting the pony shod and finding someone to repair the thatch . . . things like that. They only talk about state affairs when such matters are thrust under their noses; when something dramatic happens and there are proclamations and so on . . .'

My voice trailed away and they looked at me curiously.

De Simier said: 'Please tell us what you know, Mistress Stannard,' and Elizabeth said: 'You do know something. I can see it.'

Yes, of course she could. She knew me so well. But I could see an assignment coming up and heartily wished myself elsewhere.

'If you do,' de Simier said, 'it is your duty to explain.'

'I recall that there were one or two occasions,' I said, 'when the duke visited England – but that's nearly two years ago . . .'

'Get on with it!' Elizabeth barked. '*What* do you recall?'

'I was travelling. I and my servants were in a crowded inn and we heard some talk, some adverse comments about the French marriage.'

'How adverse?' asked de Simier.

'Quite . . . Quite angry,' I admitted. 'Resentful.'

'Threatening?' Elizabeth asked. 'Because he is Catholic?'

'Yes – both of those. From a few people.'

'He is no fanatic,' said de Simier. 'He is sympathetic towards the French Protestants.'

'I know, but most people don't fully realize these things,' I said.

This was awkward. What did Elizabeth want me to say? Did she want me to discourage the marriage or to reassure her? Or did she just want facts?

I thought about the facts, which were complicated. I knew them only because I had so often been involved in affairs of state, and also because for many years I had had my wise third husband, Hugh, to talk to.

From one point of view, there was quite a lot to be said for the marriage with Alençon. It would bring into being a most valuable treaty with France. France and England would swear to stand shoulder to shoulder if necessary to keep Spain at bay.

Which just might be necessary, though one hoped not.

Probably the reason why none of the numerous plots round Mary had ever come to anything was because her support in England was so limited, even among English Catholics. They were, after all, English as well as Catholic. They had learned that life under Elizabeth was on the whole quiet and fairly safe. Even if they did secretly yearn to put Mary on the throne instead because she would restore what they called the true faith – and in spite of a shocking Papal decree that they were not obliged to obey Elizabeth's laws and might even incur damnation if they did – a good proportion of them also realized that Mary would never succeed in ousting Elizabeth without help from abroad, which would almost certainly mean Spain.

And they *were* English. Few of even the most ardent English Catholics really wanted a foreign army trampling about on England's soil. They also knew that a Spanish victory would bring the Inquisition into England and some of them had sense enough to recoil from that. The majority of the English population were Protestant and there were still plenty who remembered the heresy hunts of Elizabeth's predecessor, the Catholic Mary Tudor. In their eyes, Mary Tudor had been bad enough; the arrival in England of the Inquisition would be unthinkable. Resistance to it would be savage.

Confronted by the prospect of the Inquisition, the larger part of the population would consider all Catholics to be deadly enemies and might well take to massacring them. The marriage with the duke could keep England safe from Mary of Scotland's ambitions, and the English Catholics safe from their fellow countrymen. But Mary did of course have supporters who didn't realize any of this. Weirdly, Mary's supporters would dislike the French marriage because they would see it as a barrier to the re-introduction of their faith, while a great many Protestants would see it as a back door by which the Catholic faith might be let in!

I tried, with difficulty, to explain some of this.

'Thank you, Ursula,' said the queen.

De Simier was dismissed. But Elizabeth, with a gesture of her slender white hand, bade me stay where I was and as soon as we were alone, said: 'I believe that of late, you too have been obliged to consider the business of marriage. Remarriage, in your case.'

I sighed. 'That is so, majesty. I don't want to marry again, but I have pursuers. I feel like a hunted deer sometimes.'

'Tell me about your pursuers.'

'I have had two approaches from Surrey gentlemen,' I said. 'Both pleasant fellows. But I have refused them. I have also had an approach from a man in the household of Sir George Talbot – the Earl of Shrewsbury, who is here at court. The man is one of his secretariat, Russell Woodley. Not as well off as my Surrey gentlemen but not a fortune-hunter either, I think. He seems to be really – well . . .'

'In love with you?'

'Apparently. He offered me heart and hand, and support and comfort. I don't dislike him. But I still don't want him. I *don't* want to marry again.'

'The choice is yours,' said Elizabeth. 'You at least are not fretted by the thought that your marriage may be necessary for the safety of the realm and that your feelings don't matter. They do. It is mine that do not. The Duke of Alençon may fear danger in our marriage. I fear marriage itself, as you well know. I like his company,' said Elizabeth. 'I long to see him again, to dance with him and talk with him. But friendship is one thing and marriage another. I think of what marriage means, and that is when I fret.'

She looked up at the study window. Beyond the diamond-shaped leaded panes, at the heavy sky. 'The embassy from Paris is definitely coming. Matters are now serious. I need to be able to speak to them truthfully of the situation here – and I want the truth to be that Alençon would be safe to proceed with the marriage. Yet, I also find the prospect of marriage and what it entails a very grey outlook. It puts an edge on my temper and my tongue, and I find it hard to sleep at night.'

TWO

Applications by a Tutor and a Groom

H ome! I had indeed looked forward to my stay at Richmond but when it ended, just ten days later, I was thankful. I had spent those days doing my best to avoid Russell Woodley and wishing that Sir George Talbot would go home and take his entourage with him. Sir George was in fact due to leave for his home in Sheffield just a few days after my own departure. Why, I asked uncooperative providence, couldn't he have gone home sooner, so that I really could enjoy Richmond, at least for a little while.

Mercifully, I had *not* been called upon to undertake any alarming assignments, and Elizabeth had not – as I had feared – asked me to stay as her moral support during the official embassy from France.

When she bade goodbye to me, she said: 'In the past, when there have been discussions about this marriage with Alençon, I have often asked you to support and advise me. But things now are so far advanced that I feel . . . I feel that the final decision must be made between the duke and myself. If you should hear of any rumour that bears upon his safety if he marries me, then you must inform me. But this is not an assignment, Ursula. Just a request to be told of anything relevant that comes your way. I thank you for all the help you have given me in the past.'

So, here I was, my disappointing visit at an end, going home with a free mind, and there ahead of me were the chimneys of Hawkswood, showing above the woods through which the approach road led. They were handsome chimneys, tall and ornamental, for I had lately had the brickwork altered. It was now patterned, very like the brickwork of the chimneys at Hampton Court.

The late March weather was still grey and cold and I was

pleased to see smoke rising from several of those chimney pots. I had sent word ahead to let my people know when I would arrive, and they had made ready for me. The hall fire had been lit and it was clear that the kitchens were busy. I hoped there would also be a fire in my favourite parlour.

Jewel, my black mare, had also realized that we were near home and no doubt had thoughts of her warm stall and a feed of bran mash. She tried to break into a trot. I checked her, because beside me Brockley was coping with the leading rein of our pack pony, and also being careful of Dale, on the pillion of his dark chestnut, Firefly. Dale had never been much of a rider. It had been a slow, prolonged journey from Richmond.

We were seen before we reached the gatehouse, and my gentlewoman companion, Sybil Jester, who had been left in charge while I was away, was out in the courtyard to meet me, a shawl thrown round her shoulders for warmth. Sybil had an unusual face, for its features looked as though they had been slightly compressed between chin and hairline, so that she had a long mouth, and long eyebrows and slightly widened nostrils. The effect was not extreme; in fact, it had an attractiveness of its own, enhanced by the fact that those same features were mobile and very expressive. Her smile of welcome was wide and beautiful. Beside her was my tall, grey-haired steward, Adam Wilder, and at the kitchen door stood the big, broad figure of John Hawthorn, my chief cook, holding up a wooden spoon in salute.

And there, running eagerly from the door that led to the great hall, was my son Harry. I was down from my saddle before anyone had time to offer me a hand, but because Harry was now nine years old and beginning to be conscious of his male dignity, I didn't rush to embrace him but let him come to me and make me a formal bow. After which he came into my arms anyway.

He was becoming handsome, I thought. He had surely grown even during the six weeks of my absence, and now it was not only his dark hair and eyes that reminded me of his father; his features too were settling into remembered shapes. Matthew had had the same bony, very slightly asymmetrical face.

Joseph Henty and Arthur Watts, two of my grooms, came hurrying to take the horses. Brockley was down and steadying Dale to her feet. 'How has everything been?' I asked, putting Harry back from me and aiming the question at all of them at once.

Sybil's smile became broader than ever. 'There have been applicants for both of the positions you wanted filled, Mistress Stannard. I had them cried in Guildford and Woking and there are three applications for the position of Harry's tutor.'

Mr Hewitt, who had held that post for nearly two years, had caught a winter chill and died, quite suddenly, just before I left for the court. I had left Sybil to assemble a list of possible replacements. 'I'll see them as soon as I can,' I said. Harry made a face and I playfully pulled his hair. 'You have to have a tutor and well you know it. Sybil, what about the stud groom's position?'

I had for some years been building up my stud of trotting horses and had had an excellent chief groom to help me. But he had also met with disaster, just a month before I went away. He had had a bad fall when training a young team to work as a four-in-hand and they had got out of control and overturned the training cart, throwing him out headfirst. He recovered but he was not young and once he was well, had announced that he wished to retire, and did so, without delay.

'We have found someone, madam,' said Arthur, who was the senior groom for the horses used by the household. 'A man called Laurence Miller. He applied, Joseph and I showed him round the stud, and he impressed us. So we gave him a trial and subject to your approval when you meet him, we feel that he will do. He has a reference from the Earl of Leicester, no less.'

'He was working for Robert of Leicester and he's left? Why?' I enquired.

'His mother was lately widowed, it seems,' said Sybil. 'She lives in Woking and he wanted to be near her if he could. He has to earn a living, which for a stud groom would mean living with his work, so he can't just move in with her. He isn't married himself.'

'If all goes well, she can come to him and share the head groom's cottage, if they want that,' I said. I turned to Joseph and Arthur. 'You say he impresses you?'

'He's got a way with horses.' Joseph was a taciturn young man but when he did speak, it was usually much to the point. 'That stallion that you bought just afore you went off to Richmond; he's a fine beast but he's temperamental.'

'He's scared of thunder,' Arthur said. 'There was a storm a week after you left, madam, and he panicked; broke out of his stall and right out of the stable, ran properly amok he did until we could catch him and get him calm. Luckily the storm were past by then.'

'Well, well,' I said. 'Let's get ourselves inside and I'll decide who I'm going to interview and when. Tell me, Sybil . . .'

As usual, there was plenty of household news to absorb. I listened to Sybil while I washed and changed out of the old riding dress that I used for journeys, and then I went to take a late dinner, not in the big hall which was such a feature of Hawkswood, but in my preferred parlour, which was the smaller of the two at Hawkswood, and very warm and comfortable.

One member of what I privately called my inner circle had not come out to greet me in the chilly courtyard, but came to the parlour before supper was served, to bring me some mulled wine. Gladys Morgan was a lame and aged Welshwoman who had long ago attached herself to me after Brockley and I had rescued her from a charge of witchcraft. Gladys was not a particularly charming person. She had dreadful teeth, like brown fangs, and a shocking habit of cursing people who annoyed her, but I had affection for her and I knew that she had affection for me. I was as pleased to see Gladys as I was to see any of my household, and the warmed wine was a pleasure. I was tired.

The meal was good. My chief cook John Hawthorn and his first assistant, Ben Flood, were clearly eager to welcome me home. Once I was comfortably full of good fresh bread and half a roasted chicken and a pie filled with preserved plums and had drunk a considerable amount of the mulled wine, I was overcome with sleepiness and went to have a rest until suppertime.

Yes, I decided as I settled down, I was pleased to be home. I didn't like the renewed talk of the queen's marriage. It had hung in the air like the mist that shrouded Richmond's pinnacles. It was putting the queen out of temper before any of the French embassy had set foot on English shores. Even if Talbot had gone back to Sheffield sooner and taken Woodley with him, with the French embassy looming like a tidal wave or a thunderstorm, the atmosphere at Richmond would still have been uncomfortable. Here at home, I could be at ease.

There are people who seem able to sense the future, but I am not one of them. I had not the least idea that my sense of ease and peacefulness was pure illusion.

In the morning, I summoned Brockley and Arthur Watts, and asked them to accompany me to the stud. To accommodate it, I had leased a couple of fields from a neighbouring farmer who was getting old and was very happy to make money out of his two most outlying fields without having to work them. I had had stabling built, with accommodation overhead for the grooms, and also a coach-house and tack-room, and a small cottage for the head groom. I wanted to take a look both at the horses and Laurence Miller.

I had several mares in foal, three generations of youngsters, the eldest ones now being broken in and prepared for sale, and the stallion, Bay Hawkswood. This was the first time the stud had had its own stallion, but I had had the idea in mind from the start and had built enough stabling to provide for visiting mares. It was expensive and I had had to fell a good deal of timber in the Hawkswood woodland in order to pay for it. Some I had sold, some was retained as building material for the stables. But I felt it was a worthwhile investment. Bay Hawkswood was a splendid animal, rich red bay in colour, with black points, a high-stepper with an arrogant head-carriage. He would command good stud fees.

'I'm proud to have such a one to care for,' said my prospective new head groom.

I considered him thoughtfully. He was a tall, lean, laconic man, and within five minutes I had realized that by nature he was as taciturn as Joseph. His long face had a dour expression; I didn't think he was much given to smiling. But he had a pleasant voice, with deep undertones, and the horses responded to it; I could see that. I asked him to harness up a couple of the better-trained youngsters and watched how he handled them, and how confidingly they nuzzled him as he adjusted their bridles and checked their hooves. I observed that they were glossy with grooming and good feeding.

'I am pleased with what I see,' I told him. 'I suggest a three-month trial. If I am satisfied, you will be welcome. You have a reference from the Earl of Leicester, I understand?'

We went to the cottage, where he had taken up residence, and the reference was produced. It spoke highly of him. It looked as though one of the two positions I wanted to fill now had a likely occupant. Next, I must see to the matter of Harry's new tutor.

Sybil provided me with the list and I examined the applicants carefully, sitting once more in my comfortable small parlour. She and Dale sat with me, so that I could talk things over with them. I was particular about the kind of man I wanted as Harry's teacher, but also aware that I shouldn't delay over the decision, because the lad couldn't be left to run wild for very long. At the moment, he was probably with Brockley, who gave him regular instruction in horsemanship and often entertained him by telling him stories of his army days. Well, all that was satisfactory, but not on its own. Habits of regular study needed to be instilled. I hoped that the three letters now before me would contain promising information.

One was from a resident of Woking, an ordained man, who apparently preferred teaching to preaching. He said he had had experience but the details he gave showed that he had been teaching younger children than Harry. I read the letter to Dale and Sybil, who both agreed with that conclusion and shook their heads at it.

'He might find Harry a handful,' Dale said candidly.

The other two letters were from Guildford. One said that his erstwhile pupil had now been sent away to school, leaving him without a post; the other said that his current post was not to his liking, but didn't say why, though he offered notable credentials, concerning a knowledge of languages, history and modern science.

'I had better see those two,' I said finally. 'I would especially like to meet the Guildford man whose latest pupil has gone away to school. That's a nice, straightforward reason for seeking a new post, and it doesn't sound as though he was teaching an infant. I think . . .'

The door of the parlour opened and Brockley stood on the threshold. I stared at him in amazement, for never in all the long years of our acquaintance had I seen Roger Brockley look like that. His expression was that of a man who had been struck on the head and left dazed. His eyes seemed glazed and he was opening and shutting his mouth as though he wished to speak but couldn't.

'Brockley?' I said.

Adam Wilder appeared behind him. 'Madam, a new applicant for the post of tutor to Master Harry has presented himself. I asked him to wait in the great hall. He . . .'

Adam himself seemed lost for words at this point. He moved alongside Brockley and glanced at him, and Brockley took a deep breath and attempted to speak. All that came out, however, was an extraordinary sound which I can best render as *Glug!*

I stood up, scattering the three application letters, which had been on my lap. 'What is this? Brockley, what on earth is the matter with you? Adam, just who or what have you told to wait in the great hall? A monster? An archangel with wings? A demon with horns and a forked tail? A unicorn with human speech and a testimonial as a skilled tutor? Will one of you please explain?'

'Brockley really should be the one to tell you, madam.'

'Brockley?'

'*Glug!*'

'*Brockley!*'

Brockley took another deep breath and this time managed it. 'The applicant isn't a monster, madam. He says . . . well, he looks like . . . he says he's my son.'

THREE
Out of Nowhere

I took control of the situation and marched us all, Sybil and Dale included, to the great hall, where we found the new arrival standing beside the central table and looking nervous. Brockley and Wilder stopped just inside the door to stare at him and their expressions really would have done justice to a two-headed unicorn, but the stranger was in fact a perfectly ordinary man, somewhere in his mid-thirties, clean-shaven, with neat, short hair and decently dressed in a brown doublet and breeches suitable for riding. A stout cloak and a black hat had been put down on the table.

Though there was one striking thing about the stranger. Except for being considerably younger, he was the living image of Brockley.

I found that I too was staring at him. There was my dear Roger Brockley, miraculously shorn of something like a quarter of a century. The light brown hair was the same, except that there was no grey in it, and there were Brockley's high, gold-freckled forehead and calm, blue-grey gaze. He smiled, a little shyly, at my amazed face and said: 'You are Mistress Stannard? I am sorry that I seem to have startled everyone. It isn't so strange, surely, that a son should . . .'

'I didn't know I *had* a son!' Brockley had now recovered his powers of speech. 'I don't understand this. This man has come out of nowhere. Who are you, sir? When were you born? What is your name?'

'I think,' said the newcomer, 'that one thing I am, sir, is your mirror image! I can see it in your face, that you have realized that. My name is Philip. I'm known as Philip Sandley but . . .'

'*Known* as Philip Sandley? That isn't your real name?'

'My real name is Philip Brockley. I am the lawful son, sir, of Roger Brockley and his wife Joan.'

'My first wife!' said Brockley.

'You remarried? Is my mother dead, then?' Philip Sandley – or Brockley – seemed disconcerted. 'I suppose I might have expected that. I was born in February 1545. I believe, sir, that when King Henry invaded France in June 1544, you were in his army. You left England before you knew that I was coming into existence.'

'Yes. I had to go. I was working as a groom for a lord who chose some of his able-bodied male employees to go with him when he joined the king's army and I was one of the ones he picked. I didn't return for over a year,' said Brockley. 'The war ended the following June. I came home in July. My wife had left me. I didn't find her for nearly two years and when I did, yes, she was dying. She didn't recognize me and certainly never said she had a child. She died . . .' an old pain coloured his voice '. . . because she had – got rid of one.'

'I see. I know that she had a husband – my father – called Roger Brockley and that she ran away with some travelling actors,' Philip said. 'Well, with one of them in particular . . .'

'Her lover,' said Brockley bitterly. I saw Dale flinch, and also saw him reach out to her and briefly grasp her hand. Without words, he was saying: *You are my wife now, my dear and faithful and honest wife. Don't mind my memories.* I saw her look at him gratefully.

'I know that much,' Philip said. His voice, too, was like Brockley's. 'The people who brought me up were a family called Sandley. They didn't hide my origins from me. I was born in February, as I said. The troupe my mother was with had been working during the winter months in the Sandley household. The master of the house was Thomas Sandley, a well-off London merchant. Travelling players always try to find somewhere to stay put during the cold weather. They offer regular entertainment for the dark evenings and for Christmas, and so on, in return for shelter until the spring returns. My mother gave birth to me there and she told the family her story. Master Sandley and his wife had no children and they were willing to adopt me. My mother thought it best, they told me. Life on the road can be hard, for a tiny child, or *with* one. She left me with them.'

'You don't remember her?' Brockley said.

'No. She left with the troupe when I was but a few weeks old. I know nothing of what happened to her after that. I stayed with the Sandleys. They were good to me. I took their name. They educated me. Master Sandley had shares in a ship that brought in spices and silks, and when I grew up, I helped him in his warehouse and his counting house.'

'But you didn't stay there?' Brockley said.

'Master Sandley died when I was twenty-three and his wife went to live with her sister somewhere. He left me a little money, which helped while I set about looking for work as a clerk. But in one house where I applied, although I didn't get the clerk's post, I was offered the chance to be a tutor to the young children of the family. So I took to tutoring and liked it. I like children. My first family outgrew me, and that's when I took the post I have just left. That was with a family called Dawes – Master Dawes is a small landowner. I was teaching twins, a brother and sister, but they are sixteen now. The boy has become his father's assistant, and the girl is to be married. I have testimonials, from Master Dawes and from the people I worked for before him.'

'Yes, we'll want to see those,' I said. I glanced at Brockley. I was beginning to take to this young man but if he was truly Brockley's son – and I couldn't suppose that he wasn't, not with those looks – then Brockley would have a say in the matter.

'Master Dawes doesn't have anything to do with court affairs,' said Philip. 'But he has a cousin who is sometimes at court. The cousin visits him now and then. I used to dine with the Dawes family, and one day, when the cousin was there, the talk turned to court affairs and I heard of Mistress Stannard, who lives not so very far from Guildford, and of Roger Brockley who is her manservant. I thought then – could that be my father? I thought of approaching you, but then I decided not to; I had my life and you have yours and I realized that you probably had no idea that I existed. But when I heard the vacancy here for a tutor being cried in the streets of Guildford . . . I hesitated at first but I do need a new post, so . . . here I am,' said Philip.

I said: 'What subjects can you teach? My son Harry Stannard

is nine years old and already has a grounding in Latin and Greek. I have also seen to it that he has begun to study arithmetic and history.'

'I can teach all those,' said Philip with assurance. 'And I have taught all ages. My first pupils were six and seven when I began to tutor them, and I stayed with them as they grew up. The Dawes children were already growing up when I took them on. I would be happy to take a pupil aged nine.'

I looked at my steward. 'Wilder, please arrange a bedchamber for Master Sandley. We had better call him that. It will be confusing to have two Brockleys in the house. See that he is looked after until his room is ready and then show him to it. Go with Wilder, Master Sandley. Brockley, Dale, I want to talk to you in the parlour.'

'Here are the testimonials,' Philip said, turning to his discarded cloak and hat, and searching an inner pocket of the cloak. He produced two small parchment scrolls and held them out. I took them with a nod.

In the parlour, I sat down to read them while the Brockleys stood by, silent and waiting. Then I looked up. 'These are good. It sounds as though he is a competent tutor and he seems to have had a good many years of experience. But the circumstances being what they are . . . Brockley, do you want your son here? And Dale, will you be happy about that?'

'I will be happy with whatever Roger decides,' said Dale loyally. 'It has to be for him to say.'

'I would like to get to know him,' Brockley said slowly. 'This has come as a shock – dear heaven, yes, a shock and no mistake. But it is a pleasant shock, though I feel I need to get used to it! As long as he really does prove to be a good tutor, I would like him to be here. On approval, perhaps, as you have done with Laurence Miller, madam.'

'Very well,' I said.

The next few weeks were most pleasant. I did not know that this was the time of stillness that so often precedes a storm.

At the end of three weeks, in the middle of April, a party of strolling players presented themselves. There were seven of them, six men and a young woman. They arrived on foot, trundling a big, heavy handcart piled with hampers and boxes and bundles containing their belongings and their props. It needed three or four of them at a time, to push and pull it along. I looked at them with interest, wondering if they had any connection with the players who had led Joan Brockley astray, but this was obviously not the case, for they were all too young.

They were striking to look at, the men in tunics patterned with big, vividly coloured squares, the woman in a bright turquoise gown sewn with glittering crystal beads and all probably related to each other, since every one of them had slightly swarthy, gipsy-like complexions and thick, dark, shoulder-length hair, except for the young woman, whose hair was red.

They all spoke with the same accent too, which sounded as though they came from somewhere north of London. The woman didn't take part in the short play that they performed for us, but she had a lute and sang songs for us, and one of the players, the one who seemed to be their leader, did card tricks. He was a tall, lanky man with very long fingers which flickered among the cards, apparently reading them by feel.

They arrived at dusk, nicely in time to ask for their pay in terms of supper and beds for the night, and we obliged. The evening turned into a jolly party. The players left the next day and our usual, orderly life resumed. We were all very happy. For nearly a fortnight, we continued to be happy, until . . .

FOUR
Into the Void

Apinl was passing and the weather had improved, becoming if anything unusually warm for the time of year. I was reading in the small parlour one afternoon without the need of a fire when Dale appeared in the doorway, to announce, in a primly disapproving voice, that Philip Sandley wished to see me, concerning future plans for Harry's education.

'I met him at the top of the stairs, ma'am, just coming out of the schoolroom. He asked where you were and I said I would ask if you were able to see him.'

'I'll be very happy to talk to him,' I said. 'It's time we consulted together. He has had some weeks now to work with Harry and find out how far his studies have already taken him, and I want to know how my son is progressing.' I looked at her unsmiling face. 'What is it, Dale? What's wrong with Master Sandley?'

'I can't like him, ma'am.'

'Why ever not? Well, I realize that he came as a shock to you, being Roger's son, but you said you were happy to have him here if Brockley wanted it. Has he upset you in some way? Surely he hasn't been rude to you. He seems such a well-spoken young man.'

Dale sighed but I looked at her and she gave in. 'No, ma'am. It's not that. It's just something about *him*. I can't explain.'

'Is it because he's part of Brockley's past and probably reminds Brockley of . . . well, things that happened then? Of his first wife? Joan?'

Dale's eyes dropped and she fiddled with her girdle. I said: 'Joan has been dead for years and years and Philip never knew her. She parted with him when he was a baby. Oh, Dale! You can't be jealous of a woman dead so long! I expect Brockley

is happy to find that he has a son. I haven't discussed the
matter with him, of course, but he looks cheerful. You surely
don't want to spoil it for him.'

'No. But I wish we . . .'

'I know.' I did know. When they were first married, there
was a possibility of having children, but it hadn't happened
and now it couldn't happen. 'Please, Dale,' I said beseechingly.
'Don't hate Philip for what he can't help. You need not have
much to do with him, anyway. He's Harry's tutor and his work
doesn't overlap with yours. Harry seems to like him. Now,
will you send him to me?'

'Very well, ma'am.'

Dale disappeared and I sat where I was, shaking my head
and thinking that keeping all the currents of a big house smooth
was sometimes a superhuman task.

Philip's arrival stopped me from brooding. He came into
the room smiling, and had evidently noticed nothing wrong
with the way Dale had treated him. His mind was entirely on
Harry. He sat down at my request, and began on a report.

'I am pleased to say that he's ahead of his age as far as
Latin and Greek are concerned, Mistress Stannard. I understand
that you started him on them quite early, before he ever had
a tutor?'

'Yes, I did. I enjoy them myself,' I said, 'and I hoped he
would take to them, which I think he has.'

'You were well taught as a child, I take it?'

'Yes.'

When my mother was sent home from court, where she had
been one of Queen Anne Boleyn's ladies, because she was
with child by a man she would not name, she sought shelter
with her brother, my Uncle Herbert, and his wife, Aunt Tabitha.
They were never very kind to her or to me when I came into
the world, but they did give us a home, and I was allowed to
share my cousins' very good tutor. I explained some of this.
I had never been secretive about it and no doubt Brockley had
told his son a certain amount.

Philip listened, and nodded. 'There's nothing like starting
young. I find him a willing pupil, in fact, intelligent for his
age. I took care to choose Latin and Greek texts that were

likely to appeal to him, and I think that's working well. For instance, he has become very interested in the Roman historian Livy's account of how Hannibal crossed the Alps with his elephants. He keeps wanting to know what will happen next. Which means applying himself to Livy's Latin! He also seems to be well taught in religious matters, not that I would presume to instruct him in those. I have heard Dr Joynings, your vicar at St Mary's in Hawkswood, preach and thought him a very sound man. He is new, I understand.'

'Yes. His predecessor, Dr Fletcher, has retired. He was a sound man, too,' I said. But I smiled, because although I had liked Dr Fletcher well enough, I also knew that he had orders from Sir William Cecil to keep an eye on me, since, as the queen's sister and occasional secret agent, I might sometimes be in danger. I knew the surveillance was for my own good but I still didn't like it. I hoped that Fletcher's replacement, Dr Sebastian Joynings, had no such brief. He was a jolly, rubicund little man and certainly an excellent preacher. Everyone had taken to him.

'There is some Catholic influence in the house, though,' Philip was saying. 'One of the maids was telling me that Ben Flood, who works in your kitchen, is Catholic and even attends Masses somewhere.'

'He does, but I don't interfere. He is a good servant to me. I can trust him. He doesn't try to convert anyone – certainly not Harry.'

'That's good. I did wonder. I am really very pleased with Harry, except for one thing. He is not well advanced in arithmetic. That's what I most want to discuss with you.'

'I taught him his figures,' I said. 'But I didn't go further than that.'

'Mr Hewitt obviously tried,' Philip said, 'but Harry clearly doesn't like the subject and has little talent for it. All the same, there are things he really must learn. I want, with your agreement, to give extra time to figurework. In particular, I would like to concentrate on aspects of arithmetic that will be of practical use in adult life. Double-entry book-keeping is something anyone should understand who is one day going to manage an estate and a stud farm. Keeping track of the accounts will be essential. But though double-entry really isn't a difficult concept to grasp, he hasn't managed it so far. Do you agree?'

'Yes, I do,' I said. 'Entirely. Please make what arrangements seem best to you. What about history?'

'History? In that, he is already quite well read. I am happy about his progress there. Is he back yet, by the way? Since I wanted to report to you this morning, I gave him some time off and told him that he could go out for a ride. I know he must learn to be proficient and self-reliant in the saddle so I gave him permission to go alone.' He smiled. 'I suggested that he should take a route that would give him a good chance of seeing some deer. Where the path towards the house called White Towers is crossed by another, if you take the right-hand track, it leads to a part of the woodland where deer often wander. You know the track I mean, I dare say. But I told him to be back in time for an arithmetic lesson before dinner.'

I nodded. The route he had described led through thick woods where there was plenty of cover for deer, both red and roe, and then continued out of the woodland to farmed country and fields whose owners, every time the corn was ripening, furiously complained of depredations. The red stags, who like Roman nobles, liked to eat lying down, were particularly exasperating, since they squashed as much as they ate. But they were beautiful animals and Harry always enjoyed catching a glimpse of them.

'Well, he must certainly have time for riding,' I said. 'That's part of a gentleman's education and he must also learn such manly arts as swordplay and archery. We mustn't forget that.' I smiled too. 'He is growing fast and your father and I have just promoted him from his little pony to a full-size horse – the one that your father himself rode before I bought Firefly for him. The brown cob with the pale nose, Mealy. He's somewhat broad in the back but Harry's legs are getting long already. His father was a tall man. And it's a good use for Mealy. We tried to train him to harness,' I said ruefully, 'but it wasn't a success.'

It had been a disaster. Nothing, it seemed, would reconcile Mealy to the idea of being fastened to a cart that followed him, rattling, wherever he went. He was a good-tempered animal as a rule but when he bit Brockley, who had stepped up to him with an armful of harness, we decided to give up.

Harry's need of a bigger mount, however, provided a use for Mealy. They were already making friends.

'I expect he'll be back very soon,' I said. 'He's usually quite obedient. I'm sure he'll be here in time for some further forays into double-entry book-keeping.'

We both laughed, and Philip's laugh was so reminiscent of his father that it jerked oddly at my viscera.

There had been a time, years ago now, when Roger Brockley and I had come near to becoming lovers. It hadn't happened, but a bond had been formed, nevertheless, of heart and mind. Sometimes there was a union of our minds so complete that we could read each other's thoughts. We were careful, because Dale was aware of the link and had at one time seriously resented it. She knew now that she had nothing to fear, but she could still be hurt and we knew it.

I rose and went to the window. The small parlour was next to the great hall and both looked out on to the courtyard, with a glimpse of the gatehouse to the right. 'Though there's no sign of him yet,' I said, turning away. 'Perhaps he went further than he intended.'

'Well, I'll leave you, if I may, Mistress Stannard. I'll go to the schoolroom and prepare for the lesson. Perhaps you would send Harry to me when he comes back?'

'Yes, certainly. Straight away. Ah!' Out in the courtyard, hooves were clattering. 'That is probably him now.' I stepped back to the window. 'He may not like arithmetic lessons very much but he's usually very good about being in the schoolroom on time . . . Oh!'

'What is it? Mistress Stannard?'

Philip had moved to stand beside me and we stared in alarm at the scene in the courtyard. Mealy was there, certainly, but his saddle was empty, the stirrups were loose and flapping, the reins were lying slackly on his neck. Brockley was at Mealy's head and our youngest groom, Eddie, was there too, stroking the cob's neck and looking distressed.

There was no sign whatever of Harry. I abandoned the window, and ran, with Philip hard behind me.

'Master Harry must have been thrown,' Brockley said as we came rushing into the courtyard. 'Though how it could have happened . . . he rides well and Mealy is quiet enough under saddle, and not given to shying. We'll have to search. Did Master Harry say which direction he meant to take?'

'You suggested a route to him,' I said to Philip. 'Do you think he took it?'

'Very likely. He really does like to catch sight of deer,' Philip said. His face was full of anxiety.

Arthur and Joseph had now appeared from the tack-room, and had joined us, also looking concerned. Brockley was paying close attention to Mealy. 'There's something wrong here, madam. This horse came in at a gallop. Look how his sides are heaving. He's sweating and he's trembling. He's been upset, frightened, perhaps.'

I was trembling too, but trying to be practical. 'We must search. We must find Harry at once. Make haste! Get the horses saddled! Everyone must come who can. Where's Simon?'

Simon was my fourth groom, a very competent young man. 'Out exercising Rusty,' Arthur said.

'All right, we'll manage without him. But everyone else! Now, quickly, everyone!'

They were quick. There was a flurry of saddling up, and in minutes, I was up on Jewel and Philip was mounting his own flea-bitten grey mare.

There were six of us: Philip, myself, Brockley, Arthur, Joseph and Eddie. We took the westward track, as Eddie said he had seen Harry set off in that direction. It led through the woods and came after a few miles to White Towers, the house that Philip had mentioned. I had friends there. If Harry had been thrown when he was close to White Towers, but had not been much hurt, he might have gone there for help. I could only hope so. They would have looked after him and perhaps lent him something to ride home on. We might meet him coming towards us on one of their horses. We might . . . We reached the place where the track was crossed with another, leading north and south. This was the place where Philip had recommended Harry to turn right. Still, we couldn't be sure that Harry had followed his advice, so I sent Eddie and Joseph off on the left-hand branch, just in case, and told Arthur and Philip to go on to White Towers. Brockley and I went to the right.

None of us found anything. The right-hand path led us northwards under a canopy of branches, now coming into leaf. It wound a good deal and round every corner I hoped to meet Harry making for home on foot, but there was no sign of him. The path was hard-packed, and would not have taken Mealy's hoofprints very well, but all the same, I kept thinking that there ought to have been something, if Harry had passed this way. There were a few damp patches that might have taken hoofprints, and had not.

In the end, we turned back and made for White Towers, hurrying hopefully towards its white stone walls and ornamental turrets, only to find Philip and Arthur in anxious conference with my old friend Christina Ferris and her husband Thomas.

Harry had not been there.

Thomas Ferris called four of his men and all five saddled up, to quarter the woods more thoroughly, without sticking to the tracks. We met Eddie and Joseph returning from a fruitless search to the south and added them to our party. Thomas organized us into groups, each covering a different part of the woods, and a fresh hunt began. We searched and searched, calling Harry's name, peering among the tree trunks for any trace – broken twigs, a piece of torn cloth, signs of trampling. All in vain.

'If only Mealy could talk!' Brockley said, gnawing his lip in frustration.

At last, we parted from Thomas and his men and turned despairingly for home. We were bewildered.

'There's a limit to how far Harry could have gone,' said Philip. 'He only left just over an hour before I came to talk with you, Mistress Stannard. We've surely covered all the ground he might have reached, even if he set off at full gallop and why ever should he?'

'He wouldn't,' said Brockley. 'He doesn't ride wildly. He

considers his horse; I've taught him about that. Besides, Mealy couldn't keep up a full gallop for all that long. He's no racehorse.'

'He'd been galloping when he came back here,' I said.

'Yes, and he was out of breath, and sweating. Something *must* have scared him. I don't understand this.' Brockley shook a puzzled head.

The afternoon was almost spent by the time we reached the house. We hadn't dined, so we were all hungry and the warm day had turned humid.

'There's a storm coming,' Brockley said glumly. I shuddered, thinking of Harry, wondering if by some awful mischance we had missed him, and he was lying unconscious somewhere among the trees. I didn't want to stop searching but I knew that we must eat and rest the horses. We could resume the hunt later.

When we rode in, most of the servants came out to meet us, along with Sybil, Dale and Gladys. Their faces were full of questions and hope, which vanished when they saw our grim expressions. I slid exhaustedly to the ground and Sybil, wordlessly, put an arm round me.

Dale glared at Philip and said: 'You were supposed to look after him!'

'Now, Fran,' said Brockley. 'The boy has to have some liberty. He has to develop independence and no one would expect him to come to harm, riding a reliable horse close to home. It isn't Philip's fault.'

'I feel as though it is,' said Philip contritely.

I had an unreasonable urge to agree with Dale. I wanted to blame someone, to shout and scream accusations. I choked the impulse down and turned instead to John Hawthorn, who was there with all the rest. 'We need food,' I said.

Hawthorn had been prepared for that. He produced stew and bread and plum tart and small ale and most of the search party, grooms included, ate together in the hall, including Simon, who had returned while we were out. Over the meal, we tried to think of further plans. Brockley, like a terrier with a bone, was still puzzling over the state in which Mealy had come home.

'He must have been frightened, if he threw his rider. He wouldn't do that, normally. I should know! But what frightened him? Did any of you see anything, anything at all that might have upset a horse?'

No one had. We planned a new strategy, involving search parties who would go all the way round the Hawkswood property, and also search within it, in case Harry hadn't ridden through the woods at all but had for some reason changed his mind and ridden round or through it instead. When we had eaten, I had Jewel saddled again and I rode to the stud premises, to ask if anyone there had seen Harry. Perhaps he had taken a fancy to look at the trotters. The three under-grooms hadn't seen him. Laurence Miller wasn't there. He had gone to Guildford, apparently, to place an order for some new harness. He hadn't returned. No one knew for sure where he was now.

I came home disappointed. But it was still light and there was time to renew our hunt. This time, we took the dogs with us. I kept two half-mastiffs, Remus and Goldie, both quite young and both intelligent. Their keen noses might find traces that we could not. We gave them some of Harry's clothes to smell and set out in hope, putting our new plan into effect by riding about the Hawkswood grounds and land, and then circling the property outside.

We found nothing and neither did the dogs.

In the evening, we all gathered again in the hall. Dusk was falling and the air was now very heavy. The storm that Brockley had prophesied was surely on its way.

Harry would be out in it. Somewhere.

Or would he? It was Brockley who said: 'There is one thing we haven't considered but it's been getting bigger and bigger in my mind.'

'What's that?' I asked.

'We've found no trace. If he had been thrown, we would have found him; we must have done. He can't have been swallowed up by the air. People just don't vanish into the void. Suppose he's been kidnapped?'

FIVE

The Stallion in the Parlour

I was exhausted and bewildered. I kept expecting Harry to appear, just to walk into the house. It was impossible to believe that he simply wasn't there, that I had no idea at all where he was. I stared at Brockley and said, 'But that's absurd. Who would want to kidnap him? Why? What for?'

'Ransom?' suggested Philip. 'If it's that, then they'll get in touch with us. At least, then we'll know what's happened.'

'Why *Harry*?' I said wildly. 'I'm not that wealthy. There are so many people who are richer than I am.'

'You . . . forgive me . . . you are a widow, Mistress Stannard. You have no husband and Harry has no father.' Philip spoke with embarrassment. 'Perhaps . . . someone thought you were vulnerable?'

'If I get my hands on them,' I said viciously, 'they will find out how vulnerable I am!'

Sybil, gently, said: 'Dear Ursula. We can do no more tonight, least of all with a storm coming.' We had had to light the candles early because of the darkening sky. 'I think Gladys should make you a potion to help you sleep. In the morning, we can search again. After all, we don't *know* that Harry has been kidnapped. But we can do no more tonight.'

She was right, of course. I was not the only one reeling from sheer weariness and we could not search in the dark, let alone in a storm. The horses had had more than enough, as well. To call off the hunt was unbearable, but we had to do it. 'We begin again tomorrow,' I said.

But as yet, no one wanted to go to bed. Feeling the need for companionship, the Brockleys and Philip and most of my grooms, along with Sybil and Gladys, sat on in the hall, except for the groom Joseph Henty. He and his wife Tessie, who had once been Harry's nursemaid, had moved into the cottage that had originally been occupied by Joseph's parents. They had died, not very long ago, within a year of each other, Joseph's father of heart disease and his mother, I think, of sheer sorrow. Since Harry had by then outgrown Tessie, who was in any case expecting a child of her own, I had offered the couple the cottage. Their small daughter was ten months old now. Joseph usually went home for his supper and Tessie would be worrying. He must get back to her, Joseph said.

I sent him off, not without an unjust and sickening surge of envy. Tessie might have been worrying but her missing love was about to return home. Mine was not.

Joseph hurried away, hoping to race the storm, which had not yet arrived though thunder was now rumbling in the distance. He had some way to go, since the cottage was beyond the formal gardens, out on the edge of the fields I had leased for the stud. He sometimes lent a hand at the stud with foaling mares. His quiet nature seemed to be helpful to them.

Gladys brought me a potion but I refused it, badly though I needed rest. I kept thinking of Harry, frightened and alone, perhaps among strangers to whom he was nothing but a means of making money. Perhaps they would ill-treat him. Oh, Harry, my Harry . . .

I had loved his father very much though I was never very happy with Matthew de la Roche. That sounds like a contradiction, but it was the truth. Our link was passionate but he was a supporter of Mary Stuart and an enemy to Elizabeth. I had lived with him for a while in France, but circumstances had caused me to visit England without him and while I was there, the queen and William Cecil had put their heads together.

I had been told that Matthew had died. So I stayed in England and married Hugh, my dear Hugh. I didn't learn until long after that I had been deceived, that Matthew still lived. He had been informed that *I* was dead. I chose to stay with Hugh, and never regretted that choice. But after Hugh had also died, and I had occasion to go back to France, Matthew and I briefly came together again. I would not stay with him; our loyalties were too divergent. But from that short reunion, Harry was born.

Matthew really was dead now. But something of him lived

on in Harry, and something of that old passion lived on in me. It always would. And to be deprived not only of my son but also of this last link with Harry's father . . .

Harry was my son and that alone would have been enough to make me desperate now. But that second dimension heightened it. I would not and could not sleep. Not yet, anyway. So I sat on in the hall, trying to be calm and not succeeding.

A fierce flash of lightning made us all jump. It was followed almost instantly by a mighty roar of thunder and then the rain came, swishing out of the sky in a deluge. The storm had broken with a vengeance.

'That's not going to do the young crops any good,' Brockley said prosaically. 'Rain's fine, but this sort of thing can flatten them.'

'They usually recover. Nature goes in for surviving,' Philip remarked, and young Eddie nodded earnestly and said: 'That's true.'

I knew they were talking in this commonplace way because they were trying to ease the tension in the room, and I longed to scream at them to stop babbling about rain and crops and *do something about Harry*. I held my tongue because I knew I was not thinking sensibly. No one could possibly do anything in such conditions. I cleared my throat and said something trite and silly about the Hawkswood lake, which had been low. It would be full enough after this.

Adam Wilder came in to ask if we wanted anything further to eat or drink. I requested a round of ale and he went away to fetch it. He looked glad of something to do.

Phoebe, my senior maid, came in next, to say that it was growing chilly now that the rain had come; should she light the fire? I said yes. She called another maid, Margery, and they went to the fuel basket that stood by the hearth and started to lay a fire with bits of wood and pieces of dried moss and tiny twigs. They were on their knees, coaxing the moss and twigs to catch light from candles, when the pounding started at the door to the courtyard and we heard Tessie's voice crying to be let in.

Sybil reached the door first and Tessie almost fell into the hall. She was holding her daughter in her arms and had flung a cloak over her head, which she had pulled round little Liz to protect her from the wet, but Tessie's skirt and shoes were drenched. 'Mistress Stannard! Mr Watts! Oh, I'm sorry, bursting in like this but we need help at the stud. It's awful!'

'What's awful? Tell us quickly!' I said. We were all on our feet, alarmed, wondering what on earth was happening now.

'It's that horrible stallion!' Tessie was in tears. 'It's frightened of thunder and it broke out of its stable. Again! It must have broken its tethering rope; I saw the frayed end. It was outside, charging about and whinnying and then it crashed right inside our cottage! The wind blew the door open! It's there inside, rearing and snorting and lashing out. Joseph tried to calm it but it knocked him down . . . no, he wasn't hurt but he's taken refuge upstairs; it's too much for him on his own . . .'

'Where are the other grooms?' demanded Brockley. He had already in a muttered aside sent Philip for boots and cloaks. 'Where's Miller? He should be able to cope if anyone can! Isn't he back from Guildford?'

'The under-grooms are frightened to go near and no, Laurence Miller hasn't come back!'

'You need not go, ma'am,' said Dale reassuringly. 'Leave this to the men.'

'It's my stud and my stallion,' I said. 'And my missing groom! Oh, dear God. Must everything happen at once? First Harry, now this! Cloak, Dale! And my boots. Someone fetch me a hat. I'm going. Brockley, Philip, Arthur, Simon, Eddie, you all come with me. Thick cloaks, all of you. Someone bring some lanterns. We'd best go on foot. The horses are tired and I wouldn't want to have them out in this anyhow. Tessie, stay here with Liz. Sybil, Dale, look after them. Get them dry; make hot possets for them.'

Out in the storm, it was frightening. The rain pounded down on us and the zigzags of lightning, striking earthwards from the sky, were like lances aimed at us by angry gods. On foot it seemed to take for ever to get to Tessie's cottage and we were all thankful for our heavy cloaks. In fact, by the time we got there, out of breath because we had hurried so, the worst was over. The rain had settled to a more ordinary downpour and the thunder and lightning were fading away towards the east. The cottage seemed to loom up suddenly, a blacker hulk against the stormy sky. Full darkness had fallen.

'What were the grooms about, letting it happen?' I panted. 'That animal needs a chain in weather like this, not a rope.'

We were almost at the door. The cottage was a simple place, with a front door opening straight into its main room, its parlour, from which a staircase led upstairs, where there were three small adjoining bedchambers. Downstairs, there was a kitchen and storeroom at the back and that was all. The parlour was well furnished, though. Its floor was deep in fresh rushes, and there was a sturdy table with benches on either side, a wooden settle and a brick hearth. It was a place where Joseph's mother, and now Tessie, could welcome women friends for a glass of ale and a gossip. It was a home for a family.

It was not, however, the right place for a horse. But the front door stood open and there inside, wildly out of place, was Bay Hawkswood. In the light of Brockley's lantern, we could see that he was terrified. His coat was soaked in sweat and his eyes were white-ringed, their pupils glinting red in the lantern light. His ears were flattened back. At the sight of us he half-reared, pawing the air with his angry hooves. He knocked his head on the ceiling and snorted with rage, presenting us with a view of flared, red-lined nostrils.

We could see that he wore a headcollar, and that from it dangled a short length of frayed rope. He had been strong enough to break it when the thunder sent him wild. He had kicked one of the benches across the room, and shoved the table aside. He looked demonic.

Two of the under-grooms were hovering at hand and came towards us.

'We're sorry . . .'

'We fetched him in when the weather turned bad, and hitched him up in a stall; fresh hay, fresh straw, water bucket, he should have been all right but the thunder started and he broke out!'

'We tried to catch him, but he turned on Jem Higgs, knocked him flying . . .'

'Would of trampled him only we dragged him clear just in
time . . .'

'Poor Jem got such a crack on the hip – he's lying on a
pile of straw in the stable now . . .'

'Caught me on the backside, kicking out . . . he's crazy!
We did try, but we daren't get close . . .'

'Where's Joseph?' Brockley demanded, not in a shout that
might frighten the horse but with an intonation that carried.
A head immediately popped out of an upper window. 'I'm
here, Master Brockley. But I dursen't go down; I'm that scared
of him; he lashes out and tries to bite and his hooves are like
hammers and his teeth are like knives!'

I had never before heard Joseph sound so loquacious.
Brockley said soothingly: 'All right, stay there. I'll see what
I can do.' He glanced round at the rest of us. 'Stay back, all
of you.' He handed his lantern to Simon. 'You take charge
of that. Light my way from behind me. Don't brandish the
lantern about; just give me a steady light so that I can see
where I'm stepping. The thunder's almost gone; that should
help. Now . . .'

Brockley had once been a professional groom and now,
it was a joy to watch him. He moved slowly forward, step by
step, talking softly and calmly.

'There we are. No thunder now, old boy. Nothing to be
afraid of any more. Come on, lad, you don't really want to
be stabled in a cottage parlour, do you? Surely not. No nice
manger full of oats in there. No hay, no bran mash. You don't
want rushes, now, do you? Come along, now, come along old
fellow. No one wants to hurt you. The nasty thunder's going
away, nearly gone now. There's a nice warm stable waiting
for you. Deep straw, fresh water . . . come along . . .'

The words, of course, could mean nothing to the horse,
but the tone did. Brockley knew exactly how to use the deeper
undertones of his voice so that they could soothe the terror
that had so maddened the stallion. Bay Hawkswood was
responding, though slowly. He was still tense, like a bowstring,
and twice Brockley stopped his cautious advance because the
horse had bared his teeth. When that happened, Brockley stood
motionless but went on talking.

Slowly, slowly, the stallion began to relax. His ears came forward to listen to Brockley's calming tones. Without turning his head, Brockley said: 'Someone bring some oats,' and one of the stud grooms said: 'I've got some here, in Jem Higgs' hat.'

'One of you has some sense, I see,' said Brockley, still in those deep, comforting tones. 'Bring it here.' The groom handed the hat to him and he gently extended it, as a peace offering. The flared nostrils were taking an interest now in the smell of oats. The muzzle dropped, warily at first and then greedily, plunging into the offering of food.

'There, that's better,' Brockley said. 'All that panic and rage makes a fellow hungry, isn't that so, now? That's it, eat it all up . . .'

A few moments later, the hat was empty and Brockley passed it back to the groom just behind him. One hand was on the dangling rope; the other was stroking Bay Hawkswood's neck. Gently, quietly, Brockley led him out of the door. 'I'll take him back to his stable, out of the wet,' he said. 'I'll rub him down. We'd better try to put the cottage right and get ourselves dry, too. But after that . . .' his voice hardened '. . . I'll want to know just where Laurence Miller has got to.'

We put the stallion first. But when Bay Hawkswood had been dried and fed and settled in his stall and Jem Higgs had been got on his feet and proved to be badly bruised and severely shaken but nothing worse, we went back to the cottage. Between us, we righted the furniture and tidied away a pile of droppings that the frightened horse had left on the floor. The kitchen fire, which had been alight when the storm broke, was nearly out but Joseph brought it back to life and lit one in the parlour too. Fortunately – because Bay Hawkswood in his panic might have kicked it, hurt himself and set the cottage on fire – the parlour fire had not been lit because Tessie was in the kitchen and had Liz with her.

Joseph, now very much our host, mulled ale for us all and called us to hang our wet cloaks round the kitchen hearth to steam. We all gathered round the parlour hearth fireplace, thankful to be warm and dry and begin to ask questions.

It then became clear that Miller's whereabouts were, quite simply, unknown.

'He went to Guildford early this morning,' the groom who had brought the oats told us. 'There's new harness needed, madam, he told you, surely . . .'

'Yes, he did. There are more youngsters to train this year than last,' I agreed. 'We'll probably need a couple of extra training carts, too.'

'Well, he went into Guildford to order the harness. He should have been back in the afternoon but he didn't come. We don't know where he is.'

I looked at Brockley and he looked back at me. 'Well, well,' he said.

'When he does reappear,' I said, '*if* he reappears, and I am beginning to wonder, I want to see him. At once.'

But nothing could be done just then. We went on talking in a desultory way and I found comfort in the fireside warmth, but when our cloaks were reasonably dry and the rain, thank goodness, had ceased and we were on our way home, the horrors descended on me again.

Where was Harry? Where *was* he? Had we somehow missed him, despite our careful searching? Was he lying injured somewhere in the woods? Helpless, in pain, terrified and alone, in weather like this?

SIX
The Trap

'Laurence Miller is back, madam,' Brockley said, coming into the hall where I was finishing a hurried and early breakfast. 'I have been to the stud to see. He arrived late last night. He said he had been to Woking to see his mother and was unable to start back when he wanted to because of the storm. I suppose it makes sense.'

'But you don't trust him? Brockley, do you really suppose he had something to do with . . . with Harry disappearing?'

'I wouldn't go so far as that. But we don't know all that much about him, do we? The Earl of Leicester guaranteed his abilities as a stud groom but said nothing about his private life. He arrives here; shortly after that, Harry disappears, and Miller also disappears for a while. I understand that it was early morning when he left for Guildford to order harness. He had all day, near enough, to go to Woking and come back, and duties to do here. Let's say, I'm wondering about him.'

'We must keep watching him,' I said. 'And this morning, we begin the search again.'

It proved fruitless, and I think I knew that in advance, but I could do no other. Anything was better than staying in the house, wondering, longing, hoping, while Harry's bed, his place at the dinner table, his schoolroom all remained empty. I took Philip, Arthur and Joseph with me this time, though not Brockley, who said he would go to Guildford to verify as far as possible what Miller had told him.

I and my three companions set out without delay and between us we quartered the woods again, and once more searched all the land within the Hawkswood boundaries and that immediately surrounding them. The woods were only on one side; on the others, there was open heath. The image of Harry was in my mind all the while, so vivid that I could not believe that he was really lost. His disappearance was like a bad dream.

In the afternoon, I rode out again, alone this time, because even in these circumstances the stables had to be mucked out and the horses groomed, and Philip had volunteered to search the grounds again, on foot 'I may be able to peer into places where a horse can't go. The thickets round the lake are quite dense.'

On returning, I found an anxious deputation awaiting me in the hall. Brockley was not yet back, but Philip was. He, Dale and Sybil were in a state of fuss and Gladys was grumbling.

'We didn't know you'd gone off alone until you had, ma'am,' said Dale reproachfully.

'You should have told us. We've been worried. We couldn't find you and never knew you'd gone out until we asked the grooms,' said Sybil, also reproachfully.

'Not good sense, no indeed,' said Gladys, in the tone one would use to a foolish child.

'You shouldn't go out alone, Mistress Stannard,' Philip said, clearly much concerned. 'Not after whatever has happened to Harry. It's too mysterious. I'm sure my father would advise against it. Mistress Stannard, if you want to go out searching – or for any reason at all – tomorrow, well, if my father is busy as I know he often is, please let me escort you.'

'I suppose you could,' I said. 'It's true that your father has many things to do, apart from investigating Mr Miller!'

'I haven't yet learned what my father's actual work is, Mistress Stannard,' Philip said. 'It puzzles me a little. Adam Wilder is the steward and my father is your manservant, but what does that mean, precisely?'

I managed a small laugh. 'Brockley's role has never been officially defined but I can answer the question. Wilder looks after the work inside the house. He oversees the maids; he talks to John Hawthorn and sees that supplies are purchased for the storeroom; he notices if any repairs are needed; he goes over the accounts with me. Brockley used to be a groom, as you must know. He keeps an eye on the stable yard and quite often lends a hand there, and he does many of the outside errands. Wilder and Hawthorn sometimes go out to buy food supplies and so on, but they are often busy with other things, so Brockley does most of that, and anything else that means riding out. He takes messages, places orders. And he is often about the grounds, just watching over things. He is invaluable. And it's true that he is kept busy.'

'Well, I have no pupil to teach just now,' said Philip ruefully. 'Unlike my father, I have no occupation. If you agree, I will be your bodyguard when you go out.'

'There's little point in it, now,' said Sybil. She had the air of one who was not saying all that she was thinking. Dale looked at her and then away. And Gladys put it into words.

'Anyone that's been lying out there injured in the forest since yesterday morning, all through that storm and rain, ain't like to be living man now, or living boy either. No good pretending, look you.'

'*Gladys!*' Dale shrieked it, horrified.

I said: 'I know Gladys is right, but still I must search. I will go out again tomorrow, and you can come with me, Philip. And the next day and the next. Until we find him, or news of him comes.'

Sybil shook her head. 'We can't search for ever, dear Ursula. There is little we can do now, except pray.'

Brockley reappeared before supper and found me sitting unhappily in the small parlour, trying to soothe my mind with a book of verse.

'Madam, I have been to Guildford. It seems that Miller really did place an order for some new harness and spent some time discussing details, but he set off early and had finished the business before noon. Woking is only about five miles from Guildford, and only seven miles from here. He was riding Blaze and Blaze is a good horse. He could have got to Woking, stayed to eat dinner with his mother – stayed quite long enough for a visit from a dutiful son – and been back here, easily, before the storm began. I really do have doubts about him.'

'Have you spoken to him?'

'Yes, madam. When I got back to the stud, I questioned him and he simply said that he had visited his mother and stayed some time there to help her arrange some new furniture she has bought. I pressed him – pressed him hard, considering the mystery about Master Harry – but he became irritated and said that even a servant has a right to his own personal affairs, and then – after I had grabbed him by the front of his jacket and rammed him backwards against the wall of the stable – he said that while he was in Guildford he had also visited a woman, a friend of his. But he wouldn't say her name or give me her direction. I didn't believe him. I could get no more out of him. But it looks suspicious. There has been no news while I was out? No one has tried to get in touch with you?'

'To ask for a ransom? No, Brockley, nothing and no one.'

'My son says he has advised you against riding out alone, madam. I gather that he has offered to escort you if I happen to be busy. Well, tomorrow I want to go to Woking. John Hawthorn needs salt and sugar and spices and I understand that Margery is sorry but all the upset made her clumsy and she dropped a pile of earthenware bowls yesterday and broke three. I can get all those things there and while I'm about it I shall try to find Miller's mother, and find out if he really did visit her when he says he did. I'll also have my ears and eyes wide open, because if Harry has been kidnapped, he must have been taken to a house somewhere. If there have been strangers in the district, I might hear of it.'

'He may have warned his mother to say he was there even if he wasn't,' I said glumly.

'If we are to find out anything, we must try *something*. I suggest that you accept Philip's offer.'

'I shall send some of the grooms out as well,' I said. 'Philip and I can go in one direction; they can go in another. We seem to be going over the same ground, again and again but somewhere, somehow, there must be a trace. There must be!'

Over supper, something else occurred to me.

'We must alert the sheriff, Sir Edward Heron,' I said. 'We've all been thinking so much about accidents, but we'd have found him by now if it had been that. We've talked about the possibility that Harry's been kidnapped but we haven't done anything about it! Please go to Sir Edward as well, Brockley. Do that first and then go on to Woking.'

'Aye, I will,' said Brockley grimly. 'What will you do, madam?'

'It may be useless,' I said. 'I expect it is. But I will go with Philip and go on searching. There are still parts of the wood that I want to hunt through again. Where there's undergrowth, and perhaps we missed a few secret places. We'll take the dogs again.'

'Very well,' said Brockley.

'I suggest,' said Philip as we started out, 'that we take the right-hand track, where I advised Harry to go. It's the likeliest direction.'

'All right,' I said. But I knew, as we started out, that it was pointless. I was simply repeating what had become a habit. I had seen the menagerie at the Tower of London and I had seen lions restlessly pacing their cage, back and forth, without cessation. I was behaving like those lions. But I couldn't help myself; anything was better than staying at home, trying to occupy myself with inspecting the work of the maids, or doing embroidery, or reading, or wandering round the rose garden that Hugh had loved so much.

Normally, at this time of year, I would be taking a keen interest in the roses, as they responded to an earlier pruning and began to put forth new growth. Now, I could not take an interest in anything.

The weather had turned sunny, as though the storm had never been. As Philip and I rode out, signs of spring were all around us. Many of the trees in the woodland were oaks, which were always slow to come into leaf, but there were also patches of beech and on them, the rain of the storm followed by warm sunshine had worked wonders. The woods were misted with green today and full of birdsong. Normally, I would have loved riding through them. Now, they might as well have been a desert.

Despondency lay heavily upon me. I would have to give up the search after this, I thought. I would have to leave it to Sir Edward Heron. I hoped he would be helpful. I didn't like him, and neither did he like me.

For the moment, Philip and I rode with care, looking from side to side, making excursions now and then, off the paths and in among the trees, to see if a patch of bushes here, or a big tree bole there, was hiding anything. Remus and Goldie ranged round us, pursuing the secret invitations that the woodland offered to their sensitive nostrils. Before starting, we had, as before, given them some of Harry's clothes to smell. If they found any trace of him, they would assuredly let us know.

The attack came so suddenly and so fast that I couldn't believe it even while it was happening. One moment we were riding, at a walk, on a track through a patch of beech trees, with some bushes in between; the next, the bushes seemed to erupt into movement, sprouting men like crazy new branches. There were hands clutching at Jewel's bridle and other hands on me, dragging me out of my saddle. There were faces, frightful faces, demons and jesters and idiot blankness, mummers' masks of course but not the less terrifying for that.

Goldie and Remus had been running among the trees and now came rushing to my rescue, snarling. A man in a demon mask had been standing back, holding a crossbow. It spat, and Goldie rolled over, howling, with a bolt through his chest, and then collapsed. The same man drew a sword and as Remus sprang at him, used it. Remus died at once without even time to howl. He fell beside Goldie and his assailant put a foot on his body to pull the sword out more easily.

I cursed and screamed, but someone clapped a gloved hand over my mouth. Tears burst from my eyes. I was struggling wildly. I heard Philip shouting and from the corner of my eye I saw that he too had been wrenched out of his saddle and thrown onto the ground and I saw a man with a clown mask looming over him, raising a club. Another was driving his speckled mare away. Jewel was rearing and plunging and the man who had grabbed my rein let her go. I heard her frightened hooves receding, following her stablemate. I knew now what had so much frightened Mealy.

My wild resistance was pointless; there were too many of them. I was pushed down onto my back, and someone was twining a rope round my ankles. Ropes were being wound round me, binding my arms to my sides, and a scarf of some sort was being pushed into my mouth. Then I was being rolled over and rolled *up*, into what seemed to be a carpet. I was being lifted. I was being placed on something hard. There were muttered voices round me. Whatever I was lying on began to move. I was being taken away, on some kind of cart.

I could not see, could not cry out. I had no idea what had happened to Philip but that club had been fearsome; he could well be dead. The horses would probably bolt home. They would give the alarm. People would come. They would find Philip – find the dogs – this was surely what happened to Harry, but he had been alone. Our party had consisted of two people and two dogs; there *must*, surely, be traces this time. This time, a search would reveal where the attack had happened, where they must start seeking the spoor of my captors. If Philip did survive, he might tell them more. Rescue might come, I thought desperately. I *would* be rescued, surely. Perhaps Harry too. Perhaps I was going to Harry.

Thinking of that steadied me a little. I wondered where on earth I was being taken. Not only could I see nothing; I couldn't hear much either, for the carpet muffled everything. But I could make out the sound of the cart's wheels and I heard when they suddenly changed and so did the motion. I thought I was being wheeled over cobbles. A horse whinnied somewhere and were those voices? But it all faded away and the motion became smooth once more. If we had been in a village street, we had left it now. I seemed to have been on the cart, if that's what it was, for a long time. I could hear plodding feet around me.

How much longer? The carpet was stifling, smelling of wool and dust and its fibres were scratching my face. I was aware of unseen objects bumping uncomfortably against me. I supposed that my captors didn't intend to kill me; they could have done that already. But there were other things to fear. First with distress and then with alarm, I realized that I needed a privy. Oh, dear God, not that as well! Oh, please God, let me hold on until we get to wherever we're going. Don't let me lose control. Did this happen to Harry too?

There was a change. I could still see nothing, but we had slowed down and around me the sounds that I could hear had changed again. We were indoors, I thought. Then I was being heaved off my uncomfortable carriage. I was lowered to the floor and rolled over, so that my enveloping carpet fell away from me. Hands were busy at the ropes that bound me. I was being helped to sit up. I was in a room, dusty and untidy but furnished like a parlour, and the faces around me were no longer masked. Staring at them in fright and astonishment, I recognized the strolling players who had entertained us at Hawkswood, so recently.

The lanky, long-fingered man who had seemed to be their leader removed his cap and said, with astounding graciousness: 'We must apologize for such rough treatment, Mistress Stannard. We had our reasons. Don't be frightened. We hope we haven't hurt you.' He gave me what he evidently thought was a conciliating smile. 'We did our best, in fact, to treat you like a queen. Queen Cleopatra of Egypt had herself brought to Julius Caesar wrapped in a carpet.'

'That was her choice. She wasn't kidnapped!' I said, and then felt panicky, wondering how I had had the temerity to answer him back. He had said *don't be frightened* but I was. I wanted to cry out *But you've hurt Philip and killed my dogs* but I didn't venture to say it, or anything further. I just stared at him.

Whereupon this oddly apologetic ringleader, as though he had read my mind, said: 'Your escort is not dead. We knocked him down but he was getting to his feet again when we saw him last. We are sorry about your dogs. We can only say that some things are more important than the lives of a couple of dogs. You will understand that shortly. For the moment, though . . .'

He beckoned to someone behind me, and the red-haired young woman came forward. She wore a cloak but as it swung partly open, I saw that she was once more wearing a crystal-sewn gown, though the gown itself was green this time, not turquoise. She helped me to my feet. I wobbled, hardly able to stand after being tied for so long. 'I need a privy,' I said to her.

The young woman promptly replied: 'Come this way,' and steered me to a door. It gave on to a cobbled yard. A glance

round me told me that this was a fair-sized house and that to
the left was a shed of the sort that was often built behind
houses for sanitary purposes.

'Go in. You'll find all you need,' the woman said, and
steadied me while I opened the shed door. I managed to
totter in on my own. On a shelf there was indeed everything
I might require for my personal needs. Someone had been
very thoughtful.

I too felt thoughtful. Some years before, I had had to seek
for a missing friend, Christopher Spelton. He was a royal
messenger who sometimes undertook secret work, just as I
did. He had a trick, if he felt he was in danger, and might
mysteriously disappear, of leaving a red chalk sign where he
hoped it might be found by anyone who came in search of
him. It would give them a chance of rescuing him, if he were
still alive; if not, to avenge him.

I found his sign and it alerted me to the presence of danger.
Since then, I had myself taken to carrying a piece of red chalk
about with me, though I had never had occasion to use it. It
was my habit to wear open-fronted skirts and have a hidden
pouch stitched inside them, where I could carry such things
as picklocks, a small dagger, some coinage and anything else
that might be useful in my unconventional existence. I had
added the chalk to the list, putting it in a little cloth bag so
that it couldn't mark my clothing. I had it with me now.

Before I left the shed, I stooped to make a chalk mark on
the wooden wall, near the floor. Christopher Spelton's mark
had been a circle quartered by a cross. I had decided on a
square with a V inside it. This was the first time I had used
it and it was quite difficult, on the rough timber of the outhouse
wall, to make the mark clear but I managed reasonably well.
I had told my friends about it, and it just might help them to
find me, if I were held for long.

I wished I had thought of asking Christopher to help in
the search for Harry, but he had left his work as Queen's
Messenger and agent to marry my former ward Kate Lake
and live with her at West Leys, the farm she had inherited
from her first husband. It was not so very far from Hawkswood
but I had not wished to disturb them.

Relieved at last, and having drawn my sign, I came out to find the red-haired woman waiting to lead me back indoors where the male members of the party were awaiting us. I took the opportunity of glancing quickly at what I could see of the house from outside. It was built of dull red brick with two storeys and an attic floor above, where two gable windows protruded from a thatched roof. The windows were small casements with square leaded panes. It was all too commonplace to amount to much. I had no chance to linger for a closer inspection, anyway. My escort hurried me indoors.

A table had been set for a meal, with a cloth and some food and drink. No one looked threatening. I took courage at last and said: 'Is Harry here? Is my son here?'

'No,' said the long-fingered ringleader. 'But he is safe. All going well, you will eventually be reunited with him.'

'*Eventually?* What does that mean?'

'You will soon know. I hope you are more comfortable now, Mistress, and I invite you to join us in a meal. You probably need one. And then – then we will explain.'

SEVEN

The Dreadful Choice

I did need food and in any case, although my captors now seemed to want to be friendly, I was still too afraid of them to argue. Therefore, I ate. There was cold meat, I remember, and bread, and some sort of almond-flavoured pudding, and small ale to wash it down. But I couldn't eat much, so the meal didn't last long. I forced a slice of cold mutton and a piece of bread down my throat, nibbled at the pudding and then thrust my platter away and said: 'Why have I been brought here? What is all this about? *And where is Harry? Where is my son?*'

The ringleader looked at me gravely and said: 'First of all, we want you to know, to understand that we are honest folk, true English folk, who love this realm and are the loyal servants of her majesty Queen Elizabeth.'

Are you indeed? I didn't say it aloud but my face said it, because he answered the question I hadn't uttered. 'Yes, Mistress Stannard, we are. We are representing ourselves as travelling players but it is only a disguise, though we have worked hard, for more than a year, ever since we formed our little company, to make ourselves convincing. Fortunately, one of us actually is a tumbler, which is very helpful, and several of us can sing, and two of us have been employed in big houses where masques were held, which they helped to plan. We learned a great deal about acting from them. We brought you here,' he added, sounding quite rueful, 'on our handcart. We were all out of breath by the time we got you here. You are not a big woman but the handcart was heavy enough already, what with our baggage and properties!'

'And wrapped in a carpet and piled on the cart along with your luggage,' I said bitterly, 'and given that you'd taken those hideous masks off by then, I could be trundled openly through the main street of a town and no one would pay the least attention! But why?'

'I promise you that we have a good reason for bringing you here. Like many others – *many* others – we worry about the future, for the times are dangerous. The danger never seems to grow less and sometimes seems to grow more. And the heart of that danger, of course, is Mary Stuart. We know that the queen keeps her close, but Mary is as cunning as a vixen and has secret supporters, here and abroad. We all know what she wants. So do you, Mistress.'

'Yes, of course. That's why the queen keeps her shut away. Mary Stuart wants to be restored to the throne of Scotland and also claims to be the rightful queen of England.'

'Quite. She is Catholic and the Catholics do not accept that the old king's marriage to Anne Boleyn was lawful. Therefore, they believe that Queen Elizabeth . . .' He paused and I saw that his fingers – they were *too* long, I thought; there was something unnatural about them – were twisting together. I could almost have believed that he was blushing. 'That Queen Elizabeth is not . . . was not born in wedlock.'

'Mary has been accused of having ordered the murder of her husband Lord Darnley,' I said. 'Her name has never been cleared and she was foolish enough, after Darnley was killed, to marry the likeliest suspect. Few English people want such a woman for their queen.'

I was repeating the things I had mentioned to the queen and de Simier. The next speaker, who was a younger-looking, slightly built man, went on to repeat more of them. I recalled that at Hawkswood he was the one who had entertained us with tumbling and juggling. He was grave and serious now. He said: 'Few indeed would want her. Which in one way makes things worse. Just because within England the support for Mary Stuart is scanty, she would if she could seek support from elsewhere. Probably from Spain. If she could, she would bring a Spanish army here. And we all know what that would mean.'

'It would be followed by the Inquisition,' said the woman and several of the others nodded emphatically. 'There's no doubt about that. And we suspect that Mary would rather have the throne of England than the throne of Scotland. She is a menace.'

'But she's a prisoner,' I said. 'I'm not sure where, at the moment, but . . .'

'Sheffield Castle,' said another man. He was big and fat and I remembered that he had taken a comic part in the little play that the group had performed at Hawkswood. He had made us all laugh and he had also sung. He had a good, resonant voice. 'She's in the charge of Sir George Talbot, Earl of Shrewsbury,' he said. 'It's a good place because Sheffield Manor is close by, where she can be moved for a while whenever the castle has to be cleansed. She doesn't have to be taken any distance, and the manor and castle are both part of the Shrewsbury estate.'

'Well,' I said, 'wherever she is, I have always understood that she was kept safely. She doesn't have visitors; she doesn't have correspondence. She can't conspire with anyone.'

'She has servants,' said the ringleader. 'Quite a few of them, as it happens. They can't be entirely prevented from leaving the castle now and then. There is little doubt that Mary can communicate with the outside world and almost certainly does. Yes, she is watched, in her daily life inside the castle, but tell me, Mistress Stannard, if you were in her place, and someone had smuggled a letter to you, wouldn't you manage to read it, even if you were watched day and night? You would, I feel sure, manage a few moments of privacy now and then. Wouldn't you? Tell us how you would do it.'

I blinked at him. 'Well . . . I suppose I might hide it in my skirts and I might read it . . . sitting on the privy perhaps. Or I might manage to slip it between the pages of a book. I expect she reads. I know I would, if allowed. Verses, psalms, travel, history, legends of fabulous beasts. They would all help to pass the time. I would need to be clever, to distract the attention of anyone I thought was watching, while I put the letter into the book but it might be done.'

'Quite. I see that you understand us very well. Our fear,' said the ringleader, 'is that we shall wake up one morning to find a foreign army in England, intent on destroying our queen

and imposing on us a religion that we don't want. Mistress
Stannard, the queen herself must fear it. And the Duke of
Alençon and Anjou certainly does.'

'The Duke of . . .'

'Yes. There are hopes, are there not, of an alliance between
our queen and the French duke, which will bring into being
a treaty between the two countries, undertaking, on both sides,
to stand together against any aggression from Spain. But the
duke is reportedly holding back because of the danger imposed
by Mary Stuart.'

They had managed to find out a lot, but there were still
things they didn't know, I thought. The queen was also holding
back, and not just because of Mary Stuart. Elizabeth had her
own private reasons. Also, as I had confirmed to Elizabeth,
many people in England didn't in the least want their queen
to marry a French Catholic. These folk might want it, but they
were probably a minority. A simpleminded and naive minority.
I did not know what I myself hoped for. I only knew that
Elizabeth was in doubt, and I pitied her.

For some reason, these people seemed to be working up to
some kind of scheme against Mary and I instinctively knew
that it boded no good to me although I couldn't think how.
But, again by instinct, I set myself to argue against the danger
of a Spanish invasion.

'A foreign army would have to come by sea,' I protested.
'We have a navy. The enemy ships would be intercepted.'

'If there were enough of them, the navy might not win.
It would on the whole be better,' said the tumbler, 'if Mary
were simply not there at all.'

'I'm sure the queen would agree with you, but Mary *is*
there,' I said. 'In Sheffield Castle. What has this to do with
me? Or Harry?'

'We know,' said the ringleader, 'that you are in fact a half-
sister to the queen. Your feelings for her and her safety must
be very strong. Your past history suggests it. We know a good
deal about you. Our company includes people who have mixed
in good society, where your name is known, where you have
a reputation. You are an ideal tool.'

'A tool?'

'We want you,' said the ringleader, 'to assassinate Mary Stuart.'

He said it as calmly as though he were proposing some commonplace thing; asking me to take a message to someone, or be a guest at a wedding, or help somebody's young daughter to choose her first formal dress, or make a choice from a litter of puppies . . .

Puppies. For a mad moment, my mind slipped into the mundane. If I ever got back home, I would certainly find myself choosing puppies. I would have to. Goldie and Remus were dead.

And, thinking of that, I clenched my fists. I couldn't speak.

'I expect this comes as a shock to you,' said the woman, quite kindly. 'But we do mean it.'

'Yes. I will repeat it.' The lanky ringleader was still using that calm, reasonable voice. 'We want you to assassinate Mary Stuart. You have a good chance of gaining access to her. You are one of the few who might. That is one reason why we have chosen you. And we have a means of compelling you.'

'You take the idea of assassination very easily,' I said, and then I found myself so angry that I was able to speak my mind. 'You have already slaughtered my dogs. What harm had they done you? They were happy, running about in the woods, and you killed them.'

'We regret that. We have already told you so. Did we not also say that some things are more important than the lives of dogs? The safety of the realm, for instance.'

'But I can't . . . I couldn't . . . I *couldn't* do such a thing, even if I could get into Sheffield Castle in the first place!'

'I said, you have a chance of access. It shouldn't be too hard. You can't get permission to go into the castle except by approaching Walsingham, we think, but if you went to him and offered your services as a spy, sent into Sheffield Castle on some pretext, but staying there for a while and watching Mary, he might well accept. You know her a little, do you not? You have met her . . .'

'Yes. I have!' I burst in. 'And the last time, we parted on unfriendly terms. I had deceived her and – to her way of thinking – betrayed her. She won't want me anywhere near her. I won't be able to *get* anywhere near her!'

'If you are in Sheffield Castle at Walsingham's orders, then Talbot will have to accept whatever Walsingham commands. So will Mary. Even if she refuses to speak to you or acknowledge your existence in any way; even if she has hysterics at the sight of you, she must put up with whatever orders Talbot gives.'

'She may very well have hysterics at the sight of me and it might not be as trivial a matter as you seem to think!'

'You can tell her that you are a Catholic convert and drowning in guilt for your past practices against her, and longing to be reconciled with her. It might work. As for Walsingham, you had better not tell him the truth . . .'

'He would like to have Mary executed,' I said, 'but legally and publicly, on the block. He would never cooperate with assassination.'

'Quite. So we will prime you with a story of something overheard, that has made you suspicious, made you think that Mary is involved in some conspiracy or other. That will be the reason why you offer to enter her service as a spy. Your reputation is that of an agent, Mistress Stannard. It is the sort of thing you might well do.'

'But I *couldn't* kill in cold blood! I could never . . .'

I stopped.

He was smiling. 'You have understood, I think. I told you that we have means of compelling you. You haven't asked what they are, but of course, you have already realized. You are not a fool. We have Harry.'

I began to tremble. The room spun. The woman looked at me with some concern and then murmured something quietly to a man who had not yet spoken (though I remembered him as portraying the villain in the play at Hawkswood, and recalled that he had a soft, insinuating voice). He went at once to a cabinet and brought out a flagon of wine and a glass, which he filled and handed to me. 'Drink this, Mistress. It will put heart into you.'

I drank as recommended. I needed it. I must keep my head. I must get Harry and me out of this, somehow. I must be cunning, wary . . .

'*Where is Harry?*' I said, in the firmest voice I could manage.

'Not here,' said the ringleader. 'But safe and well in another house, a good way away. He will remain safe and well, we trust. We are not threatening his life, Mistress Stannard. We are not murderers. In the case of Mary Stuart, we would regard her death as an execution. However, since we feared that you would be reluctant to act the headsman for us, we have to make use of Harry. No, we will not kill him. But you know, from experience, I think, that corsairs from Algiers do at times come into English waters and raid coastal houses for valuables and to capture slaves. They had a base on the island of Lundy in the Bristol Channel at one time. They have been cleared out of there, but they still come into English waters now and then; pounce, seize and flee. If you will not help us, we will deliver Harry to them.'

'You . . . no, you wouldn't, you couldn't . . .!'

'He would not necessarily have an unhappy life with them,' said the soft-voiced man. It wasn't a pleasant voice, I thought. It had an up and down cadence that spoke of cruelty and his pale eyes were cold.

He said: 'A fine young boy like your son would command a good price and would probably be bought by a man of wealth. He could do well. He might even, one day, win his freedom and come home, but that would be far in the future. More likely, of course, he would become something like a steward or a bodyguard or perhaps a eunuch in charge of a harem . . .'

'*No!*' It came out as a scream.

'There are dangers in the operation, of course.' The ring-leader spoke briskly. 'But those who survive it often do win highly rewarded and powerful positions. They are not always deprived even of natural pleasures. Some eunuchs, so we understand, can perform. They just can't breed.'

'Not Harry! Not Harry!'

'Well, there's no need, is there?' said the ringleader coax-ingly. 'If you agree to do what we ask, he will come home safely and England will be that much safer, too.'

'If Mary were murdered, Philip of Spain would probably invade at once, to avenge her!' I clutched at the idea, desperately.

'It would depend on how it was done,' said Insinuating Voice. 'Mary's health is not good. She has a recurring pain in her side and languishes when the weather is bad and she can't get into the fresh air. Talbot has to let her ride out sometimes, escorted by armed men, of course. Her death could be made to look like the outcome of illness.'

'That would protect us from Philip of Spain, I think,' said the tumbler. 'And when she was dead, you would be free to go home and you would find Harry there to greet you.'

'This has been a shock to you,' said the ringleader, in a voice now full of maddening compassion. 'You need time to think about it – and about Harry. A room has been prepared for you and Eva here . . .' he nodded towards the woman '. . . will attend you. It isn't yet very late, but I expect you would like to retire. You will want to think over what we have said. Eva, show Mistress Stannard the way.'

I was shown to a panelled bedchamber looking over the yard at the back. A washstand was there, with towels and a jug of cold water and a basin, and there was a tester bed with a plain nightgown lying ready across the moleskin coverlet. On a table beside the bed stood a carafe of wine and a glass. The red-haired young woman left me for a few moments but reappeared very quickly with a further jug, containing hot water. Then she wished me goodnight and went away. She didn't lock the door. There was no need. I was not a prisoner.

But Harry was.

I washed and went to bed but not to sleep. I don't like to remember that dreadful night. I lay staring into the darkness and trying in vain to see a way out of this morass. I drank some of the wine, hoping that it would make me drowsy, but it had no effect at all.

Harry's danger filled my mind. If Harry were to be . . . oh, God forbid . . . sold to the corsairs, in that case . . . at one point, probably about three in the morning, in a surge of fury, I swore that I would follow him to Algiers, and find him and save him. The approach of dawn, like the chill light of reason, told me that such an idea was madness; that I would never succeed, would probably end as a slave myself. I tossed from one side to the other, trying to imagine myself as an assassin, a poisoner. I couldn't. But there was Harry. Round and round went my frantic thoughts. By the time the light was full, I was even more jaded and exhausted than I had been the night before.

Breakfast was brought to me in my room. I ate it. I dressed. Then I waited, sitting wearily by the window, leaning on my hand and looking out on the yard, and realizing that there was a sunlit garden beyond. It was unkempt but dew was sparkling in the early sunlight and there were some pretty spring flowers. Deceptive, I thought bitterly. How dare the world look so beguiling? Presently, Eva came for me. She led me out to use the privy and then took me back to the parlour where, yesterday, I had heard of the dreadful choice that lay before me.

They were all there, waiting for me. The ringleader (until much later, I never heard the names of any of them except for Eva), said, again compassionately: 'I won't ask if you slept well. I don't suppose you did and we are sorry. But when the safety of a realm is at stake . . .'

'I have heard that argument before,' I said. 'And suffered for it.' Lord Burghley, Sir William Cecil, had at various times said it or implied it. So had Sir Francis Walsingham. So had my sister the queen. It was an all too familiar argument.

'We are not going to keep you here,' said the ringleader. 'There is no need, and indeed, the sooner you are free to carry out the assignment we have given you, the better. We are not going to tell you how to go about it, except that as I said to you yesterday, we have worked out a story, about something overheard, that you may use if you like, to persuade Walsingham to get you into Mary's presence.

'We suggest, in fact, that you should pretend you have heard of a plan being made by a group of young Catholic gentlemen, to collect an army on the Continent. You could have overheard one of their discussions, by chance, during your time at court, or perhaps when visiting a Catholic neighbour. We believe you have a Catholic working in your kitchen. Is that so?'

'Yes. Ben Flood. He helps my chief cook, Hawthorn.'

'But is loyal to you, is he not? Perhaps he has heard a rumour and repeated it to you. He attends unlawful Masses, I think? He could well have heard something on such an occasion. He is one possible channel through which this imaginary rumour could have reached you. You will have to decide on the details, if you use this story as your pretext. Or you may have ideas of your own. We can offer you one thing that might help.' He glanced towards Eva. 'Do you have it there, lass?'

'Yes.' Eva had a pouch on her girdle. She delved into it and produced a small phial of dark glass. She handed it to him and he in turn passed it to me.

'What's this?' I said.

'Liquid death, if you want to use it,' said Eva. 'Better keep it by, anyway.'

I examined the phial and then pulled out the stopper and smelt it. And withdrew with a snort of dislike. 'Hemlock! I know that stink.'

'Quite. Used in small doses to kill pain,' said the ringleader. 'Take it with you.'

There was nothing to be done but secrete it in my own belt pouch. I shuddered as it swung against me, a constant reminder of its contents and their purpose.

The ringleader said: 'We must warn you against setting the law on our track. If there should be any hue and cry after us – well, if necessary, we would carry out our threat, dispose of Harry, out of this land, where you cannot pursue him, and then reassemble and find another tool. It could even mean taking another member of your family.' I stared at him, shuddering, thinking of my married daughter Meg, of her children, even of Aunt Tabitha and Uncle Herbert. I was not fond of them but I owed them something and besides, they were ageing and becoming frail and . . .

'We know of no one else we can coerce,' said the long-fingered leader. 'No one who stands a chance of entering Mary's circle. We have tried to approach some of those already in it but we had to be very cautious and we met with no success. Nor have we any means of coercing any of them.'

The wretch smiled. 'You are angry with us. But that doesn't matter. What does matter is freeing England from the menace that is Mary Stuart, and freeing Elizabeth to make this most valuable alliance with France. You will need time, of course. We suggest three months. But if when three months are spent Mary is still alive, if she has not been laid on a bier with her hands folded on her breast, then . . . remember, we have Harry. He will pay the price.'

'How can you?' I said, and knew how feeble I sounded.

'Rest assured, we can. Now, we must get you home, before the hue and cry about *you* becomes too loud. It is up to you, of course, exactly how you word your request to Walsingham and how much you tell your household. In every word you say, and every move you make, you will, we trust, bear in mind that we *do* have Harry. And we have means of keeping watch on you. We will know what you are doing.'

'We shall be taking you back more or less to where we found you,' said Insinuating Voice. 'You will have to travel as you did on the way here. It wouldn't do at all for you to know where you are now. We will make you as comfortable as possible. Please don't make the mistake of resisting. We shall have to bind and gag you again, though. You might struggle free and scream for help in the hope of giving us in charge away and trusting that we will be forced to reveal Harry's whereabouts. We shan't let you do that.'

There was no point in resisting. They bound and silenced me and rolled me up again in the horrible carpet. I was loaded again onto their beastly handcart. On the way, I tried hard to work out where we were going, but I could hear very little and nothing that would help. Once again we passed through some populated place, for I heard voices and horses' hooves, but I had no idea where we were.

There came a time when I could hear wind in trees and sensed that we had entered woodland. We came to a halt. I was being lifted down. I was being unwrapped and partly released from my bonds, though they left my feet bound. Looking about me, I saw that I was in a clearing that looked somehow familiar. I seemed to have an escort of three: the ringleader, the tumbler and Insinuating Voice.

'I imagine you know where you are,' said the ringleader. 'A mile from home, roughly, and to the north of it. But you know your own local tracks. We'll be off now. You can undo your feet yourself – we've left you your belt-knife. Rub your arms and legs to get the stiffness out. The walk will do the rest.'

And then they were gone, taking their handcart with them. I found my belt-knife and cut my feet free. I got up but was so stiff that I had to spend several moments leaning on a tree. I knew the place, of course. It wasn't where I had been seized, but in a small dell, with beech trees all around, and a perfectly familiar path leading up the side of the dell. That path would take me home. I had ridden it dozens of times. I shook out my crumpled skirts and set off.

It seemed a long way, for I was very tired. But at length, I came in sight of Hawkswood's dear chimneys, and then I was walking, or stumbling, towards the gatehouse. I went through it and then Arthur and Simon came running towards me, shouting as they came, and, young Eddie was rushing into the house, also shouting, and on the instant, it seemed, Dale and Brockley and Sybil were all there, with Gladys hobbling after them, and I was being half-carried into the hall and placed on a settle.

At which point, I fainted.

EIGHT
The Queen's Advice

I came round to find myself still lying on the settle in the great hall. Someone had put a cushion under my head and removed my shoes, and Dale, with Brockley at her side, was hovering with a glass. 'Well water,' Dale said. 'Try to sit up and sip, ma'am. It may help.'

I did as she asked, and became aware that most of my household was gathered anxiously around. Sybil was adjusting my cushion. My senior maid, Phoebe, was there, looking worried, along with the other maids, Netta and Margery. Wilder was there, anxiety in every line of his long, amiable face. My head spun when I tried to sit up, and I leant back quickly. 'I'm sorry,' I said. 'I'm so tired. I didn't sleep at all last night and . . . and . . .'

'We've been frantic!' said Sybil tearfully. 'Jewel came home without you and then Master Sandley's horse and we sent out a search party – all the grooms – and they found Master Sandley blundering about in the woods, lost and dazed. They got him home but he collapsed and it was hours before he could tell us anything. Then he said you'd been carried off by madmen in horrible masks . . .'

'I was afraid Philip had been killed,' I said unsteadily, and with that, he emerged from the crowd and knelt down beside me. He had a bandage round his head.

'I was knocked flat. I had a bang on the head that dazed me. It still aches.' He put a hand to the back of his head. 'I have some spectacular bruises but no, they didn't kill me,' he said. 'But when I first got up, I didn't know what I was doing. They'd driven off my horse. I tried to get home but I got lost. I was wobbling about and lurching from tree to tree when the search party found me. Who *were* those madmen?'

'Take your time,' Brockley said to me. 'We all want to know

what happened to you after that but you must speak only when you're ready.'

'*Brockley!*' My faint had blurred my mind for a moment but it was clearing now. 'Brockley, when I went out yesterday, you were going to see Sir Edward Heron and then going on to Woking to see Miller's mother. What happened? Did you see Heron? This is important! Tell me quickly!'

'I saw him, yes. But you know what he's like, madam!'

I certainly did. Sir Edward Heron, Sheriff of Surrey, had once had me accused of witchcraft. I had proved him wrong then, and had proved him wrong on another occasion since. He regarded me as a nuisance of a woman who ought to stay out of public matters.

'*What happened?*' I demanded.

'Heron said it was sure to be a matter of a ransom demand and we should wait for that. There would be instructions about how to pay, and that might give us a chance of laying an ambush. We should let him know when the demand arrived. He had a great air of being busy and, well . . .'

'Looking as though he was thinking: *that woman again!* I can imagine.' I had steadied myself by now and was able to sit up. 'And then you came home and found I was missing as well as Harry.'

'Yes. And I didn't feel inclined to go back and report on your disappearance as well. I was more concerned – we were all more concerned – with looking for you!' Brockley looked awkward. 'Perhaps I should have gone back to him, but he made me angry.'

'Thank God for that. Brockley, we must not involve Heron any further. Now. I have something to tell you – all of you – that will horrify you, but it is also something that you must not repeat. Never a word outside these walls or to anyone except each other. Do you all understand? Oh, dear God!'

I had remembered something else. 'Brockley, when Harry was lost, we called at White Towers, looking for him! They lent men to help us search. Did they do that again when I was lost? Brockley, whatever happens, they mustn't go talking about it either, to anyone!'

'I don't think they will, madam. They did help us look

for you, but I warned them not to spread the word. Knowing the things you have sometimes been caught up in – well, I felt we should be circumspect, until we knew more. I told them so.'

'Thank God. But I must make sure. My writing things,' I said. 'Paper, ink, pen. I must write a note and you must take it to them. At once!'

A writing set was brought and I wrote the note. My hand shook as I did it. When I finished, and sealed it, I gave it to Brockley. 'Please go as soon as I have explained what all this is about. It's dreadful.' I looked earnestly at my assembled household. 'I know I can't keep it a secret from you. I can only beg you to keep it a secret from the rest of the world until, well, until there's no longer any need.'

Every head nodded and I knew I could rely on them. I trusted my household. They all knew of the strange duties I sometimes carried out and there was no one now in my employment whose discretion I doubted.

I took a deep breath and then, as succinctly as possible, I described my experiences, and the monstrous choice that now faced me. There were horrified gasps and exclamations of *Poor Master Harry!*

'It's a blessing,' I said, 'that Sir Edward did not start a hue and cry. I can't impress on you too strongly that my captors warned me that if there were any attempt to pursue them or hunt for Harry in any public way, they would carry out their threat to – sell him.'

I scanned their faces. Many had gone white. Sybil looked ready to faint. Dale and Margery were both crying. I said: 'Harry's captors do realize that I can't do anything unless I can get into Sheffield and to do that I must first visit the court and see Walsingham. I can seek him out without taking a risk, which means that I can ask his advice. In a way, my captors have put themselves in a cleft stick. They want me to murder Mary Stuart and I can't do that without entering Sheffield and I can't enter Sheffield without talking to Walsingham. Brockley, what happened about Mrs Miller?'

'I went on to Woking as instructed,' Brockley said. 'Laurence Miller's mother is a partial invalid, looked after by her servants, a married couple. Miller hadn't been there at all, lately. She hadn't seen him for weeks. He was lying. Then I returned here and found everything in chaos. You and Philip were both missing and your horses had come home without you.'

I found myself drooping again, with exhaustion truly setting in. Sybil said: 'Ursula, you must rest. Let us help you to bed. We can all discuss what to do, after you wake up.'

'I'll make a potion for you.' That was old Gladys. 'All-heal and camomile, and I'll put it in wine. You'll be off like a baby in no time, indeed.'

Brockley, putting my note to White Towers in his belt scrip, bade me farewell and departed. I let myself be taken care of. Sybil gave me an arm upstairs and she and Dale got me out of my crumpled gown – it was a durable riding dress but two journeys wrapped in a carpet and a trudge through the woods had done it no good – and slipped a clean night-gown over my head. They helped me into my bed. Cool sheets and a cool pillow received me and Gladys appeared with her promised medicine which I gratefully drank.

Dale said she would stay in the room and watch over me. She would leave the bedcurtains open so that she could see me, she said, but would close the window curtains. I nodded. I closed my eyes. And was gone.

When I woke, the light that had been filtering through the window curtains, which were not thick, had faded, by which I knew that several hours had passed. Dale was still there. As I stirred, she rose from her seat and came to me. 'Are you better now, ma'am? Rested?'

'Yes.' I even felt hungry. The body, it seems, persists in demanding that its needs be catered for, whatever else may be happening. I threw back my covers. 'I must dress. I need . . . what time is it?'

'Not quite supper-time. About six of the clock. Brockley is back. He delivered the note safely.'

'That's a relief,' I said. 'I must dress and then I need some food, something quick. And then, I will have things to talk about and decide.'

Before long, with cold meat pie and some spiced wine custard inside me, I was seated in the little parlour, along with the Brockleys, Sybil, and Gladys. I hadn't actually asked Gladys to be present; she had invited herself. But then, that was Gladys. I was used to it even though I knew she was liable to foretell disaster, whatever decisions were taken.

'I said when I got up that there would be things to decide, but of course, it doesn't amount to much.' I told them. 'My captors expect me to go to Walsingham and indeed, I don't see what else I can do. I must have his advice! *He* won't start a hue and cry. He'll understand why he mustn't. I don't like Walsingham very much but I can trust him for that. He likes to work in the dark, anyway.'

'Will you seek his permission to go to Sheffield?' asked Brockley.

'I will have to ask him that. But I must do something! I can't abandon Harry. And I can't see either how I can possibly do what these people have told me to do . . . well, as I said, I need Walsingham's advice.'

'If I were you,' said Brockley, 'I would go to the queen first. She is caught up in this, after all. It's her possible marriage with Alençon that is at the heart of it all. Your captors seem to think that the marriage would be a good thing.'

'Yes, and I don't agree with them, though it's her business, not mine,' I said. 'That doesn't mean I don't realize that Mary is a menace. She's been that for years! But to . . . to murder her! I can't!'

'Maybe someone else could,' said Dale, quite matter-of-factly. I supposed that over the years, my people had become inured to strange and even violent situations. From her tone, Dale might just as well have been saying, *Perhaps, this time, someone else could make the pastry, rub the mare down, bring in the washing.* 'Maybe Walsingham could arrange it,' she said. 'It wouldn't matter who, surely, ma'am.'

'I'm quite sure he'd do no such thing!' I said. 'He's a man for the law. Really, Dale!'

'It'd be a way out,' remarked Gladys.

I began to fear that contact with me and my curious calling had contaminated my associates. More desperately than ever, I needed advice, but it had better not be theirs.

'I will have to see him, or the queen, or both. Yes, that's

clear enough. I'll go to the court tomorrow. I believe the queen is at Greenwich just now.'

'There's something else,' said Brockley sturdily.

'Yes?'

'Well, wouldn't it be best of all if we found Harry ourselves and rescued him? I think we should try.'

'They said they had ways of keeping watch on me,' I said.

'Are you thinking of Laurence Miller?' Brockley asked.

'Yes, I am. Though we can't be sure. He lied about Woking but maybe he really was just seeing a paramour in Guildford.' I rubbed my forehead. My brain felt as though it needed encouragement. 'He can't keep a very close watch on me, can he? He doesn't live in this house, or even come close to it very often.'

'No. But he knows those who do. He can learn, in a casual fashion, a good deal about your movements. He may well be our man.' Brockley ran a tired hand over his gold-freckled forehead. 'If only we could be more certain. Bullying him won't work. I've already tried it! I will try to make sure someone keeps an eye on him.'

'Well, he's welcome to know that I have gone to Greenwich,' I said. 'Walsingham is usually with the court; if Miller is a spy, and through him that news gets back to Miller's unpleasant employers, they'll suppose I went to see him to arrange a visit to Sheffield and that's what they want. If I go to Greenwich, that should keep Harry safe for the time being, at least. Let Miller, if he is the spy, do all the reporting he likes. For now.'

'Tell me, madam,' said Brockley, 'how long was the journey between the house where you were held and our woodlands? And could you sense the direction? That might give us a start.'

We mulled that over, but without any very definite result. Gladys gave me another potion that night, and once more, I slept.

In the morning, with Brockley as my escort, and Dale once more uneasily perched on Firefly's pillion, I set off for Greenwich.

* * *

I was not expected and so could not be sure that we could be accommodated. Therefore, we found an inn not far from Greenwich Palace, left the horses there and continued on foot. We found that I had guessed right. As the queen's half-sister, I was a privileged person to some extent, but no, there was no accommodation for us, and worse, neither Elizabeth nor Walsingham could see me yet, either. The French embassy had arrived, complete with a full suite of aides and servants, and were still with the court.

I decided to see Elizabeth first, if I could, but I had to wait another three days before I was granted an audience.

On the morning of that third day, I saw the French visitors take their leave, by river, a major operation with a string of ornamental barges and numerous servants carrying baggage down from the palace. On the following morning, a message came that the queen would receive me. She saw me alone, as she usually did. Dale and Brockley were left to wait in an anteroom while she had me shown into her private study. It overlooked the river, though the leaded window had such thick glass panes that it had to be open before one could see out of it. There were numerous candle-stands, so that Elizabeth could work there after dark if she so wished. There were some tapestries, and a spinet, and a polished wooden floor, and a settle as well as a desk and some chairs. She sat down on the settle and I remained standing until she waved me to a chair.

'Well, Ursula. What news? I gather that you have been persistent in seeking to visit me, so I take it that something is on your mind.'

I told her my tale. She listened without interrupting, her eyes searching my face as though trying to read more in it than I was telling her with my tongue. When I reached the dreadful errand that was the price of Harry's freedom, she nodded.

'I wondered what was coming. It seemed plain, before you actually said it, that Harry was to be a lever to force something on you. I thought at first that they were going to ask you to assassinate me! So their target is Mary. Well, well.'

She got up and walked restlessly about the room. I twisted on my chair, to follow her with my eyes. Once again, she was wearing loose, informal clothes, but her skirts, of ash-grey brocade, swept the floor as she walked.

Abruptly, she said: 'Mary is a fool, with her ambitions. Her health is not good. Suppose she did manage to have me murdered and managed to seize my throne? How long would she live to occupy it and who is to come after her when she dies? Unlike me, she has an heir of her own body, a lawful son. But he is in Scotland, being brought up as a Protestant and at the moment he is *my* heir as well as hers. What use is Mary to the Catholic world if she cannot pass her religion on to her successor? The woman has no sense at all.'

'But she does still have her ambitions,' I said grimly.

Elizabeth was silent then for some moments. She went to the window and pushed it open, letting in the smell of the river and the cry of gulls that had flown upstream from the sea. There were always ships at anchor close to the queen's riverside palaces, and where there are ships, there are pickings in the water for hungry seabirds. I watched my sister in silence, wondering what thoughts were in her head.

Eventually, without turning round, she said: 'The French embassy are anxious for the marriage to go ahead, and they did indeed express fears about Mary. Suppose the wretched woman did seize my throne. She would need outside help, which has to mean Spanish help. Which would mean war. She could not take the crown without it. And suppose she then reigned, re-imposed the Catholic religion on England, and in due course died, as we all must. What do you imagine would happen then, Ursula?'

I was puzzled. 'Her son would be her heir.'

'Her Protestant son. How would Spain react to that, I wonder?'

'Dear God!' I suddenly saw what she meant. 'I think Spain would intervene. If King Philip were still alive, he might try to take England over himself. But if Mary's son James had supporters . . . there would be another war!'

'There would indeed.' Elizabeth swung round and looked at me with an extraordinary triumph in her golden-brown eyes and suddenly I had a horrible feeling that I had somehow walked into a trap.

'My marriage with Francis *would* be a protection against Mary,' Elizabeth said. 'But he seems to feel that if he pursues the matter, he would need protection against *her.* The French government seem to agree – the embassy I have just hosted asked innumerable questions about her; how close she is kept, whether visitors or letters or gifts are allowed to her. De Simier has returned to France. His visit here was private and he left before the French embassy arrived – to tell his master what you told me at our last meeting. As I said, his government want the match but it remains to be seen whether Francis will come to me – or not.'

'Do you want him to?' I found myself asking.

She had turned back to the window. 'One cause of anxiety is removed. It is no longer at all likely that I can conceive a child. That time is probably past. I am forty-seven and already . . . well, shall we say that certain things have largely ceased though not entirely as yet. That being so, one of the reasons for me to marry is, well, fading, and I wonder now whether Francis will wish to pursue his suit, with or without the threat of Mary, for I believe that he wished for an heir. As do my council,' she added dryly, 'but they are now resigned to disappointment.'

I said nothing. Still gazing out at the river, she said: 'I miss Francis. He is the most interesting, amusing, *intelligent* man I have ever known and he is attractive. Despite his pockmarks, he has magnetism. In me, he rekindled a fire that I thought was dead for ever. It seems that there was still an ember and he has blown it once more into flame. And yet . . .'

She was implying that there had been an earlier flame. I did not ask who had lit that, for I knew. It had been Robin Dudley, of course, now the Earl of Leicester, handsome, flamboyant, adventurous, her playmate in childhood and still her best friend. For the first time, I found myself wondering whether, if only his wife Amy had died naturally, in her bed, Elizabeth might after all have married him.

I doubted it, though. She feared marriage. Her father, King Henry, had condemned her mother to death, and later on, her young stepmother Katherine Howard. Elizabeth had been too young to understand her mother's terror, but she had witnessed Katherine's, and would surely have understood it then. To her, marriage meant placing one's very life in the hands of a man. And then Amy had died, not peacefully and in accordance with nature, but mysteriously, of a broken neck at the foot of a stair.

And Robin Dudley had been suspected of arranging it.

It was not true. I knew that and Elizabeth knew it too but nevertheless, the suspicion had been aroused, and uttered, by a good many people and the old demon had been awakened. *Marriage is dangerous. Men sometimes kill their wives. To be a wife is to be in peril of one's life.*

The demon had never gone back to sleep. Elizabeth might well desire the attractive Duke of Alençon and Anjou. She came, after all, of lusty stock on King Henry's side, and her mother, Anne Boleyn, had by all accounts been nervous, tense, like a well-bred horse, but not cold. But fear could be stronger than desire, and Elizabeth was at times as nervous, as high-strung as her mother had apparently been.

King Henry was my father too, but I had never known him and he had not murdered my mother. I had escaped the fear that haunted Elizabeth.

She swung away from the window and came back to the settle. 'Your captors have tried to simplify things too much. They are as foolish as Mary. They seem to think that with her out of the way the road is clear for the marriage between me and Francis but they are wrong. There is still the feeling in the country, as you yourself have made clear to me. There is the possibility of his hesitation because, as I said, he desires an heir. And there are my own . . . private doubts.'

She paused but I did not speak. I knew what she meant by private doubts but it was not for me to enlarge on them unless she did so first. I waited, listening to the plash of oars on the river and a couple of boatmen shouting to each other.

In a curious, tight voice, Elizabeth said: 'Mary is a menace to me and my entire realm. If she were not there, she couldn't make secret plots with Spain. And there would be no need for this marriage.'

'Majesty, what are you saying?'

But I already knew. I had indeed walked into the trap, with

my too-farsighted vision of England's future if Mary prevailed. Elizabeth had had the same vision. She had meant to lead me into acknowledging it. Into acknowledging the true extent of the danger Mary Stuart posed.

Her fear of marriage was still there. I could see that quite plainly. She might miss Francis, might long for his company, but she wasn't longing for his bed. She was afraid of it. And it was principally Mary who was pushing her towards it.

Her attitude would be a sorry disappointment to my captors. To those who were threatening my son.

Still in that curious voice, as though her throat were constricted, my half-sister, Elizabeth, queen of England, remarked: 'I really wouldn't mind at all if something happened to Mary.'

'You . . . I can't!'

'Your captors are right to wish for it, even though they haven't looked as far ahead as we have,' Elizabeth said. 'She is a danger to all England. If she were to plot successfully and get England invaded by her friends, then our green fields would be soaked with blood twice over. The same applies if she were to be openly murdered. That could draw avengers here. It would have to look like illness or accident.'

She still didn't look at me. 'We certainly don't want Spain arriving with a punitive expedition. But Mary's health isn't good. Something could be arranged, no doubt, and I'm sure you are clever enough to arrange it, Ursula. Think: it would save your son. Walsingham will get you into Sheffield. I will tell him that I wish to install you with Mary to find out what she is or is not doing; how much of a danger she truly represents, to me or to Francis. I shall say it is because of Francis' fears and the embassy's questions that I wish to do this. Walsingham will grumble, because he doesn't approve of my marriage plans, but he will obey. Talbot will be told the same and will be ordered to have you included among Mary's entourage. He has charge of her. He can insist. He will invent some suitable purpose for you.'

She might have been one of Harry's captors. She sounded just like them. I sat there. Silent. Trembling.

She still wouldn't meet my eyes. But she said: 'If you return to Greenwich Palace at this time tomorrow and go to Walsingham's office, the necessary documents to get you into Sheffield Castle will be ready for you. If you choose to use them. You are free to choose, naturally.'

NINE
Playing For Time

When the court was in or near London, Sir Francis Walsingham, Secretary of State, often lived at home and attended court by day. But when it was in the more outlying palaces, such as Greenwich, he went with it, to avoid wasting time on daily travel. In all the palaces, he had an office, usually consisting of an outer room where his subordinate clerks worked, and an inner sanctum where he could have privacy. His suite was always very workaday, full of dusty documents and cupboards which often strained at their latches because of the books and maps and paperwork thrust inside them.

I was at his Greenwich office promptly the next morning, though I was tired. I had had a bad night and had been afraid of having a migraine attack. In times of serious conflict or anxiety, I was liable to such things. However, so far it hadn't happened. I arrived at Greenwich Palace when the dew was barely off the grass and was ushered in without delay; though the Brockleys were not allowed to come with me and were once more left behind in an anteroom.

Walsingham was at his desk, dictating to a clerk, who at a signal from his master withdrew, leaving us alone. Walsingham himself stood up politely to greet me.

He looked as usual, tall, dark of hair and eye, swarthy of complexion, black-robed, intimidating. The queen, who never minded making personal comments about her associates, called him her Old Moor because of his dark skin. He looked tired himself, and I remembered that his younger daughter, Mary, aged seven, had died not long ago. Walsingham, the terror of the queen's enemies, was in private a loving husband and father.

I dropped a curtsey and was waved to a seat. We looked at

each other. Like the queen, who had been known to throw things at him, I trusted Sir Francis Walsingham but didn't like him. In turn, he didn't like me. He didn't consider that women should be engaged in secret missions. Like Sir Edward Heron, he considered that I should put my mind to my stillroom and my needlework and stay out of masculine affairs. The fact that I wished very much to stay out of them but kept on getting forcibly pushed back in never seemed to weigh with him.

I sat down, and said: 'The queen bade me come to you. She said you would have documents ready for me.'

'I have,' said Walsingham grimly. 'Extraordinary ones. The queen, whom I know, at heart, is averse to marriage, nevertheless seems anxious to remove certain barriers to this one, to the Duke of Alençon and Anjou, and because he – and his government, apparently – harbour fears connected with Mary Stuart, you are to be planted in Sheffield to find out how justified these fears are. They would all do better to be afraid of the English Protestants, many of whom greatly desire,' said Walsingham, with savage humour, 'to eat the duke for dinner. They don't at all like the idea of the queen marrying a French Catholic, even a tolerant one. I am not a fool, Mistress Stannard. I smell something amiss here. Something I am not being told. A secret, hidden purpose. *What is going on?*'

I looked at him in alarm. I had not expected this, though perhaps I should have done. He was both experienced and subtle; he could sense, as if through his skin, when something was being kept from him.

'You don't answer. Listen,' said Walsingham, 'I have enough problems to worry me. I don't regard this project of the French marriage as a means of keeping Spain at arm's length; I think it's more likely to provoke King Philip into some kind of attack on us. I also think it's not, at heart, what her majesty desires, and yet I am supposed to promote it. I lie awake at night, sometimes, haunted by these things. And now, the queen is indulging in mysterious moves of her own and not confiding in me. I insist, Mistress Stannard, that you tell me what you know. Otherwise, I will brave the queen's wrath and not release the documents I have for you.'

He was trustworthy. I knew that. I told him.

He listened without interruption and then, when I had fallen silent, said: 'Have you reported your son's disappearance to Sir Edward Heron?'

'Yes. He advised waiting for a ransom demand.'

'He would! Have you reported this further outrage – your own kidnapping?'

'No.'

'Dear heaven, why not? We could have the tale cried in every town in the country! Every honest citizen could be turned into a spy, searching for Harry. We would find him in no time at all! Someone would come to say that a house near them had been hired by strolling players who trundle handcarts about. You were apparently transported in broad daylight! You would have your son back in a week, most likely! What kept you silent? I will order Heron to set it in hand at once!'

'*No!*' I had kept my explanation brief and not mentioned the full details of the hideous threat to Harry. An angry, brazen alarm bell now clanged in my head. 'No, Sir Francis, you must not. You must not! Harry's plight must not be cried in the streets.'

'Why not?'

'They warned me. The people who hold him. I think they are quite ruthless. They call themselves honest citizens and think they are patriots but they are ruthless; I fear them. They warned me that at the first sign that I had put the law on their track – and Harry's abduction being announced in public would be that – they would get him away and carry out their threat to . . . to sell him as a slave, beyond hope of recovery. I don't know what they'd do then, but most likely they'd disperse. They're not really players. I suspect they would just split up and go back to their everyday lives – and then come together again and next time kidnap and threaten someone else, perhaps another member of my household! They threatened that, too. After all, it's me they want to use, because I just might be able to get into Mary's household.'

'I see. Yes, I do see.' Walsingham put his fingers together, placing his palms in an attitude of prayer. He was silent for a few moments, thinking. Then he nodded, as if concluding some private conversation within his head. 'It seems to me,' he said, 'that there are two lines to pursue.'

'Yes?'

'One is that you should play for time. Appear to fall in with their wishes. That means going to Sheffield, though not too hastily. Delay a little if you can. Meanwhile, I will see that Sir Edward Heron does not try to investigate the matter further, or make it public. That is what you want, I imagine?'

'Yes! To protect Harry!'

'And to gain time for you. When you get to Sheffield, make a great show of trying to win Mary's confidence.'

'That could be difficult,' I said dryly. 'The last time I encountered Mary, I prevented her from making a bid to escape from Elizabeth's control. She won't welcome, or trust me.'

'You were obeying your queen's orders. Mary herself is a queen and knows very well what a subject's duties are. You can play on that. Talbot will see that you are placed close to her, somehow, and the rest is up to you. Besides, it is only a pretence. You won't,' said Walsingham, 'actually *need* to win her trust. There is no question of you carrying out your unpleasant task.'

'No, there certainly isn't!' I agreed, earnestly.

'You will need to be careful, though. They may have a spy of their own in Sheffield.'

'They said they had ways of keeping watch on me.'

'Yes. That could mean in Sheffield as well anywhere.'

'Then why,' I said angrily, 'can't their spy carry out their nasty assassination plans?'

'He may be afraid. The penalty would be severe; after all, she is the queen's cousin and under Elizabeth's protection. If the assassin were caught, Elizabeth might have to make an example of him. Or her.'

'Thank you!'

'That, of course, is partly why the queen insists that Mary's death, should it occur, must seem like illness or accident. It isn't just fear of reprisals from Spain; she also wants to protect you.'

But she's still prepared to use me.

I ought to be used to it, but I didn't think I ever would be.

'In seizing Harry,' Walsingham said, 'your captors are employing about the only lever they can think of, to make you risk performing the deed. However, as I said, there is another line to follow, and knowing your past experience and that of your man Roger Brockley, it is perhaps more hopeful than it sounds. That is for Brockley – mostly him, because if you are in Sheffield you can't take part – to find Harry and rescue him and identify his captors, so that the authorities can seize them.'

'Brockley himself has said that. He will set about it the moment we return home.'

'It's a tall order,' said Walsingham. 'But it's our best chance. Whatever happens . . .' and here he studied me very gravely '. . . and whatever the queen may wish, Mary must *not* be assassinated. Any suspicion that her death wasn't natural might indeed bring reprisals.'

He got up and prowled about the room. 'Believe me,' he said, 'if Mary could be caught out, getting herself involved in a serious plot to harm the queen, to bring a foreign army here and snatch the crown, then we could execute her openly and even Philip could hardly complain. He is a king and knows the meaning of treason. One day, I sincerely hope . . . Mary is dangerous, but assassination in the dark isn't the answer.'

Sir Francis Walsingham was shrewd and experienced but although this was not apparent until several years later, he was not quite right. He underestimated Philip's devotion to his religion, and his family feeling, and his dislike of Elizabeth. Once, when she was young, Philip had sought to marry her, but she had refused him. Looking back, I think that he never forgave her. From then on, she was the heretic queen of England, whose mother had ousted Katherine of Aragon, his own relative, from her marriage and her throne. But on this spring day in 1581, the future remained hidden. Mary had not as yet laid herself open to an official executioner, and Harry remained in terrible danger, unless he could be rescued in time.

I said: 'I will do as you say. Go to Sheffield but delay if I can, and set Brockley to the hunt.'

*   *   *

On the way home, I talked earnestly to the Brockleys. 'I see,' said Brockley when I had finished. 'So the queen is sending you to Sheffield to assassinate Mary . . .'

'I shan't *do* it! I can't assassinate anyone!'

'Walsingham says you must gain time as best you can, while I and what helpers I can find have got to find Harry before you are forced into an impossible position. Three months, they said, didn't they?'

'Damn them, they did,' I said.

'And you think that it would be too dangerous to take the obvious route, to let Edward Heron have the news cried in town streets. He'd do that if Walsingham ordered it.'

'And *they* might . . . harm my son,' I said. 'No. *Would* harm him. They meant it. It's Harry I'm thinking of, afraid for, all the time.'

'Oh, ma'am!' said Dale miserably, jolting along on Brockley's pillion.

'All right.' Brockley was frowning, thinking. I looked at him gratefully. He was a reassuring man to have at one's side in an emergency. After a moment, he said: 'I could always try beating Laurence Miller up until he tells what he knows, but I am not at all sure that he *does* know anything. We could be wrong about him.'

He was silent for a while, and we let the horses walk quietly while he ruminated. Then he said: 'Madam, when we found Philip, he was lost and reeling about and he hasn't been able to tell us exactly where the attack took place but we found it when we searched for you, because we found the dogs.'

'Our poor dogs!' I said, and the tears sprang into my eyes.

'We brought them home and buried them,' Brockley said gently. 'But I am wondering, if we were to go to the place where you were seized, you might remember something useful. It's a long chance, but perhaps you would. Can you take us there? Now? And have you any idea, anyway, of which way you were taken – north, south . . . whatever. Could you hear anything that might be a clue?'

I thought, and then shook my head. 'I could hear very little, on either of my journeys on that handcart. The carpet I was wrapped in was too thick.' And stifling and horrible. I wrinkled my nose at the memory. 'I heard faint sounds – hooves, wheels, voices once or twice, but nothing . . . nothing distinctive.'

'Never mind. I think,' said Brockley, 'that we had better go at once to where you were snatched and see if anything stirs your memory. Now, as I said, before we go home.'

I knew the woods round Hawkswood very well and it was easy for me to lead us to the place where disaster had struck. I guided us along the track through the stand of beech trees. I drew us to a halt and pointed at some bushes on the right.

'They sprang out from there,' I said. 'And *there* . . . they dragged me from my saddle and Philip from his and they killed the dogs here! They told me that some things – matters of state, they meant – were more important than the lives of dogs. I think the lives of Goldie and Remus were more important than the lives of those vile plotters!' I swallowed hard. 'We will have to buy some new dogs, and look after them better!'

'I suggest, madam, that you enquire if your friend Mistress Ferris, at White Towers, has any young dogs for sale. I believe she and her husband are breeding half-mastiffs in a serious way, these days.'

'Yes, they are,' I said distractedly. Christina Ferris was a very old friend. I had helped to promote the marriage between her and Thomas Ferris, and that was the occasion on which I had first met and crossed swords with Sir Edward Heron. And yes, of course we must replace the dogs. I hoped that the Ferrises would be able – and willing – to help over that. My unusual way of life had caused the death of a dog before, and that dog, too, had come from White Towers. I was beginning to feel that I was a dangerous person to be attached to, whether one was a dog or a servant – or even a son.

But just now, I must think only of Harry. I brushed away my tears and leant over Jewel's shoulder, staring at the ground. It was noticeably trampled on both sides of the track, which was no help at all. Brockley, however, was moving slowly on along the track, looking at the ground. 'There's something here,' he called.

I followed him, and came up beside him. 'What have you found?'

'Sign,' said Brockley, and pointed. 'It's a different time of day from when the woods were searched for you,' he said. 'That was late morning; this is late afternoon. The light is different. No one saw those marks then, but they're there.'

He was right. The traces were very faint, but the sunlight filtering through the trees was now at the right angle to light them up. There were trodden weeds on the edge of the track, one or two barely discernible footprints, and yes, one unmistakable wheel-mark.

Brockley looked up and around. 'The traces lead north. What's north of here? The village of Priors Ford . . . Did you go through a village, would you say? Madam, please *think*.'

I tried. I did remember a few things. 'I believe we did, yes. We went over cobbles, I think. Not for long, but I'm sure we did. It could have been Priors Ford.'

'And how long were you on the cart after that?'

'Eternity,' I said.

Brockley smiled, but grimly. Dale said: 'Oh, Roger, you mustn't harass the mistress so!'

'He has to,' I said, dragging at my memory. 'It seemed a long time. But ten minutes would seem a long time to anyone wrapped in a carpet and jolting along on a cart. And when we did get to the house where I was held, I never saw the outside of it, not the front, anyway. I did see the back. It was very ordinary but I think it was fairly big. If we could find out what houses have been bought or rented lately, in an arc round Priors Ford . . . we might not have gone straight on northwards. I couldn't tell about that.'

'Adam Wilder was born at Hawkswood,' Brockley said. 'He knows the country for miles around, has known it all his life. He knows every house for miles, as well. If you agree, I'll consult with him and take him with me, and my name isn't Roger Brockley if we don't find the right place soon. Though it will probably be empty,' he added. 'Having got rid of you, I doubt if they would stay where they were. They evidently had another base, since you say they told you that Harry was in a different house.'

'Yes,' I said.

'But we might find out something about the enemy's further

movements,' Brockley said. 'A party of strolling players with
a handcart would surely be noticed by someone. Well, we can
but try. Meanwhile, let us make for home.'

Once we were home, I was overtaken by exhaustion and told
Dale that I wished to retire at once. It was already nearly
supper time. Dale saw me to bed. I settled under the covers
and abruptly, taking even myself by surprise, burst into tears.

Dale sat down on the edge of the bed and put her arms
round me. 'Ma'am, please don't. Don't take on like this. It
will be all right. Roger will find Harry and bring him home,
I am sure he will. Try to believe that. Do please try.'

'It's a nightmare!' I tried, through my tears, to explain. 'I
can't kill someone in cold blood! How can I? It's impossible,
I could never make myself do such a thing, not in a million
years, and even if I could, I wouldn't dare. If I couldn't make
it look natural or accidental, then I would be brought to justice.
This is England! The law would have to be upheld. The queen
couldn't let it be publicly said that she had connived at murder.
And yet, there's Harry and what will happen to him if we
don't rescue him in time! I feel as though I'm going out of
my mind. I'm being attacked by a weapon of many prongs.
Whichever way I turn . . . whichever way I turn . . .'

'I am going to fetch Gladys,' said Dale with decision. 'She
must give you one of her draughts, to get you to sleep. That's
what you need, ma'am, most of all. Sleep.'

She fetched the draught and I drank it and not greatly to
my surprise or anyone else's, woke up in the morning with
the migraine I had been fearing and expecting. I usually
managed to overcome these attacks within one day but this
time, although Gladys brewed me a whole series of soothing
potions I only threw them up. It took me a full two days to
recover.

Brockley said he had let it be known as widely as possible
that I was ill; in particular, he had let Laurence Miller know
it. He hoped that the news would reach the ears of my captors,
so that they would understand that for the time being I could
not travel to Sheffield or anywhere else. It would gain us time,
just a little time.

Meanwhile, he and Adam Wilder were going to the district north of Hawkswood, to investigate houses. After some thought, I sent my youngest groom, Eddie, with them. Eddie had come to work for me five years before, when he was only sixteen. Then, he had been shy and nervous, though not of the horses. But those five years had changed him. He was twenty-one now, a vigorous, bright and even, on occasion, a slightly saucy young man. He kept his dark hair tidily short but because it was wiry hair, it tended to stick up in unexpected spikes, which somehow reflected his nature.

He was also athletic and strong, and quick-thinking. Eddie could well be useful, I thought.

TEN

A House Without Dogs

They were to work discreetly. Even through the agony of my headache and the turbulence in my stomach, I managed to make that clear. Brockley and Wilder must find the house if they could but the idea that its tenants – or recent tenants – were criminals must not be bruited about.

'I shall be amazed if they're still in the house where I was taken,' I said. 'But we have to begin somewhere. You had better make enquiries – at inns and so on – about strolling players. Say that we want to find them again to ask for a repeat performance because we enjoyed their show so much. Ask if anyone knows of a house that was occupied by strolling players for a while. Say they gave the impression that they had a base out towards the north of Hawkswood. But make sure that you only make such enquiries from people who don't know who you are.'

'And if we find the house and they *are* still there?' Brockley asked.

'I doubt it,' I said. 'I doubt that very much. But if it happens . . .' My voice trailed off for a moment. My head felt as though a hammer were pounding it, just over my left eye. Thinking was painful. 'If they are still there,' I said, 'I want them watched. Eddie can carry reports to me while you and Wilder stay on guard. It will need two of you for that. Find a room or an inn nearby, and then one of you can watch the house by day and the other by night. If you see them preparing to move, follow them. They may lead us to Harry. Go armed. Just in case. You and Wilder can handle swords; find a dagger for Eddie.'

The three of them set off, and I rested on my pillows and strove to recover. They returned that evening, having had no success, and rode off again the next morning. During that second day, my headache did gradually subside and I stopped throwing up. Once more, they came home with no success to report, but there was a good deal of ground to cover and quite a number of possible houses not yet investigated. Perhaps the third day would be bring good luck.

That night, I slept fairly well and woke feeling better. Migraine, once it had gone, sometimes left me feeling weak, but this never lasted. Normal health would reappear with astonishing speed. I took some breakfast and not only kept it down, but wanted it. Having eaten, I felt a desire for fresh air and went outside, into a bright May morning, taking with me a carrot to give to my mare, Jewel. I found the groom Simon wisping her. Her coat was glossy and becoming glossier still under his ministrations but his face was unhappy.

'These are sad times, Simon,' I said, as I presented the carrot. 'Wilder, Brockley and Eddie are out on a search for Harry and we hope we may find him, but . . . we are all drowning in worry.'

'All the worse for losing the dogs, madam,' Simon said gloomily. It was usually his business to feed them. 'Bad enough about Master Harry, but the dogs as well! Arthur and I saw to burying them, madam; a sorry business. And now – well, a house without dogs isn't properly alive, to my mind.'

'You're right.' I had felt it myself as I crossed the courtyard and no lively canine friends had come bouncing to meet me as they usually did. Yes, something must be done about that. And although I had written to the Ferrises at White Towers, I ought to see them for myself. 'Simon, finish Jewel as soon as you can. I shall need her.'

'I will, madam,' Simon said earnestly. I smiled at him, though smiling at all, at anyone, for any reason, was an effort. I returned to the house and paused in the hall, thinking. Then I went upstairs to the room that had been – no, was – Harry's schoolroom. I had guessed right. Philip Sandley was there, sitting at the table, busy writing. He looked up as I entered.

'Mistress Stannard! I was just . . . well, my pupil isn't here but I can at least be ready for him when he comes back. I am roughing out a series of arithmetic lessons for him.'

'How are you now?' I asked. 'How is your head? I see you've got rid of your bandage.'

'I am all right, I think. Perhaps still a little shaken, but the headache has gone. It faded quite quickly.'

'Could you manage to ride, do you think? Slowly, at ease. But I want to visit the Ferrises at White Towers – where we went when we first searched for Harry, if you remember. The Ferrises breed dogs and nearly always have some for sale. We need dogs here. And since Remus and Goldie . . .' My voice shook.

Philip smiled, but in a kindly way, and for a moment, I saw his father, the young Brockley, look out of his eyes. If the world had been different, if circumstances had been different, Brockley and I, who had once so nearly become lovers, could have had a son like Philip. I pushed this foolish thought away. 'I should like company,' I said.

He stoppered his ink jar and laid his quill aside. 'Of course I'll come,' he said.

It was good to be mounted and riding gently through the woods. Dread and sorrow gnawed at me but when all was said and done, Harry was not dead and somehow – I was determined on it – we would get him back home. Remus and Goldie were gone, which was painful to think about, but there would be new dogs soon, to love and play with. Things would come right in the end, said the bright, cool May sunlight and the piping of blackbirds, the murmur of wood doves and the soft thud of hooves on leaf mould.

At White Towers, Christina came hurrying out into the courtyard to meet us. I looked at her with affection. She had been married for over ten years now and had three children. Two others had died in babyhood, which was a common misfortune, but the trio of survivors were thriving. Her marriage to Thomas Ferris had put an end to a long-standing feud between their two families, and she had in fact chosen well, for big, broad-shouldered Thomas was a kind and sensible man.

During their courtship, Christina had had smallpox, which had spoiled her face, but where many young men would have turned away from a girl so badly pockmarked, Thomas appeared hardly to notice. He had merely told her that she still had her beautiful beechnut-brown hair and sparkling dark eyes and that they were enough for him. She had them yet, and her pocks seemed to have eroded with time. They were much less noticeable than they had been. Now, as she came quickly to greet me, it was the look of welcome and question in her expressive eyes that I noticed.

She burst into speech as soon as Philip and I had dismounted. 'Ursula! We had your note, so we knew that you were safe home again. Knowing that you are sometimes involved in secret matters, we guessed – we had already guessed – that you wouldn't want idle talk. There has been none. Thomas and I have made that clear to all our household. But oh, Ursula, what *happened*? Is there any news of Harry? Come inside. We can't talk easily out here in the courtyard.'

We followed her into the great hall, where she invited us to sit down. The big hall of White Towers had changed a lot since I first saw it, years ago. White Towers had been a legacy from Thomas's parents, who had had ambitious notions and had made their hall pretentious. It had had little colour in it, for they thought bright colours frivolous, and the furniture had been over-impressive, the table and sideboard so massive that there was hardly enough room to pass between them. Somehow, they made even the air feel heavy.

But the older generation of Ferrises had died, and Christina and Thomas had a cheerful attitude to life. The walls now were bright with tapestries of hunting scenes, showing gaily dressed people on bay and chestnut horses riding through a woodland full of light green leaves, and the furniture was smaller and more convenient and veneered in some golden coloured wood. The weather was bright but not so very warm, so there was a fire, round which the three of us now gathered.

Christina said: 'You can trust our discretion. But please, tell me what you can.'

'We can't, or very little,' Philip said. 'Isn't that so, Mistress Stannard?'

'Yes, it is,' I said. I looked frankly at Christina. 'I was seized, and then released, and please forgive me, Christina, but I must not tell you more because if I do, I could put Harry in danger.

Please leave it there. I came today to make doubly sure about
your discretion, but also about something quite different. When
I was seized, the dogs that were with me and Philip here were
killed by my attackers. Remus and Goldie. They were lovely
dogs. We need replacements. I was hoping you had a suitable
litter and were willing to sell.'

There was a pause, before Philip said kindly: 'We do take
care of our dogs. What happened to Remus and Goldie was
just . . . an unexpected tragedy.'

'I do lead an unsafe life,' I admitted, recalling the previous
occasion when one of my dogs had died because of my work.
'But I will do my best to make sure that nothing happens to
any more dogs of mine. Can you help, Christina? I don't want
small puppies, but young animals just out of puppyhood.'

Christina smiled. 'We know you care for your animals. All
your dogs and horses look well fed. I was just thinking over
the possibilities. In fact, we have two different litters where the
puppies are now at the right age to leave home. If you have
one from each, a dog and a bitch, they won't be related, and
you can breed from them. Oh, Thomas!'

Clad in breeches and boots and a loose jacket over an open
shirt, her husband had just come into the hall. He removed
the dashing green hat he was wearing, bowed to us, and after
throwing the hat onto the table, pulled up a stool and came
to join us by the hearth.

'You want new dogs? I heard you, just now. I'm sure we
can help.' His eyes searched my face. 'Is there any news of
Harry?'

'Brockley and Wilder are pursuing enquiries. But as I said
in the note I sent, it is essential that as few people as possible
know about either Harry's abduction or mine. For Harry's own
sake. I can't say any more.'

'I understand. But if we can help in any way, please call
on us.'

Philip said: 'Mistress Stannard, could we not at least ask
about the strolling players?'

I rubbed my forehead, where, for a moment a twinge had
reminded me of my recent migraine. 'I suppose so.' I looked
at Thomas and Christina. 'Without going into details about

why I am asking, could you tell me, earlier this year, did you
by any chance have a visit from a group of strolling players
– all quite young, and one of them a red-haired girl? We did,
and I would like to find them again.'

'Good heavens!' said Thomas.

'What is it?' I asked.

Christina turned to me. 'They did indeed come here, some
time ago now. And we know where they are now,' she said.
'We have let my great-uncle's house to them.'

I looked at the two of them in astonishment. 'Your great-uncle's
house? I didn't even know you had a great-uncle! What do
you mean?'

'Those players came here,' said Christina. 'In April some
time. They performed for us one evening. They were staying
in a Woking inn but they said their quarters were cramped
and they wanted to hire a house somewhere within fairly
easy reach of Woking and Guildford and Leatherhead. They
said that was how they went about things – choosing a
district, establishing a base in the middle of it and then
working through all the possible households, before moving
on. Isn't that right, Thomas?'

'Yes. And as it happened,' said Thomas, 'we could help
them, because of Christina's great-uncle Robert.'

'He was my mother's uncle,' said Christina. 'He died only
a few weeks ago. Most of his money went to his manservant
and there were small bequests as well to people who did the
garden and cleaned, but I was his only surviving relative, so
he left the house and its contents to me. We never saw much
of him when he was alive; he wasn't married and he wasn't
sociable, either. He lived alone except for the manservant. We
were still wondering what to do with the house when these
players appeared, and we saw a way of using it.'

'If we let it to them on a temporary basis,' said Thomas, 'it
would be occupied, and we would make some money from
it, and we could take our time over deciding what to do with it
eventually – sell it or keep on renting it out. It might be useful
for one of the children, later. So we offered to lease it to the
players for three months and they accepted gladly. I think they

moved in almost at once – the place was furnished, you see. We had been to see it but we didn't remove anything.'

'What is it called?' I asked. 'And where is it?'

'Heath House, it's called,' said Thomas. 'It's in a dip in those low hills between Ashtead and Epsom. It isn't old. Christina's great-uncle only bought it three years ago – isn't that right, Christina? It was newly built, then.'

'That's so,' said Christina, nodding.

'We'll find it,' said Philip. 'It shouldn't be difficult.'

'Oh, we can give you directions,' said Christina easily. 'About halfway between Ashtead and Epsom – the market town; you know it, I suppose – there's a track leading off to the left. It goes uphill and down dale and across some common land and then it forks. The left fork goes to Priors Ford and the other straight on to Heath House.'

She rose to her feet. 'But I imagine that you won't be rushing off there instantly! You must stay and dine with us. And, of course, you have to choose your new dogs.'

She moved towards the door and as she did so, because she wasn't wearing a farthingale, I noticed her waistline. 'Christina!' I said. 'Are you expecting again?'

She and Thomas both laughed. 'In the autumn,' said Christina. 'We hope for a son.' Her face grew suddenly sad. 'I have Edward and his two sisters, but the two that died were both boys. Well, you know what happened. All the children had the scarlet fever together. Edward and the girls pulled through; Johnny and Hal did not. They were the youngest, too small to fight back, perhaps.'

'I hope you'll get your wish,' I said and Philip said kindly: 'We will pray for you.'

We rode home in the afternoon, accompanied by a weather-beaten, heavily built man who was the Ferris kennelman, and two young half-mastiffs, one dog and one bitch, from different litters, as Christina had said. They were both very beautiful. The young bitch had a coat the colour of ripe wheat – 'Thomas and I both heard stories about the Vikings when we were children, so we decided to call her after a Viking goddess of fertility,' said Christina, laughing. 'She answers to Freya.

The dog is called Prince. He has a princely bearing, don't you think?'

He did. His coat was an unremarkable brown and had some dark stripes, but he had a proud walk. The kennelman came with us on a pony, carrying a basket with spare collars and leads and the toys and blankets that Freya and Prince were used to, so that he could see them settled into their new home.

As we rode back, the pair were allowed to range, just as Goldie and Remus had done on their last day. This time, no one attacked us. I watched my new acquisitions running among the trees and sniffing at roots and undergrowth and felt what I always felt when dogs died and had to be replaced: a wrench at the heart. The transition of affection couldn't take place without that.

Once home, there was the pleasant bustle of introducing the pair to their new kennel and showing them to the grooms, especially Simon, who would be feeding them. The kennelman gave precise instructions about the kind of food that would suit them best. Then we gave him some ale and sent him back to White Towers, and played with Freya and Prince a little, to make them feel at home, and waited impatiently for Brockley and Wilder and Eddie to come back.

They were late and dusk was falling by the time they rode in, looking dispirited and with nothing to report, Brockley said, as they came into the hall, where I was sitting with Sybil and Dale. Philip's headache had returned just after we reached home, and he had gone to his room to rest.

'But we have something!' I announced. 'Sheer chance but what good luck! We know where the house is and what it's called.'

They all looked amazed, including Eddie, who had come into the hall with the others though as he was not indoor staff, he was hanging politely back.

'Heath House,' I said. 'In the hilly common land between Ashtead village and Epsom!' I explained about Christina's legacy from her great-uncle, and the way she and Thomas were now using it.

'Heath House?' Wilder was puzzled. 'I've never heard of it,

and I thought I knew most of the houses in that district. That's odd.'

'Well, we know how to get to it,' I said, and repeated Christina's instructions.

While I was talking, Eddie's eyes were widening. 'I know it! I'm sure I do! I called there once, on a hot day, to ask for a drink of water. I was exercising one of the horses! We haven't been to that part of the district yet, madam, but . . .' he turned to Wilder '. . . it's quite new, only built a few years ago and it wasn't called Heath House to begin with. It was Vale House at first.'

'Vale House!' Wilder beamed. 'Oh, yes, of course. I do know it! Or used to. Maybe this great-uncle changed the name when he moved in.'

'We had better go and look at it,' I said. 'If we find it and I think it's the right place, we must find out if they're still there and if so, keep watch. If they are gone, perhaps we can get some news of the direction they went in – someone might know, someone who did the garden or delivered food supplies there, or did building repairs. But we *must* be discreet. They mustn't know we are trailing them, because that could be so dangerous to Harry.'

ELEVEN
Dead End

'That must be it,' said Brockley.

We had halted on the crest of a low hill, having advanced warily, using the cover of a woodland patch. We were still under the shadow of the trees as we drew rein, looking down into the small valley below us. Wilder, Brockley and Eddie were my companions. Philip had wanted to come, but had admitted to being headachy again, and Brockley had discouraged the idea.

'You never know, with bangs on the head. You'd better rest until you're properly well again, son. You shouldn't have ridden to White Towers.'

I was a little amused to see how completely Brockley had accepted the responsibilities of fatherhood, and how well the pair of them were getting on.

'Does it look like the right place, madam?' Wilder asked.

'As far as it goes,' I said. 'Thatch, red brick and I can see gable windows. All that's right. It's also ordinary. There are thousands of houses just like that. From what Mistress Ferris said, this ought to be the place but I wish we could risk a closer look.'

'There's no chimney smoke,' Brockley remarked. 'And I can't see anyone in the grounds.'

'It's a warm morning,' said Eddie. 'I could do as I did before – call and ask for a drink of water. That time, I spoke to a manservant; must have been the old great-uncle's man. He'll be gone by now. If anyone is there at all, it won't be him. But it might be the players. Anyhow, I think I could find out.'

'All right,' I said. 'Go along, then. Be careful. You're out exercising one of my horses and you're thirsty. That's *all*.'

'I wonder if we're wise.' As we watched Eddie ride off, Brockley was uneasy. 'They could have seen that lad when they came to Hawkswood. If they're there, they *might* recognize him.'

'He can still be out exercising a horse and feeling thirsty,' I said. 'I doubt if they'll harm him unless he shows too much curiosity and I think he has more sense. But . . .' a new idea occurred to me '. . . if they do recognize Eddie as a Hawkswood man, well, that might make them decide to move. And if we're on the watch and follow them – we just might find Harry. One has to take a chance sometimes, and seize a chance if it offers.'

'You, madam, have taken chances so often that I often wonder you're still alive!' said Brockley candidly.

Wilder said: 'I hope that lad comes back safely, that's all.'

He need not have worried. Eddie was back in a very short time, shaking his head. 'There's no one there; I'll take my oath on it. No answer to my knock, no sounds from inside. I put my ear to the door and yes, I did venture to peep in at a window. There was a room inside with tables and benches and things and a hearth, but no fire in it, not that that's odd, on a warm day like this, but everything looked somehow – like it wasn't being used.'

I considered for a moment and then said: 'Let's go closer. If I can, I want to make sure that it really is the right place.'

'*That's* taking a chance,' Brockley demurred.

'Not so much of one, with you three beside me,' I said. 'And we're all armed.' As I spoke, I touched my riding skirt, and felt the hidden pouch, and the outline within it of my own small dagger.

'True,' said Brockley. And then his eyes gleamed. It was as it had so often been in the past. Brockley was protective of me and did not really approve of my way of life, and yet, when it came to the point, he would suddenly spark into adventurousness. 'And if by chance we do find any of them there . . . yes, I suggest herding them at sword-point into one room and locking it, and keeping just one of them – the ring-leader you told us about, madam, if he's there – in our hands, and making him talk, also at sword-point.'

'I fancy he will,' Wilder agreed, glancing thoughtfully at Brockley.

'Oh, he will. He'll spill beans in abundance, like a kitchen maid who has tripped over the kitchen cat,' Brockley assured him.

'Assuming she's carrying a crock of beans and not a bowl of eggs!' remarked Eddie. 'That would just make a mess!' Whereupon we all laughed and as one, we urged our horses on and went at a canter down the sloping path before us.

Heath House was surrounded by a fence, which by the look of it embraced not only a small front garden but a fair-sized garden at the rear. I recalled that the room I had slept in during my captivity had had a view of a rear garden. To the right of the house, there was an open archway which seemed to offer access to the property. We rode through.

We found ourselves in a small stable yard. There were no horses to be seen. Another open archway to the left led us into a paved yard, with the back garden to the right, and the back of the house to the left. Glancing at it, I saw the windows I recalled, including the gable windows peeping out of the thatched roof. Such things were certainly features common to many houses but there in front of me was the shed which was the necessary house. Pulling up, I slid out of my saddle, handing my reins to Eddie.

'Wait here.' I went into the shed. It was dim inside but I left the door open and stooped to look at the right-hand wall, low down. My red chalk square was there. I backed out and shut the door after me. 'It's the right place,' I said. 'I left a mark. Do we go in? Maybe they've left a window unlocked somewhere.'

Wilder, however, had also dismounted and had been trying door and windows. 'They haven't, madam,' he said.

'We can try,' I said hopefully. 'I have my picklocks with me.'

But the picklocks failed me. I tried them on the back door, but though the lock turned, the door remained fastened, and felt as though it had a bolt inside. However, there was a fairly big mullioned window giving on to the room where I had been a reluctant dinner guest and been told of my hideous assignment.

I peered through the glass and said: 'There's a latch here and if we can just get at that, we can probably open this window. I think we should. This is serious business, to do with saving Harry and an assassination plot. Go on, Brockley.

Get us in. If anyone pounces on us, it will most likely be *them.*
We have no need to justify ourselves to the people who have
kidnapped Harry and we can pay the Ferrises for any damage
we commit.'

'Very well, madam,' said Brockley and without hesitation
used his sword-hilt to break one pane of glass so that he
could put a hand in and lift the window latch. We left Eddie
to hold the horses while the rest of us climbed in. I was
wearing a very simple dress, not too full, with no ruff or
farthingale, and with Wilder's help I was able to manage the
scramble quite well.

Inside, the house was silent. We had made a good deal of
noise when we broke in, but if anyone were lurking indoors,
they hadn't come to investigate. Keeping together, we moved
from room to room, finding nothing but basic furnishings,
mostly in need of dusting. The ground floor was empty and
there didn't seem to be a cellar. Cautiously, we climbed the
stairs.

We found the room where I had slept. The bed was stripped
of coverings, though its hangings were still there. By the
look of things, the players had taken away whatever items
they had brought with them, but left the things they had
found already there.

It was much the same in the other bedchambers. We found
a half-used candle beside one bed and a jug containing some
stale water beside another but nothing to suggest present occupation. We went up to the attics, where the windows poked
out of the thatch. These were not furnished as bedchambers,
but seemed to be storerooms. One had some spare bedlinen
on shelves and some stools and benches roughly stacked
together; the other was empty but had scuff marks in the dust
on its plank floor. It had perhaps been used to house some of
the players' equipment.

There was no one to be found, and nor was there any indi-
cation of where the erstwhile tenants might have gone. I poked
and peered, looking under pillows and pallets and in drawers,
in case I might find a forgotten letter or sketch map or other
document in which there was useful information but there was
nothing.

'We've found the house,' Brockley said at last. 'But it can't tell us anything at all. What now, madam?'

'We go home,' I said. 'And I think I must go to Sheffield and at least give the impression of . . . preparing to do as I am asked.'

I was silent for a moment after that, remembering that Sheffield Castle was where Sir George Talbot, Earl of Shrewsbury was living, and where I would once more encounter his amorous clerk Russell Woodley, who might, quite possibly, pursue me again. Well, I would just have to cope with him. I had more important matters on my mind.

'Somehow or other, before it's too late,' I said to Brockley, 'you must – you *must* – find Harry!'

TWELVE
Sheffield Castle

I t was over a hundred and seventy miles to Sheffield. My late husband Hugh had, when young, travelled a good deal in England and had left maps that gave useful information about routes and distances. It took six days to get there, though that was to the good, since every one of those days represented another stretch of time during which Brockley and Wilder just might manage to trace Harry.

One thing that helped to slow the journey down was the fact that I took Hugh's old coach. Coach travel is always slower than horseback. Though I didn't take the coach just to provide time; it was a practical necessity. Dale was to come with me but nowadays she wasn't equal to a long journey on horseback, still less in the wet and windy weather which had now set in. She was apt to take cold.

Besides, I must take my court dresses, since I was paying a visit to a noble house and would have to attend on Mary Stuart, who was a queen, albeit a dispossessed one. Some of my gowns were therefore elaborate, especially the ones designed for the open ruffs which were so much in fashion. I never felt that they suited me very well, but they were certainly elegant and a good way to display one's necklaces. I would have needed the coach for the luggage, anyway. I also wanted to take ample funds with me and was glad enough not to have to carry a heavy money-bag personally. I felt reasonably sure that even the most suspicious of secret watchers could not wonder that I had encumbered myself with a coach.

In my luggage too, tied into a leather pouch and hidden at the bottom of a packed hamper, was the phial of hemlock that my captors had given me. Just in case.

Brockley must remain behind, to continue the search for Harry, and of my four grooms, Simon and Joseph were married with small children and would not want to be taken away for too long, while Arthur Watts, the senior groom, was getting on in years. Eddie, however, was young and fit. I told Simon that he must now assist Brockley and Wilder in their search for Harry, while Eddie came with me as groom and coach driver. The coach had only Dale as a passenger, for I intended to ride my mare Jewel. But I decided that we only needed a two-horse coach team. That way, Eddie would not have too many horses to look after.

The weather also helped us to keep our journey slow, for we were plagued on the way with all the bad-weather hazards of coach travel, such as wheels getting stuck in muddy ruts and flooded fords where one had to take detours to find better ones, or bridges. However, the wind and rain relented on the sixth day and we arrived at Sheffield on a sunny May afternoon.

So here we were at last, rolling up the final stretch of track towards the castle, which reared above the town, menacing in its power. It had been founded by Norman barons and they knew how to create castles that could dominate. Yet it had pleasant surroundings. Two rivers met close by and the castle stood on the west bank of one and the south bank of the other. Sheffield town was below it on one side but otherwise there was parkland all about, with trees and meads and grazing cattle and, in the distance, the square, grey shape of the modern manor house, with the tall, ornamental chimneys which I had learned – from Hugh, who had taught me so much – were an architectural signature of our times.

I was jogging along beside the coach and now leant down to tap on the window. Dale opened it and looked out. Her face was wan. Even travelling by coach tired her. 'Are we nearly there, ma'am?'

'Five minutes away, no more.'

'Thank goodness. I hope they let us in without a fuss. I can't abide fusses when I'm tired,' said Dale.

'I have the credentials Walsingham supplied,' I said.

'You know what some people are like,' grumbled Dale. 'They peer and examine and tell you to wait while they consult someone else. It's all meant to show how important they think they are.'

'I hope that won't happen this time,' I said with feeling. I was tired too and I could tell that the coach horses, Bronze and Rusty, were just as weary.

We need not have worried. Walsingham had smoothed our path for us. We were admitted without difficulty. Eddie went off to see the horses unharnessed and stabled, while Dale and I were met by a dignified steward, passed promptly to a page, and taken without further delay to the presence of Sir George Talbot.

As we were escorted through the castle, I caught glimpses of the world I was about to join. We passed a doorway into a fine great hall, with a lofty painted ceiling and a big stone hearth and a long, polished table in the middle. I caught sight of a couple of ladies seated at it and examining lengths of fabric.

A narrow stair opposite the doorway vanished upwards and round a corner to somewhere out of sight. The page, a bright-eyed and freckled lad of about sixteen, smartly dressed and barbered but with a marked country accent, seeing that I had paused to look at it, said respectfully: 'That do lead to Her Grace Mary Stuart's quarters, madam. We address her as Her Grace. Up there's her private rooms. She do have a household of her own. There's thirty folk here to serve her. She do be a queen, after all.' He sounded impressed.

We were shown up a different staircase and into a small, cluttered, badly lit room. Like many castles dating from stormy past centuries, Sheffield had some immensely thick walls with small chambers hollowed out of them, and this was an example. Sir George Talbot seemed to be using this one as a study, since he was sitting at a table with a branched candlestick at his elbow to improve on the light from the two narrow windows, and writing figures into a ledger.

'Mistress Stannard and Mistress Brockley, sir,' said the page, with his accent carefully moderated, and with that, he left us. Talbot stood up and bowed. We curtsied.

'So here you are.' He recognized me, for we had met at court, more than once. I didn't know his age but he looked as though he must be in his fifties. He was tall and thin, with a long, melancholy face, solemn hazel eyes, a thick brown beard and – which was usual with him – a most expensive doublet. This one was white satin with a small, busy pattern on it in silver thread. He looked round him, for all the world as though he didn't quite know what furniture he had in his own study, noticed a padded stool and signed to me to sit down. Dale remained standing beside me.

'Welcome, Mistress Stannard,' he said. 'I was expecting you. And this is . . .?' He looked vaguely at Dale. He had seen her before, of course, but obviously hadn't paid much heed to my attendant.'

'Frances Brockley,' I said. 'My personal maid and also my friend, Sir George.'

'Who else is with you?'

'Only my groom, Eddie Summers. He is tending our horses.'

'Just the three of you. That's a mercy. What with Her Grace's retinue and my own people, this castle is bursting at every point.' He sat down again. 'Mistress Stannard, I don't know very much of what this is all about. I have received – well, orders – from Sir Francis Walsingham. My wife, the Countess of Shrewsbury, has also received orders. Bess is to declare that you are here at her invitation, and to bring you into contact with Her Grace, Mary Stuart. In fact, I understand, you are here to act as a spy on behalf of the queen. There is some new suspicion surrounding Mary Stuart, apparently. Sir Francis has given me no details.'

I nodded, impressed by Walsingham's ingenuity. I was to be brought into contact with Mary, apparently at the request of the Countess. All sociable, normal and open, whatever Mary might think of it.

'I would have preferred,' said Sir George huffily, 'to be given more details of this new suspicion, but if Sir Francis Walsingham doesn't see fit to supply them, I know there is little I can do.'

Carefully, I said: 'Walsingham gives his orders and that's that. I know little more than you.' I was sure that he had given orders to Sir Edward Heron as well, as indeed, he had said he would. I had heard nothing from Heron, which suggested that he had taken no action. He might not like me, but the disappearance of a young boy was serious and if no ransom demand was forthcoming then he would surely have taken steps of some kind eventually. If he hadn't, Walsingham was almost certainly the reason.

Talbot was nodding. 'My wife and I will do our best to carry out his orders. Though I can't speak for Her Grace. As I understand it, you and she have met before but did not part on friendly terms. She may not welcome you and there is little that either the Countess or I can do about that. My wife is here at the moment, again on Walsingham's orders. Bess . . .' he smiled as he used the informality of her first name '. . . usually prefers to be at her own house, Chatsworth. It's much more comfortable than this castle, but when Walsingham commands, even Bess must comply. But though we may be able to insist that Her Grace accepts your presence at times, we can't compel Her Grace to speak to you. I really don't see what you expect to achieve. Or what Sir Francis expects you to achieve, either!'

'That has been thought of, Sir George. I could present myself as a penitent, begging her forgiveness, assuring her that I have now seen the truth of the Catholic Church and realize that I should offer my allegiance to her, and not, any longer, to Queen Elizabeth. Or I can plead that last time we met, I was obeying the orders of my queen, just as Her Grace would have had her own subjects do. Sir Francis suggested that.'

'So, you think you may be able to make yourself acceptable?'

'I might,' I said. 'At least, I can try.'

'Yes. You can try.' Again, he smiled. He had an unexpectedly sweet and understanding smile. 'Her Grace is still full of charm,' he remarked, 'though not, these days, of so much beauty. Her health is not good. And nor, I think, is her judgement. Well, she never did have good judgement. To marry that spoilt young peacock Darnley, allow herself to become one of the suspects when he was murdered, and then to marry the *principal* suspect . . . essentially,' said George Talbot, and now he became authoritative, 'she is a foolish woman. Emotion sways her. It doesn't sway Elizabeth! That is why Queen Elizabeth really is great, and Her Grace Mary Stuart is not. One of your ploys may succeed. Anyway, I must leave it to you to cope with her. Have you been offered any refreshments, by the way?'

'Er . . . no, not yet . . .'

'Tch!' He rose, went round his desk, put his head out of the door and shouted, a manoeuvre that produced a scurry of feet on the stairs outside, and the reappearance of the page.

'Wine and pastries!' snapped Talbot, and then shut the door again.

He was mercurial, I thought, swinging from absent-minded, to comprehending, to barking orders, all in the space of a few minutes. Which was the real Talbot? Or perhaps they all were. He had a formidable wife, for Bess Hardwick, whom I knew slightly, was a lady with a commanding presence and a powerful intellect. Perhaps her partner needed to be a man of many facets. A simple bucolic soul wouldn't suit her at all.

Because I was thinking about Bess Hardwick just then, it startled me when Talbot suddenly said: 'You will be wondering why my wife, who is supposed to have invited you, has not been informed that you are here, and come to welcome you. She will soon do so, but at the moment she is with Her Grace. I can't exactly say that they have made friends; they are not kindred spirits by any means. We were ordered to accommodate Her Grace; it was not a matter of choice. But they do share a great interest in embroidery – designing patterns as well as making them. Are you interested in such things, Mistress Stannard?'

'Yes, Sir George, though I am not so very gifted in designing.' Sybil was, and for a moment I wished that I had brought her. I had left her in charge at Hawkswood, however, and in view of Talbot's remarks about the castle being full to bursting, perhaps it was as well.

'I look forward to meeting the Countess,' I said neutrally and at the same moment, Talbot cocked his head.

'I think I can hear . . . yes, here she is. Bess, my dear, Mistress Stannard has arrived. But this is not a particularly comfortable place for the two of you to get to know each other in. Do take your guest to your parlour, Bess. I have accounts to finish.'

'Of course. You are welcome, Mistress Stannard. We have met at court, have we not? Do come this way,' said Bess Hardwick, Countess of Shrewsbury, my hostess.

In the pleasant parlour which was the natural setting for the castle's chatelaine, seated over the refreshments which had been sent after us, we took stock of each other.

Bess, as a girl, had surely been winsomely pretty. She had delicate features, with high cheekbones and a nice pink colour in her cheeks. Her dark eyes were beautiful, and though she was surely in her fifties, there was no trace of grey in the glossy waves of hair, richly brown with just a tinge of red, that showed in front of her hood.

There was nothing winsome about her now, though. This was a woman accustomed to wealth and power. I knew quite a lot about her. She was very wealthy indeed, especially as a result of her third marriage (Talbot was number four). She had been widowed three times. The first marriage, I had heard, had been a childish affair, arranged by the parents of the two parties. The bridegroom had been a boy of thirteen, Bess herself only sixteen or so, and the groom had died shortly afterwards. It was generally assumed that they were never really man and wife. Later, though, by her second and third husbands, she had had several children. I wondered, as we exchanged conventional greetings, how much she had actually loved her various partners. She didn't, just now, look as if she had ever been vulnerable to the softer emotions.

But whether she had loved them or not, she had no doubt been a good wife. She had known her duties and performed them, with dignity and no doubt with intelligence. Every line in her face spoke of a strong and well-informed mind.

'I am to introduce you to Mary Stuart,' she was saying, 'as a friend I have asked for a long visit. That is what Sir Francis Walsingham requires. But I have to say that I can't understand why, or what you are expected to do. Can you enlighten me?'

'I am to watch Mary. I am to form an extra guard on her. Since she has unhappy memories of me, well, I hope to get round that. One way would be to pretend to be a newly converted Catholic. I know the – er – rules,' I said. 'I was brought up by a Catholic uncle and aunt.'

'Not by your parents?'

'My mother was with me when I was a child but she died when I was sixteen. My father . . .'

'Is the rumour correct? That he was King Henry?'

'Yes,' I said shortly.

'So rumour speaks truth.' She was appraising me, with interest, I thought. I hoped it wasn't with dislike. Bess was the sort of woman whose dislike might well have teeth. 'I had better take you to her as soon as possible,' she said. 'The sooner this rather difficult introductory meeting is over and done with, the better, I feel! I wish you luck. Frankly, I doubt if you will have any!'

In fact, I wasn't taken to Mary's rooms at once. Bess took it upon herself to show me my room, so that I could change my riding dress for something more suited to a queen's guest. The baggage from the coach had been brought up and Dale was able to unpack without delay. Bess left me for a while to change in private, and Dale said: 'Have you really decided to pretend to be a Catholic, ma'am?'

'I'm not sure, Dale. There is an alternative approach. I shan't know for sure until I meet her. Pretending to be a convert could be a good way of getting close to her. She's all too likely to be difficult, for she has no pleasant memories of me. But I know her religion means a great deal to her, and I may succeed by exploiting that.'

'Would I have to pretend as well?' asked Dale miserably.

I looked at her with sympathy. I knew how Dale felt about this particular form of dissembling. It went back to a dreadful experience she had had, long ago, when she had been with me in France, and nearly been executed as a heretic.

'No, Dale,' I said gently. 'No one will question you on the matter if I can help it, and if they do, you can tell the truth. Say that you remain true to your own faith but don't question that of your mistress.'

'All right, ma'am,' said Dale, still miserably.

'Come,' I said. 'Help me with my hair. I must look fit to be seen.'

Bess, when she reappeared, considered my tawny over-dress

and cream satin kirtle with approval, unaware of the hidden pouch and its curious contents. The amber jewellery that I wore with the outfit was not costly but very handsome.

'Her Grace does not yet know you are here,' she said. 'I gave her no chance to say that she wouldn't admit you to her presence. We will take her by surprise. Your woman had better remain here, or she can go down to the hall and make herself useful to Mistress Seton and Lady Livingstone. They are there, choosing dress lengths.'

I nodded to Dale, who left the room. Then I followed Bess, down many stairs, and then up the narrow staircase I had noticed before, and into the presence of Mary Stuart.

She was sitting in a window seat, working at an embroidery frame, with an open workbox at her side. She was alone. In the old days, she had had four close attendants, all called Marie, and usually had some if not all of them with her. She looked up when the sentry at her outer door announced the Countess of Shrewsbury, with a guest, and then, seeing me, tensed sharply. I felt myself cringe.

As we rose from our curtsies, Bess said: 'Good afternoon, Your Grace. See who has come to pay me a visit! An old acquaintance from my days at Queen Elizabeth's court. I believe you have met her before, have you not? Here is Mistress Ursula Stannard.'

'*You!*' said Mary venomously.

She had changed greatly. She had been so beautiful, once, but her face now was lined. Her skin was dry and her dark red hair, I realized instantly, was a wig. The hands grasping the embroidery frame were beginning to be wrinkled and I saw liver spots on them. Only the golden-brown eyes, much the same colour as Elizabeth's, were unchanged, except that they now met mine with anger, a more powerful anger than I had ever seen in her before.

She was a complex being; I knew that. She had a brave, adventurous side. She had been on a battlefield, she had made wild rides in times of emergency, been hounded and hated and involved in elaborate escape plans, made frankly insane marriages. But she also had a very female desire to be protected, taken care of by a trustworthy and loving man.

Twice, she thought she had found one, and twice she had been disappointed. She was a poor judge of men, but that was a misfortune, not a sin.

All at once, I abandoned any thought of pretending to be a Catholic convert. Suddenly, I was embarrassed by the reason for my presence here, and sorry for her, and it seemed to me that she was entitled to some sort of honesty. The other alternative was the right one. I stepped forward and fell on my knees in front of her.

'Madam, I know what you think of me. After our last meeting, you felt I had betrayed you, and in a way, I did. But I did so because it was then my duty as a subject of Queen Elizabeth. Who is also, as you no doubt know, my half-sister. I had no choice. I am not here now with the intention of doing anything against your comfort, only as a guest of your hostess, the Countess of Shrewsbury. You too are a queen. You must many times have expected loyalty from those who are your sworn adherents or your servants. I also know that you were often disappointed, in ways that caused you great distress. Please don't condemn me for giving loyalty where it was my duty to give it.'

Mary stared down into my uplifted face. I kept my eyes steadily on hers. The fury died slowly out of her. 'Yes. I see,' she said. There was a pause and then she held out a hand to me. I saw, close up, that despite the wrinkles and the liver spots, it was still a shapely hand, and would have been even more wrinkled than it was, except that it had been well tended with creams. A faint perfume rose from it. I kissed it, as she clearly wished me to do.

'You may rise,' she said. 'I can recognize honesty, I hope.' She glanced past me, to Bess. 'Well, my friend, you have brought me a surprise companion, it seems.' She turned back to me. 'Lady Livingstone and my dear Marie Seton will be here presently. Marie Seton has always stayed with me, and Lady Livingstone was once another of my Maries. She and her husband have become part of my household here. So I have two of my Maries here in Sheffield. Bess, I have begun on the embroidery pattern we worked out yesterday. I have chosen to do the version with the pale green leaves. I leave the autumn tints to you. Do sit down, both of you.'

Bess and I seated ourselves. I found myself listening to a discussion about embroidery patterns and the choice of silks. It was a smooth, ladylike conversation, with Mary and Bess deferring graciously to each other's opinions. But I noticed that neither smiled or made even the smallest kind of quip, and I sensed that I was in the presence of two noblewomen who did not greatly like each other though they knew how to behave as great ladies should.

Presently, the door opened again and in came Lady Livingstone, whom I realized was one of the women I had glimpsed in the hall, and Mary Seton, who had been the other, though it was only now, at close quarters, that I recognized them. I had of course met them both in the past. Both had aged, like Mary herself. Lady Livingstone was elegantly dressed in silvery grey with a peridot necklace and earrings but Mary Seton was austere in a nun-like black gown and her face was stern, though when she spoke her voice was low and musical, just as I remembered it. Both she and Lady Livingstone eyed me with suspicion, but Mary disarmed it by repeating to them what I had just said to her.

'Who am I to disdain honest loyalty, even when it is given to a queen other than myself?' she said. 'Nor may I be discourteous to the friend of my hostess. Let us all be comfortable together.'

I asked if they had seen Dale, and learned that she had offered her services to them, and had accordingly been set to work with Lady Livingstone's maid, to begin cutting out sleeves from some of the fabrics the ladies had been looking at in the hall.

I was offered an embroidery frame and a carefully drawn pattern of leaves and flowers on a piece of fine white wool fabric. I accepted, and we all settled down to what should have been several innocent hours of needlework and cool, well-mannered chit-chat.

It wasn't quite like that, however, for after a while, Mary remarked: 'This pattern reminds me of something. You said, madam, that these embroideries were to be joined together to make a wall-hanging for your great hall. Surely, there is a tapestry in the hall that has the same pattern, on a larger scale. I remember seeing it when I dined with you last week.'

'Yes, Your Grace. It's new,' Bess said, holding a needle up to the light to thread it. 'It arrived from Flanders only last week.'

'You have a generous husband.'

'Oh, I used some of the money my third husband left me. Sir William St Loe. He left me a great deal of wealth and Sir George has allowed me to retain sole use of it. A tapestry here or there is nothing. I have been fortunate in my marriages.'

The one before Sir William had actually left her in debt but clearly Bess didn't intend to mention him. Nor did Mary. Instead, she said: 'Were you – are you – in love with any of them?'

'Marriage is a business partnership as much as anything,' said Bess calmly, setting a stitch with a steady hand. 'It is also a form of friendship that brings children into the world. I have always, since I became free to choose for myself, tried to bear these things in mind when approaching matrimony, rather than be guided too much by emotion – or fleshly desire – and I feel that I did right.'

For one mad moment I almost opened my mouth to ask if there was a cat in the room. I could have sworn that somewhere close at hand, I had heard a faint, soft *meow.*

'You may have missed something, all the same,' Mary said gently. She sighed a little. 'The summer lightning; the glory of passion. Whatever else has befallen me, I have had that.'

Mary's smile was as sweet as a dish of honey.

With a wasp in it.

Looking up, I caught Mary Seton's eye and knew that she had heard and seen what I had. It was Mary Seton who said: 'I don't think our green silks are an exact match for the tapestry in the hall, but they're near enough. After all, the new hanging is to go on the opposite wall, is it not?'

'Yes. It won't be right beside the tapestry,' said Bess smoothly.

'That is true,' said Lady Livingstone. 'And the light will fall differently. Things that are the same colour will look different if they are seen in different lights.'

The four of them began a ladylike discussion about dyes and daylight. I stitched in silence. It was now very clear indeed that Bess and Mary didn't like each other. I was going to have an uncomfortable stay, by the sound of it.

Not that it mattered. It wasn't my business. I didn't like to think about the business on which I was *supposed* to be here. Every time that came into my mind, I shivered.

That night, in a small bedchamber high in one of the castle towers, with Dale on a truckle bed next to mine, I fell into a heavy sleep, for I was very tired. But in the night, I awoke with my heart pounding. I sat up. The sunny afternoon had been only a respite, it seemed, for a fierce gale was now blowing. But it wasn't the gale that had woken me, but a dream. I couldn't recall the dream, but it had left a dreadful thought pulsing in my mind. *I was supposed to be here to assassinate Mary. I had pretended to agree because Harry was threatened. I did not intend to do it, but I had gone as far as pretending. What if* Elizabeth *had been the victim I was supposed to kill? Would I, even for Harry's sake, have as much as pretended to agree to that?* Could *I?*

I realized that I didn't know. Was it possible that there might be things, situations, that were – might be – of such huge importance that they might have to come even before Harry? It was an appalling idea. Surely, as a woman, I should put Harry first, always, no matter what the consequences. Surely, to protect my child, I should be ready to betray my country, commit a murder, even . . . *Elizabeth*?

I tried to find a way out and could not. Defeat the foe by guile? Take one's own life? Even now, I have found no answer.

I tried to command myself. *It hadn't happened.* I had so far managed to put up the pretence, to make an attempt to save Harry without committing any kind of crime. Except that I was expected to commit one. Even Elizabeth seemed to expect it. I couldn't see how and even if I could, I couldn't imagine how I would bring myself to do any such thing.

I had been given three months.

Feverishly, I wondered what use I could make of those months. Could I make a feint, create a failed attempt at murdering Mary? I tried to think of some kind of seeming accident that would look convincing but wouldn't actually harm her. I couldn't do that, either. I remembered my interview with Walsingham and his suggestion that there might be someone here in the castle who was keeping watch on me, waiting for me to act. It was a most unpleasant idea.

What were Brockley and Wilder doing? Had they achieved anything?

I should have put more trust in Harry. He, as it proved, had guile aplenty.

THIRTEEN
Word From Home

Next day, the gale continued to blow until nightfall, and there was heavy rain, but after that, things improved and the sun came out again. It made no difference to the fact that for me, life was miserable, and stayed so for the whole of the week that followed.

It was plain, very quickly, that Mary, although she was putting up with my company, and theoretically understood why I had once betrayed her, still wished I wasn't there.

She used me as an errand runner. I was required to fetch and carry (*find my riding gloves, will you, Ursula; Ursula, I've mislaid my big workbox, look for it, please; fetch me my fur cloak, Ursula*). I was asked to tune her lute (but not to play for her); to applaud when she practised dance steps with Mary Seton and Lady Livingstone but not to join in; to thread needles for her; to wash her little black and white terrier, Timmy.

Because I was good at embroidery, I was sometimes allowed to help with that, but I was discouraged from taking part in the conversation that usually went with it. I was treated, in fact, like an unattractive poor relation. It made me feel like one.

At the end of that week, however, things improved a little, and that was due to Timmy. He was a lively little dog, sometimes given to slipping away to explore on his own, and on that seventh morning, Mary caught sight of him disappearing out of her parlour door, and told me to go after him.

I hurried out, saw his little piebald rump vanishing down the stairs, and gave chase. He glanced back once, realized that he was pursued and mischievously led me a dance, through a part of the castle that I hadn't seen before, down some more stairs and straight towards the castle kitchens.

He was a fast mover and kept ahead of me, so there was time, before I caught up with him, for a noisy uproar to start beyond the kitchen door. I broke into a run and found myself in the hot, steamy cavern that is the usual kind of kitchen to be found in a castle, staring at two men dressed as chefs, one brandishing a most alarming carving knife and the other anti-climatically flourishing a bronze spatula. They were face to face and shouting, while Timmy cowered in a corner, whimpering.

'You don't kick Her Grace's terrier! No one kicks Her Grace's pets! You should have . . .'

'I'll kick any blasted animal except the kitchen cat that sets a paw in this place!' bawled the chef with the carving knife. 'And I wouldn't put up with the cat except that it catches mice!'

He was a big man with a red face, though this was possibly due to the heat. There were four huge hearths and all of them contained roaring fires, where capons were sizzling on spits and cauldrons were bubbling. Both chefs and all their under-lings – who had one and all stopped what they were doing in order to gape – were sweating heavily. 'I am sick,' Red Face announced, '*sick* of hearing about Her Grace!' He managed to infuse the title with loathing, as though he were talking about the smell from a midden.

'Her Grace,' said the chef with the spatula, 'is the guest of Her Majesty and in the care of my lord of Shrewsbury . . .'

'And there's folk enough in this land would be glad to be rid of her!' Red Face became redder than ever. 'It's bad enough she has an altar in a private room and a Catholic chaplain reciting illegal Masses for her, polluting the air with her blasphemies, but as well as that, I have to put up with her minions taking over one of my hearths, and a spit and a trivet and all them pots and pans that I ought to have the use of, so as she and her folk can have whatever dainties they like, cooked in *my* kitchen, elbowing me out of the way as if I'm nothing. You just get out of my territory and . . .'

I gathered that Mary had a cook and kitchen staff of her own and a part of the castle kitchen set aside for their use and that the castle chef didn't like it. And that he had kicked Mary's dog. I also saw that the castle chef, knife upraised, was now advancing on the man with the spatula – Mary's cook, presumably – and that the situation was about to become really ugly.

'*Stop!*' I shouted. They hadn't realized I was there, and were sufficiently startled to turn and look at me. I swooped forward and picked Timmy up. He cowered in my arms, pressing himself against me and then whined a little as I gripped him. I realized that he had indeed been kicked and was probably bruised.

I stroked his head to soothe him and said sternly: 'You two gentlemen would do well to behave with more dignity. I presume that whatever arrangements have been made for Her Grace's cook were reached after discussion with Lady Shrewsbury or someone appointed by her, and it is your duty to abide by them. You!' I stared hard at Red Face and his knife. 'What is your name?'

'What's it to you? Who are you? Never seen you before!'

'His name's Master Tallboy,' said one of the younger cooks, who was standing by a table with a wooden spoon and a mixing bowl in his hands and an array of jugs and small dishes in front of him, no doubt ingredients for whatever he was blending in the bowl. 'New here. The old cook left to run an inn with his brother.'

'And you hoped to take his place!' snarled Tallboy. 'You, Jim Randal, half my age and with half my experience! Hold your tongue!'

'I am Mistress Stannard, and I have just come from visiting Her Grace's apartment, at her and my lady of Shrewsbury's invitation,' I said coldly. 'And I am not concerned with the internal politics of this kitchen. But I am concerned that Her Grace's pets should not be hurt, and I am also concerned to find such an offensive attitude to Her Grace. You had better be the one to watch your tongue, Master Tallboy. And also, watch what you do with your feet. I will have to report what I have heard. I shall now take Timmy back to his mistress.'

I turned away and left them to it. I heard curses from Master Tallboy, rude laughter from Mary's chef, and exclamations and recriminations among all and sundry break out behind me, but I ignored them. I returned Timmy to Mary and told her what had happened. I did not repeat Master Tallboy's objectionable remarks but I did tell her that he had apparently kicked Timmy and that I had spoken very sharply to both chefs.

Mary, gently petting her bruised Timmy, thanked me most sincerely. I did report the matter in more detail to Bess when I was able to speak to her without anyone else listening, and I heard later that Master Tallboy had been dismissed and that his chief assistant, Jim Randal, had after all been promoted.

Castle gossip informed me that the rest of the kitchen staff were relieved, as they hadn't liked Tallboy. Randal, apparently, was both competent and popular, and quite able to manage the kitchens even when one hearth and a lot of equipment had been given over to Mary's cook and his aides.

After that, I was treated more pleasantly by Mary, was even, sometimes, invited to join her and her two Maries over wine and pastries. I was closer to her now. Then I found that I wished I was not.

For one thing, I felt uncomfortable when, arriving to join them a little ahead of time, I found a thin, black-gowned cleric with what I would call a fastidious face, reading to them an account of someone back in the days of the boy king Edward the Sixth, who had been martyred for his Catholic faith. I could do nothing but obey Mary's signal to sit down and listen but I remembered the three hundred or so Protestants, decent people nearly all of them, judicially and sadistically murdered for their faith in the days of Queen Mary Tudor, and I did my best to listen instead to the birdsong outside the window. And to block out Mary's sighing remark that it must be wonderful to die for the honour of God.

That was the time when I noticed that one of the tapestries in Mary's parlour was drawn aside and that behind it was a half-open door, through which I could see a little altar and a huge crucifix on the wall above it. It was the only time I ever glimpsed Mary's chaplain or her secret chapel. I never desired a closer look and I never actually exchanged even a word with her chaplain.

But I had other reasons for disliking my new closeness to Her Grace. There were certain drinks and dishes that only Mary took and it would not be too difficult, I thought, remembering the phial that seemed to me to be burning a hole in the drawer where I had hidden it, to put venom into one of these. I had been presented with opportunities that I didn't want.

Everyday food and drink apart, another possibility had now shown itself. Mary did indeed suffer from a persistent pain in her side and had a painkilling medicine which I learned, from casual talk with her ladies and her physician, contained traces of hemlock. I might well, I thought, manage to doctor that. Perhaps enough to make her ill . . . as though I had misjudged the dose . . .

But no. The thought was unbearable. I couldn't. I *couldn't*! Not even as a pretence, without doing any real harm. Oh, dear God, give your blessing to Brockley's search. Find Harry before it's too late! Find him! I can't bear this much longer.

I tried to reassure myself that there was no very great urgency. I had been given three months and it would be reasonable for me to be careful, and not make any kind of attempt until my position was well established, and I would not so easily be suspected if Mary were to fall ill and die.

And yet, wouldn't those who held Harry expect me to act, for his sake, as soon as I could? I was always tired those days, for I never slept much at night.

Far from home, without news, I was becoming more and more afraid, not for myself but for Harry.

I became obsessed with the idea that somewhere in the castle, someone was keeping watch on me, waiting for me to act. I tried, as the days went on, to make acquaintances, hoping to discover who was doing the watching. I cultivated the freckled page, whose name was Walter Meredith. He was cheerful company and I had discovered that he was a great gossip. The castle steward, whose name was William Cropper, would have been a good source of information too but he was so very dignified that I could form no kind of friendship with him; he might as well have been a Greek god visiting from Olympus.

Of course, there was Sir George Talbot's clerk, Russell Woodley, who had proposed to me at Richmond. He too was knowledgeable and although I had refused him firmly enough, I knew at once that he had not given up hope. He kept on seeking my company, not obtrusively, but with an air of quiet determination, and now that I really wanted all the information I could get on the inhabitants of the castle, I allowed it, up to a point.

He was an excellent dancer, which presented me with plenty of chances to talk to him without attracting much notice, and I soon realized that he was not just well informed but *very* well informed indeed. He knew all the ins and outs of the castle and those who lived there, who liked or disliked whom; what love affairs were brewing; how the two households worked. He was a useful, if embarrassing contact. Quite apart from wondering if there was a spy in the castle, I had to be prepared in case I really did have to make a pretence at trying to attack Mary. I needed to know all I could about how her meals were prepared, and what her daily routine was, who was and who was not one of her servants, who was and was not allowed into her presence.

A third person with whom I more willingly made friends was Lady Alice Hammond, a pretty young thing who was one of Bess of Shrewsbury's junior attendants. She too was well primed with castle gossip and she was good if giggly company. She was wholesome fresh air and I needed that.

One man I would have liked to cultivate but couldn't do so easily was John Grey, captain of the castle garrison. I sometimes watched him drilling his men and saw that he was one of those quiet, competent men who can command without difficulty. If Brockley had been with me, I would have asked him to make friends with Captain Grey, but Brockley wasn't there and Eddie hadn't status enough to hobnob with the garrison captain.

On the twelfth day of my stay at Sheffield, carrying my workbox and the piece of embroidery on which I was currently working, I made my way to Bess's apartment because, keeping up the pretence that I was there as her guest, she regularly asked me to join her for part of the morning before going on to Mary's rooms.

As I approached her door, I was startled to hear cries – indeed, wails and sobs – of anguish coming from beyond it. Worse, I thought I could distinguish Alice's voice. One of Bess's senior ladies, whose name I did not know, opened to my knock and admitted me without a word, and with a completely blank face. She let me precede her inside, but I stopped short at once, distressed to see poor Alice, with tears in her eyes, leaning against the wall, as though she had been flung there, and holding a hand to the side of her face. As she saw me, the hand slipped a little and I saw that her left cheek was crimson. And Bess, breathing hard, was standing a few feet away, hands on hips and glaring at her.

The other ladies stood round, watching. Some looked upset, but no one was daring to protest. I swung round to the senior lady, who was just behind me. 'What . . .?'

'Lady Alice scorched a ruff. She was supposed to be pressing the pleats. She is careless, and chatters while she works and doesn't attend properly to what she is doing,' said the lady coolly. She was a middle-aged person, with a bearing as stiff as the buckram lining of her brocade bodice. There was no sympathy in her face.

'But . . .!'

'What a fuss,' said Bess. 'Really, Alice! I barely tapped you. In future, take more care with my belongings. You look surprised, Mistress Stannard, but I have no doubt you have seen the queen herself deal with poor service in a similar way. Alice, stop crying and take the spoiled ruff away. I shall not wear it again. The rest of you, settle down and get on with your sewing. Do be seated, Ursula. One of my ladies will play the lute for us.'

It was perfectly true that I had seen Elizabeth chastise her ladies as Bess had just chastised Alice. There was nothing unusual about it. I still hated witnessing it. I knew all too well how it felt. The uncle and aunt who brought me up had been free with their blows. I had never let Harry's tutors beat him because of that.

Alice, still sobbing, went to the back of the room and picked up the damaged ruff. Ironing was done elsewhere, so I supposed she had brought the disaster in to show Bess and apologize.

'The world hasn't ended. I have plenty of ruffs,' said Bess. 'But I expect certain standards of service from my household. In future, Alice, I trust you will take more care. You may go.'

Faint signs, not of contrition but of a weary kind of understanding, then appeared on her stern countenance and she added, addressing the lady behind me: 'Lucy, see her to her chamber and send for some wine for her. It will revive her. Stop that whimpering, you silly girl. It was all your own fault. The wine will restore you. Now *go.*'

Alice blundered past me, and the lady who I now knew was called Lucy went after her. I found that I was trembling. Bess glanced at me, unconcerned.

'I don't allow carelessness in those whose business it is to wait on me,' she said. 'No doubt Alice will grow out of her foolishness, but I don't propose to wait for nature to improve her. I mean to see that she becomes as responsible and reliable as she should be, *now.* I have ordered a small mid-morning collation for us all – a glass of wine each and some almond pastries.'

Bemusedly, I took the seat she indicated. This was a side of Bess I hadn't seen before and it didn't appeal to me. I opened my workbox, threaded a needle, with difficulty because my hands were trembling, and began on a half-finished oak leaf. Bess sat down beside me, and also picked up some work.

The other ladies followed her example. It was a cold day, bright as the month of May should be, but with a sharp wind that made itself felt even indoors and I had felt chilled as I made my way through the castle to Bess's apartment. However, there was a fire in the room, and the warmth, and the comfortable cushions on the settle to which she had waved me, slowly calmed me. My trembling stopped. I hoped that Lucy was being kind to poor Alice. Accidents with irons did happen; Alice had been roughly treated in my opinion but since I was here as Bess's guest, and needed to be here, I had better not irritate her.

When the door opened to admit the freckled Walter and

Bess, smiling at me, said: 'Ah, here is our collation,' I managed to smile back and say: 'How pleasant.'

But Walter was not carrying a tray. He made a brief obeisance to Bess but then said: 'Mistress Stannard, I have a message for you. Your man Roger Brockley is here and wishes urgently to have speech with you.'

'Brockley!' I turned to Bess. 'My lady, I must go to him, if you will excuse me.' I swung round again, to Walter. 'Where is he?'

'He has been taken to my lord of Shrewsbury, who has sent me to fetch you.' His cheerful freckled face was alight with interest. 'I heard Master Brockley say it was about your son. Perhaps he has been found!'

'*Walter!*' Bess was outraged. 'What is this?'

Walter looked alarmed. 'I . . . I am sorry. Have I spoken out of turn? My parents live in Woking, and in their last letter to me, they mentioned a rumour in the district that Mistress Stannard's son had run away from home. If I shouldn't have said anything, I beg your pardon, Your Grace. I . . .'

'You have been warned before about gossiping,' said Bess. Her voice shook with anger. 'Unless you take heed and learn to watch your tongue, I will have you whipped.'

Walter went white and after what I had just witnessed, I could understand why. I was also embarrassed, because I had myself been encouraging Walter to gossip, though I certainly didn't want him spreading rumours about Harry.

Nervously, I smiled at both Walter and Bess. 'It's quite all right.' Better to assuage curiosity than to feed it. I did not know for sure, but I didn't think that either of the Talbots knew of Harry's disappearance. Walsingham had most likely just told them that I was to spy on Mary, and nothing else. 'Walter, my son has been – er – has been – away from home, but some things are private. I don't want it talked about. Please respect that. Please ask no questions and do *not*, please, discuss the matter with anyone else. My lady . . .'

'Yes, yes, you must go to your servant. I will not ask questions, either,' said Bess. 'Walter, show Mistress Stannard the way. And remember what I have said!'

I made for the door and Walter, visibly trembling, his

usual blithe insouciance quite gone, led me away. I was thinking that this business of keeping Harry's disappearance a secret was more difficult than I had realized. I couldn't of course have hoped that no word of it would get round our district. Harry had made friends with other boys of his age, sons of various people in our locality, including youthful relatives of our servants, who must have enquired after him. The news was bound to get out. I had been slow. I should have thought of some convincing lie. Perhaps I could do so even now, and send word home that this or that story was to be put about. I had now told Walter that Harry was away from home – which wasn't the same thing as missing. I could enlarge on that, say that Harry had gone on a visit, perhaps . . .

Or perhaps . . . a most unpleasant thought had entered my mind. I had been trying to find out who might be watching me on behalf of Harry's captors. Could that someone be Walter? He had obviously managed to take charge of Brockley and talk to him. Could nice, naive freckle-faced gossipy Walter be one of their minions?

I didn't want to think so but once the idea had entered my head, it wouldn't disappear. It was possible. I must be careful. *Very* careful. I had better stop gossiping with Walter.

While I was thinking about all this, Walter was guiding me through the castle, to the study where I had first met George Talbot. He was not there now, but Brockley was standing by the window. I walked in ahead of Walter and as Brockley started towards me, I put a finger to my lips and then turned to wave the page away. 'Close the door after you,' I said sternly. He did so. And then I forgot about imaginary visits, forgot everything except that here was Brockley, with news, which I instantly demanded.

Brockley's grave face broke into a smile. 'Madam, I have had a message from Harry! Your son, for all he's only nine, is growing already into a most resourceful lad! Here!'

He held out a little roll of paper, which I fairly snatched from him. On the outside was my name and a direction to Hawkswood; on the inside, when I unrolled it, was a letter. The writing was Harry's; I knew it at once.

*I am imprisoned in a big house. Don't know where. It
took three days to get here. It's grey stone with a slate
roof and ivy on the walls. There's a wall round the house
and garden, and there's a front courtyard. It's lonely. I
can look out of windows and see over the wall but I can't
see any other houses. The people who hold me are those
players who called at our home. I am in health and
treated quite well but I know they want you to do something and what will happen if you don't. There is a man
with a soft voice who has threatened to hurt me if I try
to escape. Try to find me, I beg you. I will try to slip this
into the gear of a man who has called to mend the roof.
I hope he will pass it on. I send my love – Harry.*

Then, evidently as an afterthought: *There are dogs.*

'He may be only nine years old but he has plenty of good
sense,' Brockley said. 'He knows what details we need to
know.'

'Yes. Between us, we have taught him well,' I said. I was
hurting inside, moved beyond bearing by the courage and the
resourcefulness that had enabled Harry to get his message to
us. And I was shuddering at the thought that he had been
threatened by the man with that soft, cruel voice and the Arctic
eyes. Please God, let us find Harry and save him before
anything more befalls him!

'The man who presumably repaired the roof did send it on
to Hawkswood,' Brockley said. 'He hired a courier. The courier
came from Stratford, well north of London. He hadn't met his
client before – said the man gave his name as Master Ashley.
The courier rode off; I spent the rest of the day thinking things
out and then started for Stratford the next morning. When I
got there I couldn't hear anything of anyone called Ashley
living there. I heard of two roof menders in the town but
neither was an Ashley or had employed a courier recently – or
ever, in one case. *Who'd I be writing to, away from here? All
my folk are here and always have been and I can't write,
anyhow*, he said to me. Nor could I hear of a house matching
Harry's description. I tried the vicarage and I tried the landlords
of the inns.' I nodded.

'But it's the first lead and the only one we've got,' Brockley said. 'Madam, I spent a day at Stratford and then came straight on here, as fast as I could. Stratford's over eighty miles from here – nearer ninety. I left Firefly after the first stage when I left Hawkswood, and then used hirelings. Rotten slugs some of them were, too. I rode all day yesterday and finished the journey this morning. I did my best.'

'We're all doing our best, Brockley.' The worry I had felt when Walter Meredith revealed how widely the news of Harry's disappearance had spread suddenly reasserted itself. 'I have a new anxiety,' I said, and explained it. 'We ought to have put out a story of some kind,' I told him. 'I must think of one and write to Sybil . . .'

'Oh, that!' Brockley laughed. 'Madam, it has already been seen to. Mistress Jester and my son Philip both thought of it independently and came to me, Mistress Jester first, and Philip two hours later. We have already told the household that they are to spread the news that Harry has gone on a visit to his married sister, Mistress Margaret Hill, your daughter, in Buckinghamshire. That rumour should already be flourishing, and Mistress Jester wrote to Mistress Hill in case any hint of it should reach her. Arthur Watts took the letter. It's all been attended to.'

'I'm well served!' I said appreciatively.

'It's difficult to quash rumours,' Brockley said, 'unless there's something to replace them with but I think we've done it. It's hard to think of everything at once. I was going to tell you but somehow, telling you about Harry's letter came first.'

He yawned suddenly and swayed a little and I saw with compunction how very tired he was. He was no longer young. 'You need to rest,' I said. 'Dale is in my chamber, seeing to some sewing. I will take you there. She will look after you. And I'll send for some food and wine for you. But when you have rested, we must confer. The first thing to do is to find that house! It is surely not far from Stratford.'

'I didn't bring Wilder. He didn't feel able to travel so far on horseback or at the speed I meant to go,' Brockley said. 'Philip's better now and he wanted to come with me, but I sent him to Guildford to try, once more, if he could trace

Laurence Miller's movements there. He was quite cross about it, but I think it's important. Miller's a valuable man, but I am very suspicious of him.'

'Brockley, I know you're doing your best. Come with me now, and we'll find Dale.'

The next part of the story belongs to Harry. I will let him tell it, as eventually, when we were at last reunited, he told it to me.

FOURTEEN
Harry's Tale

We heard his tale, of course, a great deal later, when much had happened and he had been rescued. Yet it seems natural to repeat it here.

'I was out riding, just out riding,' Harry said. 'And they jumped out at me when I was going through the wood. They were horrible, all wearing ugly masks, with devils' faces and clowns' faces, but cruel clowns, nasty ones. I struggled all I could – I really did . . .'

He sounded almost fearful, as though he thought he would be accused of not trying to resist. 'We know you would have struggled,' I said. 'Don't worry about that. Just go on. What happened next?'

What happened next, it seemed, was exactly what had happened to me. He was trussed, wrapped in a carpet and trundled for a long time on a handcart, and finally unloaded in a house which from his description was the one where I had been taken. He was given food and drink and allowed to relieve himself and he was able to look at his captors, who had removed their masks.

'They were the players who came to our home,' he said. 'All seven of them, except that there were others as well – nine or ten altogether, all men except for the woman with the red hair.'

Then he was told why he had been seized.

'They wanted me to write a letter to you, Mother, saying what would happen to me if you didn't do what they asked. I was t . . . terrified!'

Brockley and Dale were among those present. 'We can well understand that,' Brockley told him.

His lips were quivering. I held him firmly. 'It's all right. It's all right, Harry. I'm here and you're here. You never wrote that letter, it seems.'

'No, I said I wouldn't.' His lip still trembled. 'But they said they could make me, and I knew they could, if they really wanted to. I was so *frightened*. The man I remembered as the player with the very soft voice – his name was Lucas and he was the villain in the play – he looked as if he did want to. Well . . .'

'It's all right now,' Brockley said. 'You need not talk about him or remember him. Don't think of him at all.' He spoke in the deep, calm voice that I had so often heard him use when quieting a nervous horse. It seemed to steady Harry as well.

'So why was the letter not written?' I asked.

'They weren't all in agreement about it. It sounded as though they had been arguing already – Lucas said to one of them, *Oh, you keep on saying that but we have to make contact with Mistress Stannard somehow!* But the man who was the leader – he was the one who did card tricks at Hawkswood – said that in his opinion it could be too dangerous. Someone would have to deliver the letter. A courier would be needed. Yes, and *he* said, *I keep on repeating this*, so they must have been arguing beforehand. It seemed that none of them wanted to be the messenger. It would be so risky for whoever it was. Lucas said messengers could be hired, who need not know what the message was, but the woman said that hired couriers could be traced and questioned.'

'They sound like a muddleheaded set of conspirators,' Dale remarked.

'Conspirators often are,' Brockley told her. 'All full of exalted ideas and not much common sense.'

Harry said: 'Next, they talked about just leaving a letter where the Hawkswood people would be sure to find it, but well, once more, no one wanted to do that in case they were caught. I think some of them were afraid of what they were doing! They argued and argued, but in the end, they decided to keep to another plan, what they called their alternative. That meant . . .'

'Snatching me instead,' I said. 'Yes. That's what they did.'

'Mother, I can't bear to think of you . . .'

'It's all right, Harry. It's over. I'm safe and so are you. Go on. What happened next?'

'I spent the night there but next day I was trussed up again and blindfolded this time, and then wrapped in that beastly carpet, and put on a cart of some sort, only horse-drawn this time, and taken away. It was a long journey – we were two nights on the road. There were breaks in lonely places where I was allowed to get out and walk about, to ease my aches, but I was kept blindfolded.'

'How dreadful!' Dale was appalled.

'It was horrid,' Harry said. 'I don't know where we spent the nights. Once was in some sort of hut, I think; it smelt of fodder and I had to sleep on a pile of hay. I could hear wind in trees and bird calls close by. The next night, I think we were in a ruined building. I could hear how voices echoed, and the sound of wind whining in a chimney. But in the end, we got to the house where you found me, and they freed me and took off the blindfold. There were two men, and neither of them were from the group of players. They weren't masked. Why did the players bother with masks? It doesn't make sense.'

Brockley said: 'They couldn't have been sure of catching you alone. They must have been lying in wait, ready to seize any chance of snatching you, but if you had had a companion who got away, they wouldn't want anyone to recognize them who might set a pursuit on their trail very quickly. Once they were a good distance from Hawkswood, it wouldn't matter so much.'

'I see. I suppose that would be right.' Harry agreed, and then burst out: 'Those masks were so horrible! It was like being with demons! Things from hell!'

Brockley and I calmed him again and he said: 'The two men weren't bad. They made me fairly comfortable, with a room, and quite good food, but they were very watchful, and . . .' He shivered. 'They said I'd regret it if I tried what they called any funny business, but I was too frightened to try anything. The players joined them later.'

'Having stayed behind to kidnap me,' I said grimly.

'Yes. Once they'd come back, the first two went away. The players guarded me instead.' Again, he shivered, his memories still bearing hard on him.

'It was all horrible,' he said. 'They told me they wished me no harm, but that some matters of state were more important than my life or freedom. They made me feel as if I was nothing – just a pawn on a chessboard. That was one of the most horrible things. It made me feel ashamed, somehow. They said that as your son, I ought to understand that because they were sure you did.'

'I do,' I said, with feeling. I had often been sent into danger by Cecil or Walsingham on behalf of the queen, because they held the same belief.

Harry said: 'I tried to take note of them. There was Lucas, for one. I hated him. He had such a soft, cruel voice. There was the leader; he did his card tricks to amuse me. There was the big fat man, who sang for us at Hawkswood – he was called John – and one, his name was Jeff, who was a tumbler and a juggler. I remember him doing tumbler's tricks at Hawkswood and once, from a window, I saw him practising in the garden. There was the woman, who was called Eva. And two others of the seven who weren't special, somehow, except that one spoke like a man from the north country. I can't remember what the two were like who guarded me while the rest were away. I never heard their names.'

'They will be found,' I said, and once more heard how grim I sounded.

'They let me out into the open air each day,' Harry said, 'though always with someone to guard me. I was allowed to help weed the garden at the back, and to play with a ball in the front courtyard. I played with the dogs sometimes. I made friends with them. But I never had a chance to escape. I did begin to think about it after a day or two. I was frightened – so frightened – but I was more afraid of what might happen to me if I didn't escape than what they might do to me if I tried and failed!'

'You were brave,' Brockley told him.

'The wall was high,' Harry said, 'and there were only two gates, one in front and one at the back, at the end of the garden, and they were always padlocked except when a cart was coming in or out – fetching supplies, usually. There was a stable yard beside the courtyard, with an archway in between, but I was never allowed near that.

'I tried, though, to see how the days went, who came and went and so on. To see if I could make a plan.' I saw now that he was remembering that he had tried to plan, that he was remembering the things that didn't make him feel ashamed, and his voice had steadied. I looked at my son with both admiration and astonishment, for he sounded older than nine; already, a man was beginning to take shape within the boy.

'Go on,' I said, since he had paused, collecting his thoughts.

'There never seemed to be any outsiders,' he said at length. 'Once there were some repairs done to a drain, but the people who were in charge of me saw to that themselves. I never saw the back gate unlocked and the front one was only unlocked to let carts in and out, as I said. If a cart arrived and wanted to come in, the driver would blow a horn. If I was outside at those times, I was called in. My bedchamber had a view – I think I said something about that in my letter, didn't I? – but I couldn't see any other house or any smoke from a village though there must have been a village or a town somewhere because the supplies must have come from somewhere.'

Brockley said: 'There is a village within easy distance. And a farmhouse. But they would both have been screened from you by woods and by folds in the land. So, you tried to plan. What happened next?'

A pained look appeared on Harry's face, a line between his young brows. 'Once, when a cart came out of the stable yard as I was playing ball in the courtyard, I was left there, as though I had been overlooked. The cart stopped, and the driver – it was the fat man, John – got down and went back through the stable yard arch as though he had forgotten something. I thought: now is my chance! There was a leather cover on the cart – they used to draw it over the goods when they brought them back. I got under it, quick as a trout darts! And then I heard John come back and there were shouts and running feet and the cover was thrown back and I was dragged off, by the woman. She slapped me and John stood there glaring at me and saying, *Yes, we thought you might try to escape. We decided to test you. So now we know!*

'It was a trap.' His mouth shook again. 'They marched me indoors and up to my room and John held me down and Lucas

. . . he beat me. It hurt . . . it hurt so much . . . and I think he enjoyed it. He . . .'

I felt a surge of rage. I had never allowed Harry's tutors to beat him; I never wanted him to know what I had once, miserably, known myself. I wished that the soft-voiced brute was here, bound and at my mercy. I would make him cry for it.

To Harry, I said: 'Don't brood about it. It's all over now. Go on. How did you get that letter out?'

'Well, it was just after that, that the drain had to be mended. The next day, I think. It was Jeff, the tumbler and juggler, who saw to it. He came in from doing it, and I was there, downstairs in a dark little dining chamber, eating some pottage. The woman was watching me, and Lucas was there too. I wasn't taking any notice of them. I hated them!'

His voice rose in bitterness. He swallowed and then said: 'Jeff came in, not into the room where I was, but into a sort of vestibule adjoining it. I heard fat John's voice, asking if he'd done the job all right, and Jeff said yes, and it was a good thing they were all fairly handy with little jobs because they shouldn't need to call in anyone from outside.

'But that night,' said Harry, 'there was a gale and a couple of slates crashed off the roof. It gave me a fright, I can tell you, because the slates came from just above my room! And next day it was clear that one job none of them felt equipped to do was climb on to the roof and put the slates back. I thought it was odd; they're all so . . . so good at physical things, but not one of them felt safe on a roof. So they had to bring someone in from outside, because the roof was leaking into the attic just above my room and I heard Jeff say that other slates looked loose, too.

'They locked me up when they were planning to get the roof mended but it took them all day to find someone and one of them – yes, it was the leader, the one who did card tricks, said that if I wanted something to pass the time, why not do some study? Had I been studying Latin? I said yes, and he brought me some books and said see if you can translate any of this into English! One of the books was the one by Livy that I was working on with Master Sandley, the one about bringing elephants over the Alps. I said all right, I would.

They gave me some paper and a quill and some ink. Then I got the idea that I could write a note and somehow get to speak to the roof mender and ask him or trick him into taking it. I wrote the letter and rolled it up. I used my belt knife to cut a lace from my shirt and tied it with that. And I waited and hoped and I was lucky. I never came face to face with the man – there was only one – who came to do the work but he left a jacket hanging on a ladder leaning against the wall near my window. The window was narrow . . .'

'Yes. Very old-fashioned,' I said.

'But I'm thin. By twisting sideways, I did manage to get halfway out and get hold of the jacket and drag it in. It had a pouch inside, like the pouches you have in some of your over-dresses, Mother. I put the letter into the pouch. I couldn't get the jacket back to the ladder but I just let it fall, as though it had slipped off. And then,' said Harry simply, 'I prayed.'

'And the workman – Master Ashley – found the letter and sent it on, from Stratford,' I said thoughtfully. 'He must have wondered how the scroll came to be in his jacket!'

'Your name was known to him, madam,' Brockley said. 'You are known to many now as a relative of the queen and trusted by her. Well, he did send it on. He probably felt as though it would burn a hole in his jacket if he didn't. And we have Harry safe.'

FIFTEEN
Old House With Ivy

B ut all that was later. For the moment, as I led Brockley
to the room where Dale was repairing the hem of my
favourite tawny gown, my son was still lost to me, and
in danger. All I knew, or guessed, was that he was in an old
house, with a slate roof and ivy on the walls, and that it was
probably not far from Stratford.

'I'll have to find somewhere for you two to be together,' I
said to the Brockleys, as Dale cast aside her work and went,
tutting, to divest Brockley of his cloak and remove his travel-
splashed boots. 'Look after him, Dale. I will try to make some
arrangements for you.'

I went in search of Bess and found that she had left her
ladies, withdrawn to the study and was conferring with her
dignified steward, William Cropper. I explained that my man,
who was the husband of my maid, had arrived with news for
me, and that they would need – were indeed accustomed to
– accommodation of their own. Cropper suggested a room in
the same tower as me, just above me, in fact.

'It isn't used often, being up such a long stair, but it can
be made quite comfortable. I will have it prepared if you wish.'

Clearly he wasn't going to recommend more convenient
accommodation for two mere servants, and neither was Bess.
However, they would be near me and they would have some
privacy. I agreed and the steward went off to give the necessary orders. I asked to see the room, however, whereupon Bess
shouted for a page and when Walter Meredith appeared, told
him to show me the way. And as I followed him up a spiral
stone stair that would certainly get Dale out of breath, the
irrepressible Walter asked if I really had had news of my son.

'As a matter of fact, Walter,' I said dampingly, 'your parents
have it all wrong. My son is on a visit to his married sister,

my daughter Mistress Hill. But I really don't want my private business shouted to the wide world.'

I had been sorry for him when I saw how frightened he was of Bess of Shrewsbury's threats, but it was possible that she had a point. 'Please hold your tongue! And do go slower! These stairs are like a precipice!'

The stairs explained all too well why the room at the top wasn't much used, but the room itself was quite sizeable. In the early evening, however, when Brockley had had a sleep and I had been graciously allowed to share a game of cards in Mary's apartment, I brought the Brockleys to my chamber. I closed the door and as so many times before, we were in conference.

'What next?' I said baldly.

'I think,' said Brockley, 'that I must go back to Stratford. My enquiries there, after a roof mender called Ashley, were no use, but we have to find that house and the best way *is* to find the man Ashley. He may be a Warwick man – Warwick is only eight miles or so to the north of Stratford and is a bigger town. I would have pursued more enquiries there at once, except that I wanted so much to get to you, to give you Harry's letter. I shall go back to Warwick now and see what luck I have there. I'll have my eyes wide open for old houses with walls round them, too.'

He looked at me gravely. 'I don't think you can come on this hunt, madam. You have to stay here and – pretend about things, don't you?'

'Yes, except that I don't see how,' I said worriedly. 'I can't think how I can *pretend* to try to kill Her Grace! I daren't do anything at all in case it goes wrong – how awful if I arranged a riding accident or some food poisoning and *did* kill her, by mistake! The queen might be pleased,' I added bitterly. 'But I wouldn't. I'd never forgive myself and suppose I were caught! The law would have to be upheld, I think. Even Walsingham might find it difficult to get me out of it.'

I wondered if he – or the queen, or Cecil – would actually sacrifice me and realized to my horror that although it wasn't likely, it wasn't impossible, either.

'But if I don't make a move soon,' I said, 'I endanger Harry. We have to find him! We have to find that house!'

Brockley ruminated and then said: 'Is this perhaps the moment to go to the county sheriff – or to Sir George Talbot? To get official help?'

'I'd like to,' I said. 'But there's the threat to Harry if there's a public hue and cry. If a number of men begin making enquiries about lonely houses and roof menders called Ashley, the news might reach the wrong ears. I have a bad feeling about this . . . this gang. I'm afraid of them, and that's the truth. For Harry's sake, not mine.'

'So I must do my best,' said Brockley. 'Very well, madam. I will find that house if it's humanly possible. I promise.'

We were interrupted then, because Walter Meredith came tapping at the door with a message from Mary. Would I attend on her and Lady Shrewsbury? I left the Brockleys and went to Mary's rooms, where I found that the new wall-hangings had now been completed and the pieces stitched together, and that Mary and Bess were shaking out lengths of silvery satin and discussing what to embroider on them.

'I think just one colour, blue. Blue on silver,' said Mary, 'would be very charming for a kirtle.'

'With sleeves to match,' said Bess. 'I have an idea about the pattern. Bluebells, some in silhouette and some filled in . . . I have a rough drawing here . . .'

We settled down to the feminine task of planning the pattern. I found it hard to concentrate.

It was too late for Brockley to set off again that day. When I was free to go back to them, I told him to rest again, bade Dale take the greatest care of him, and arranged for food to be brought to them so that they need not run the gauntlet of curiosity and questions in the castle dining chamber. I went to supper as usual. I tried to appear normal but must have had a worried air, just the same, for, to my annoyance, Russell Woodley came to my table, sat down on the bench beside me and asked me, with an air of concern, how I did. 'For you look pale, Mistress Stannard. Are you not well?'

'I am a little tired,' I said. 'Nothing more.'

'You are sure? You look troubled to me. You can't tell me what the trouble is?'

His blue eyes were scanning my face as if hoping to read

there the news I wasn't telling him. He was about the same age as me and I recognized, all too clearly, the warmth in his gaze. Well, I could only blame myself. I had gossiped with him, hoping to learn something useful – perhaps some little detail that could point to whoever might be a spy on behalf of Harry's captors, and he had interpreted that as encouragement. I now regretted it very much. I was so very, very tired of being pursued. After Hugh's death, as a woman of substance with money and two good houses, royal connections and the possibility, still, of bearing children, it was inevitable that I should be, but I didn't enjoy it. I wanted to remain, to live and to die, as the widow of Hugh Stannard, and leave it at that.

It was true that since Hugh's death, I had had that one extraordinary reunion with Matthew de la Roche, the husband I had before Hugh. From that, Harry had come and I could not regret that. But I didn't want to repeat it, either. It was also true that in another world, Brockley and I might have been a couple – might have had a son like Philip – but that other world did not exist and never could. It was further true that I had once, briefly, considered marrying my friend Christopher Spelton. But Christopher had changed his mind, had instead fallen in love with my ward, Kate Lake, and was now married to her and very happy with her at West Leys, their farm not far from Guildford, and with his little stepson and his own tiny twin daughters, and I had found on thinking it over, that I didn't regret that either.

I did not want Russell Woodley. I was through with passion. Nor, I felt, was it becoming in a woman of my age. I was nearly forty-seven, after all.

The queen was older, and was locked into a half-betrothal to the French duke, Francis of Alençon, and, I knew, was half in love with him and half desperate to escape. My personal view was that escape was the right thing for her. There comes a time when loving and mating are things of the past.

I didn't answer him, but he seemed to be good at guessing. 'You are a half-sister to the queen. I know that,' he said. 'That relationship may well be a burden at times.'

'And too many people know of it,' I said waspishly.

He nodded. 'I will say no more.' He frowned. 'Is your hidden trouble something to do with your son? I believe he is missing, or some such thing?'

'There is too much tittle-tattle in this castle,' I said with irritation. 'Has young Meredith been tattling?'

'He is a terror, that way,' said Russell. 'Well, yes, he has. He always seems to know a lot. Don't be anxious. I shan't talk about it if you don't want me to. I understand the meaning of the word discretion. But, Mistress Stannard, believe me, if there is anything I can do to serve you, I will gladly do it. I am here if you have need of me.'

'My son is not missing,' I said patiently. 'He is visiting his elder sister, my married daughter. If he were missing,' I added righteously, 'I would hardly be likely to be here, now, would I?'

Brockley, dear Brockley. May God speed your search.

In the morning, before Brockley left, I went to the stables and inspected the hired nag he had arrived on. It was a depressing animal, with hairy heels, a goose rump and a massive roman nose. One at least of its recent ancestors had assuredly been one of the heavy horses formerly bred to carry knights in plate armour. Returning to our rooms, I gave Brockley some money from the hoard I had brought and recommended him to buy a good horse before he left Sheffield.

'If you're going to make for Warwick,' I said, 'I know it's nearer than Stratford, but you still have a long ride ahead of you, and then God knows how far the trail will lead you.'

'It's a good eighty miles from here to Warwick,' Brockley said. 'If one were a crow, at that.'

'So you need a good, reliable horse under you. The grooms here will know the best dealer,' I said. 'Tell me which Stratford stable produced that dismal animal, and Eddie will take it back. He can lead it and ride one of our coach horses.'

Brockley departed on this errand and was back within three hours, bringing with him a good-looking bay gelding, with the deep chest needed for stamina, a good tail carriage to round off sturdy hindquarters and the dish face that meant Barbary blood. It carried its head well, too.

'He's called Jaunty,' Brockley said. 'On account of the way he holds his head and tail, apparently.'

'A pleasant name,' I said approvingly. 'And a good horse, I fancy. You must miss Firefly!' I gave my old friend and retainer a smile and then said: 'Brockley! You haven't shaved today!'

'Madam, if I find the house, I may also find some of those players who came to Hawkswood and they might recognize me. I have been thinking of ways to change the way I look. Growing even the start of a beard might help.'

'So it might. That was well thought of. Well, Brockley. Godspeed!'

And now, once more, I must hand over this narrative to another person for I dared not leave Sheffield. This part of the tale belongs to Brockley.

SIXTEEN
All Unknowing

Since he wasn't using remounts, Brockley did not reach Warwick until almost the evening of the second day. Jaunty was a very good horse but Brockley didn't want to press him over-hard. Time mattered, though. Every day that Mistress Stannard had to stay at Sheffield without taking action to please the enemy increased the danger to Harry.

The weather, however, was not too kind. On the first day there was a short but fierce downpour which soaked him thoroughly, despite a good cloak and a stout green hat. The inn where he spent that night was not good, either. His supper was poor and his bed lumpy. He set out on the final day of his journey in an irritable temper.

In the late afternoon he was approaching Warwick and was relieved at it because he was beginning to feel shivery, the result no doubt of his soaking the day before. He was thankful that the sun was now out, and could warm him a little.

He was interested, as he rode, to notice a fine black and white house on the left-hand side of the track. Its white plaster and jet-black beams looked as though they had been newly refurbished, and there was a man on the roof, apparently putting on new thatch. Old thatch lay in heaps in front of the building, and the thatcher was aloft, working busily, with a big basket of thatching straw tied to a chimney, and a long ladder behind him, reaching to the ground. Brockley pulled up, wondering suddenly if this, by any unlikely chance, would turn out to be Master Ashley himself. He was about to shout to the thatcher when another, younger-looking man appeared round the side of the house, peered at the ladder and began to adjust it, whereupon the thatcher shouted to him to let it be, it was properly positioned already.

'But it b'ain't, sir,' the second man, presumably an assistant, shouted. 'One foot's on a loose stone; it'll likely slip if you put your weight on it! I'm making it safe!'

The thatcher retorted with a fierce statement that he had been positioning ladders since before you were born, you young idiot; what do you mean by interfering? After which, his voice subsided into angry muttering and Brockley changed his mind. This was the wrong moment to interrupt with enquiries about identity and besides, he was really beginning to feel ill. He wanted to reach shelter. He could come back tomorrow, after all. He rode on.

The castle, looming up on the west bank of the river Avon as he rode towards it when evening was drawing near, was in sight before the surrounding town was, a mighty structure of walls and towers. It drew Brockley's eyes at once. Well, tomorrow he could try going back to talk to the thatcher, but very likely the castle would be a better place to begin. Castles were the sort of building that often needed repairs, including roof repairs. Well, he would decide tomorrow which to do first. For the moment, he wanted to find an inn. A good one.

This was not difficult, but he found that he had little appetite for the excellent supper he was offered. He was glad to lie down, on what this time was a comfortable bed.

He woke in the morning with a violent sneeze and a raging sore throat and a fever.

He cursed, but in vain. The landlord's wife was kind and brought him broth and hot possets, and the fever left him by nightfall, but he was horribly weak and his nose felt as though it were made of rock. Two clear days passed before he finally woke in the morning to find that he felt capable of getting on his horse. Luckily, he had always been strong and he always did throw colds off quickly. This one, however, was very ill-timed.

The thatcher had probably finished his job by now. He had better start by going to the castle. Crossly blowing a red, sore nose, he set out, to find its main gate.

*   *   *

Here, despite the ominous appearance of the castle from a distance, he met with an unexpected air of hospitality. The gates stood wide open and people were going freely in and out. There were guards and they did ask his business, but civilly, and without any air of wishing to exclude anyone.

'I need to make some enquiries about a man who may at some time have done repair work here,' Brockley said, balancing frankness with discretion as best he could. 'I wish him no ill; in fact, my mistress may want to employ him. I would like to speak to a suitable person.'

'My lord Ambrose of Warwick isn't here just now,' one of the guards said. 'He's visiting the royal court and half his household are away with him, and that includes his steward. He's expected back tomorrow or the next day but if you are in a hurry, there's the under-steward. You'd best talk to him.' He stepped back into the gatehouse, calling for somebody named Barty, which produced another guard, a young one with an amiable pink face.

'Take this fellow to see Master Devereux,' said the first guard. 'What's your name, fellow?'

At this point, Brockley hated himself for not thinking properly ahead. He didn't want to give his proper name to all and sundry in case the wrong ears heard it, but of course, he was bound to be asked for it here, and he must not hesitate. He snatched at his son's surname and said: 'Roger Sandley.'

It sounded reasonable and was accepted as such. He dismounted, let the pink-faced Barty take Jaunty's bridle, and followed him across what seemed like acres of cobbles and greensward to a small doorway. A groom appeared to take charge of the horse, while Barty went inside to ask after Master Devereux. The under-steward was evidently not at hand but Brockley was finally allowed over the threshold and found himself in a vestibule leading to what, judging by the savoury scents emerging from them, were kitchens. A large man, rubbing greasy hands on a leather apron, came out, looked him up and down, and pointed to a stone bench. 'You can wait there.'

He did wait there, as patiently as possible though the

vestibule was cold and the stone bench very hard. After what seemed like a long time, Master Devereux appeared. Brockley, accustomed in my company to visiting the court, rose politely to his feet, and was not surprised to see that the under-steward bore himself sternly erect, had a neatly barbered beard, was finely dressed, with a gold chain of office, and looked much more like a guest of the house than any kind of servant. His eyebrows were thin and shaped like Norman arches and now, looking at Brockley, he raised them, which gave him a very supercilious air.

'Well, fellow? Barty from the gatehouse says you wish to enquire after someone who may have been employed here at some time. But first who are you?'

Brockley had had time now to consider the difficult problem of his identity and concluded that complete discretion was not possible. This man was visibly trying to intimidate him with his air of power and dignity. He would have more authority and more chance of learning what he sought to know, if he was frank up to a point.

He said: 'I am the manservant of one Mistress Ursula Stannard. The name may perhaps be known to you. She is related to her majesty. My own name is Roger Brockley. I gave a different name at the gate because I am here on Mistress Stannard's business which is also the queen's business and have been asked to preserve secrecy as far as possible.'

'I have heard of Mistress Stannard, of course.' Master Devereux looked surprised but his air of deliberate intimidation softened just a little. 'My master, Sir Ambrose Dudley of Warwick, is the brother of my lord Robert Dudley of Leicester and is often at court. Well, what is this enquiry?'

'We – that is, my mistress – need to find a man whose business is that of repairing buildings, especially roofs. His name is Ashley and he may live in Warwick or near it. I am not at liberty to say why Mistress Stannard needs to find him, except that no harm is intended to him.'

'My good fellow!' Devereux looked quite pained. 'This is an earl's castle. We have a full staff of men whose business is to maintain the castle and its outhouses in a good state of repair. We do not hire outside help, and none of our permanent maintenance staff bears the name of Ashley. You have wasted your time in coming here. I should try an innkeeper or some such person . . .'

His voice, though, faded, and a frown between his eyebrows removed the supercilious expression. He was thinking. 'But I have heard that name not so long ago . . . that's strange. I can't remember . . . wait!'

He withdrew, apparently into the kitchen, as a waft of heat came out of the door through which he had gone. Presently, he reappeared, accompanied by a large woman whose dun-coloured working dress was dusted with flour. She was perspiring, as kitchen workers usually did.

'This is Mistress Prentice, one of our pastry-cooks. I thought I remembered that the name Ashley had something to do with her and she says he's some sort of relative and that yes, he repairs roofs and has been here, which surprises me. Tell this man about it, Mistress. And tell me, as well! I thought we never brought in outside workmen.'

'We don't as a rule, Master Devereux,' said the woman, 'but it was after that storm a couple of weeks ago when the roof came off the coach house and half the tiles off one of the stable blocks, and the horses had to be moved out and it was a mercy there were empty stalls in the block that are kept for guests' horses, for where they could have been put otherwise . . .'

'Her son,' said Devereux to Brockley, 'is one of the grooms here.' He turned back to Mistress Prentice. 'Never mind all that. How your tongue runs away with you! I've had to speak to you before about working harder and talking less. Now, however, we wish you to tell us about your relative, Master Ashley. What relation is he to you?'

'He's the husband of my second cousin,' said Mistress Prentice primly. Brockley, amused, thought she was using exactitude in retaliation for being reprimanded before a stranger. 'John Naylor that's head groom said the roofs must be put right as quick as could be and there weren't enough men to get it done as fast as he wanted. There'd be guests coming when my lord came home and there wouldn't be enough stabling fit for use, so Master Jefferson that is in charge of the repair men, he said, better bring in some extra help, and I suggested my cousin's man, Daniel Ashley, for I know he's a fine craftsman for thatching and tiling. Master Naylor said yes, call him in, and Master Jefferson sent for Daniel and he came along and did a fine job, from what I heard. It all took a couple of days to arrange because Daniel was working somewhere else, and . . .'

'Yes, all right. So he's probably the man you want, Master Brockley. Where is he to be found, Mistress Prentice?'

'Little cottage out on the Stratford road, to the left, just beside a stream that runs into the Avon. It's called the Thatch and it has the best-looking thatched roof you ever saw. Daniel says it shows the world his work. He lives there with my cousin Ellie and their children, three lovely children they've got, and . . .'

Brockley said: 'I'll find it,' and pressed a gold coin into the talkative Mistress Prentice's floury hand.

He didn't know where the stables were, so he went back to the gatehouse and Barty was despatched to fetch Jaunty. In another ten minutes, he was setting off to find The Thatch.

A cottage called the Thatch, on the left-hand side of the Stratford road, by a stream. Brockley was well on his way before he realized that he had omitted to ask how far along the Stratford road he would need to go. However, he came to the place quite quickly. It was quite unmistakeable, for the stream crossed the track by way of a watersplash, and there was the cottage, surrounded by a trim garden, and a recently thatched roof, golden in the spring sunshine. Smoke rose from one of its chimneys.

And its front door was wide open, men and women were standing in the front garden and moving in and out and every one of them was dressed in black.

Dismayed, Brockley pulled up. A man standing by the gate turned at the sound of a horse, and then came up to him. 'Are you here for the funeral, sir?'

'I . . . no,' Brockley said. 'I have business with a Master Ashley, a roof mender. I was directed to this house . . .'

'This is indeed Daniel Ashley's house. I am his brother,

Will Ashley.' He spoke with a local accent but a correct command of English. 'But if you have business with Daniel, sir, you are over-late.' He nodded towards the cottage door. 'Daniel . . . is being brought out now.'

Brockley turned. A coffin was being carried out, on the shoulders of six men. A handcart was being wheeled to meet them and while Brockley watched, the coffin was loaded on to it. A woman, in black but not veiled, appeared in the doorway and was watching, though she came no further. Brockley thought he glimpsed some children behind her.

'What happened?' he asked.

'Daniel was a roof mender, as you say,' said Will Ashley. 'He had an accident. He lost his footing on a roof where he was working – in Warwick town – three days ago and killed himself falling. His was always a hazardous profession. I am in the building trade myself, but I don't do roofing.'

Brockley hesitated. In the normal way, business or no business, he would never have attempted to intrude on a family in mourning.

But there was Harry, in a form of danger that made the blood chill in Brockley's veins, for he had once, himself, been in peril of becoming a corsair's prey, and on top of that, he was my man and owed a duty to me, a duty in which he was determined not to fail.

He looked gravely at Will Ashley. 'Sir, I would not for the world disturb this sad occasion but I am charged with a task that – is of more importance than I am free to explain. I take it that Mistress Ashley – there is a Mistress Ashley, I believe – will not attend the burial?'

'Naturally not. She will remain in the house until we return. Does that matter to you? Do you propose to intrude on her regardless?'

Will spoke angrily. Brockley shook a placating head. 'No. I do not. I ask, instead, if I may leave my horse here and attend the burial myself, as a mark of respect to your brother. Afterwards, if you permit, I would be glad to return to the house with everyone else, offer my condolences in the proper way, and then, yes, perhaps ask her a very simple question, concerning the whereabouts of a house where her husband worked recently. That is all. I will then take my leave.'

Will Ashley frowned. Brockley, however, slid his feet out of his stirrups and quietly dismounted. He had recognized the kind of man Will Ashley was. He was a solid workman, experienced and successful in his trade, sure of himself accordingly, and knowledgeable enough in the ways of the world to recognize what kind of man Brockley himself was. He would know that Brockley would not press such a matter, here at Daniel Ashley's very funeral, without a good reason.

They stood face to face for a moment, studying each other. Then Will said: 'Your name?'

'Roger Brockley. I serve one Mistress Ursula Stannard, who in turn serves the queen.'

'Mistress Stannard, eh? I have heard that name. Daniel has worked at Warwick Castle and heard talk. I see. Very well. I will ask Mistress Ashley if you may join us.'

He made his way to the woman who was still in the doorway. From a distance, Brockley saw them speaking together and saw her nod.

Will, returning, showed him the stable behind the cottage, where Jaunty could be stalled alongside the cob that Daniel Ashley had used. Then they joined the procession that led from the cottage, along the track a little further and then off to the right on another, well-used track, and after a short distance, into a small village with a church.

Brockley never did learn the name of the village. It was very small indeed and so was the church, which was completely filled by the mourners. There were benches, but several people were left standing at the back. A number of them seemed to be customers who had used Daniel Ashley's services and been pleased with them. No one took much notice of Brockley. The coffin was placed on a trestle in the centre aisle and the service proceeded, after which the coffin was borne out again, taken to a newly dug grave and lowered reverently in while the vicar, a large, amiable man with a good speaking voice, recited the committal.

Then came the return to the cottage, not a procession this time but just a crowd of people walking together. When they entered the cottage, Brockley found himself impressed. It was plainly furnished, as one might expect, but it was nevertheless the home of a man who had been successful in his trade and adequately paid for his work. The walls might be unadorned stone but the two matching walnut settles had beautifully carved lions' feet and on one wall hung a clock, with black metal hands and Roman figures on a round cream-coloured face, enclosed by a glossy wooden case. And on the opposite wall hung a small but brilliantly polished silver mirror.

The table in the centre of the room was spread with a white cloth and set with cold meats and fresh bread, fruit patties and ale, which Mistress Ashley, bravely in charge despite her mourning gown, was dispensing. With her were two young girls, probably aged about twelve and ten. They were red-eyed and visibly unhappy but she was encouraging them to help her. A little boy, just a toddler, watched, thumb in mouth, in the care of another woman.

Will caught his eye and led him over to the table. 'Sister-in-law, this is Roger Brockley, of whom I told you. I explained, I think, that he serves Mistress Ursula Stannard, who serves the queen.'

Mistress Ashley nodded. She had a rosy, mature face, tired just now through the stresses of grief and busyness combined, but she gave him a small smile and told the two little girls to take up the plates of patties and offer them to the guests.

'Your daughters, madam?' Brockley asked politely.

'Aye, so they are. Mary and Cath. Good girls both. And the little one is my son Johnnie. Will said you had something to ask me, and that you were sorry to intrude but the matter is important. He said that the name of Ursula Stannard made it so. I know nothing of such a name but Will is very knowledgeable about the world and so was . . . so was my husband. I will help if I can.'

'It's very simple,' said Brockley, silently blessing the fact that the name of Ursula Stannard was becoming well known. 'By the way, I was encouraged to seek out your husband by your cousin Mistress Prentice, in Warwick Castle. She evidently didn't know of his accident.'

Mistress Ashley made an angry face. 'I wanted to tell her. I'd have liked her to come to the funeral but I know that just now, with my lord Ambrose due home so soon, she would never get permission out of that snooty under-steward. He'd have said, no, not for just the husband of a second cousin. He'd only give her the time off for a close relative. Them's his rules. She says he's a proper slave-driver. If I'd told her before the funeral, she'd only have been upset. I'd have sent word very soon. I hate that under-steward. He thinks anyone below him is dirt beneath his feet. My cousin will understand why I didn't worry her until it was all over. But that surely wasn't your question?'

'No. The truth is that I need – I truly and genuinely need – to find a house where your husband did some work – let me see, it would have been just before he was called to work at Warwick Castle – just after the time of the big gale. He was repairing a slate roof that was damaged in the wind. The house was lonely, and I believe had ivy on its walls, and had a high wall all round it, shutting the grounds in. It was occupied by a number of people, not an ordinary family. Did your late husband speak to you of such a place, or tell you where it was, or its name – or anything about it?'

Mistress Ashley folded her plump, capable hands and gazed into the distance, evidently thinking. Then she said: 'Yes, he did go to such a house though he didn't say much about it. Just after the gale, it were, and just afore he went to the castle. Yes, he said it was to repair damage as the weather had done. There were slates to replace. And he said the place was lonely. It was some way off, must have been, for he went for two days running and left so early each morning, and came back late.'

'He never gave it a name?'

'No.' She shook her head. 'He were fetched by a messenger, someone from the house. Came here, asked for him special.

Folk do that – he had a good name for his work, my Daniel did.'

Her voice wavered. In his very best and most soothing voice, the one he used for calming nervous horses, Brockley said: 'I am very sorry to learn of his passing, and not just because I wanted to talk to him. I am truly sorry for your loss, madam, and for your children's loss of their father. And also for the world's loss of a man I think must have been a fine workman.'

'He was that. And how he ever come to fall off that roof, a roof where he's done repairs half a dozen times before, and he's never slipped on any roof at all that I know of . . . He was working on a fine house just outside Warwick; it was being done over, new plaster, black paint on the beams and all, and new thatch. His ladder slipped when he was coming down to fetch more straw.'

'But . . . I think I saw the place on my way to Warwick! I'm almost sure of it! Black and white, a big house, on the left as you come towards the town.'

'Aye, that would be it. You saw the house, you say? And him?'

'Yes.' The idea that now thrust itself through Brockley's brain, was as sharp as a blade. He made his next comment with caution. 'What a dreadful thing to happen. Did he not have an assistant to hold ladders steady for him?'

'Oh, no, he always worked alone. He said that assistants could be more trouble than they were worth,' said Mistress Ashley.

Oh, dear God. That was Daniel Ashley, it really was. But if he was working alone, then who was the man who came and fiddled with his ladder? He shouted at him not to interfere! Was the younger man not an assistant but an intrusive passer-by? The thatcher had been very angry with him.

And had that young man . . . moved a safe ladder and made it unsafe? Had Daniel Ashley not died by accident, but . . .?

Did I witness it, all unknowing?

Mistress Ashley said sadly: 'They said at the inquest that Daniel didn't fix a ladder rightly, so when he put some weight on it, it slipped and tipped him off the roof, but Daniel didn't do things like that. Twenty years in the business, he'd been! I couldn't believe it.'

Nor did Brockley. Too many things were fitting together, and the pattern they made was not pretty. But here and now was not the time or place to speak of his suspicions. He put a gentle hand over one of hers. 'Such things do happen. Try not to think about it. I hope . . . I hope you have been left provided for.'

'Oh yes. Daniel had savings and I can get work at the castle and there's neighbours who'll look after little ones while I'm there. My elder girl might get work there as well. There's usually work for women and girls in a place that size. Even if we do have to put up with that there under-steward whenever my lord is away.'

'One more thing. Did your husband recently seek the services of a courier?'

'Why, yes, sir, he did. Said he'd come across something that he ought to let someone in the south counties know about. He was a bit mysterious. But it happened that he met a courier, a man from Stratford, in an inn, after work one evening, and was able to hire him for the job. I thought it was all very strange. He carried on as though the business made him nervous but he wouldn't tell me anything.'

'Just one more thing. Mistress Ashley, you are sure your husband never told you where the walled house is – or its name?'

'No, he never did.'

'Then,' said Brockley, 'when he rode off to go to his work there, did you see which way he turned?'

'Oh, yes. Left, and then right again after a little way, towards the village where you've just been. One of those days, I was upstairs, tidying and I looked from the window and saw him turn off.'

'And . . . madam, forgive me for letting my one question grow into so many . . . what time he was supposed to be at the house?'

'Eight of the clock or thereabouts, he said. And he left,' said Mistress Ashley, who had clearly grasped the point of the question, 'at seven. We have a clock here,' she added proudly, and pointed to the one that Brockley had already noticed. He looked at it again and estimated that it was not only handsome but probably accurate as well. An hour's ride away, then, and he had a direction.

That was something.

SEVENTEEN
Glimpsed At A Window

Brockley stayed long enough at the Ashley house to eat a midday meal. He talked quietly to this person and that; fitting in and not drawing attention to himself. It was easy to remain unobtrusive when so many of the gathering were the late Daniel Ashley's customers, and were strangers to each other.

Then he bade farewell to Mistress Ashley and her brother-in-law Will, collected his horse and took his leave. While preparing to set off, he gave some thought to his next move and he did not at once ride off in search of the unknown walled house. He had been gripped by a terrible anger. If his suspicions were right, then Harry was in the hands of people who were prepared to murder others besides Mary Stuart. They had said they wouldn't kill Harry himself; they clearly had some limitations, but Harry was a child. Daniel Ashley, a grown man, had by the sound of it had less claim on their sense of humanity.

If they had any idea that he had carried a message from Harry, they might well have decided to silence him. If some unknown spy – Laurence Miller? – had told them that such a message had reached Hawkswood, then Daniel was an obvious and probably their only suspect.

But he must be careful. In the light of this, careful of himself, for if they could slaughter poor Master Ashley, they would probably slaughter Brockley just as willingly. His rage was like a stone in his chest, but he must be wise, and wary.

He had taken a glance or two at his reflection in the little silver mirror and concluded that though his nascent beard had certainly changed his appearance, it hadn't gone far enough. Someone who had seen him when the players visited

Hawkswood might yet see through the disguise. He needed
to do better. He turned his mount back towards Warwick.

It was late afternoon by then but it was still sunny and the
east gate of the town, by which he entered, was busy with
traffic. Carts, horsemen, pack animals, folk on foot were going
purposefully in and out and the streets inside were populous.
He made an enquiry or two and found what he wanted at the
second attempt.

'Wanted for players up at the castle, would it be?' said the
man he had accosted. 'Allus having masques and the like up
there, they are and my lord's due home from the court any
day so there's likely to be some entertainments soon. Wigmaker,
he do a good trade in this town. Straight along there, then a
lane to your right. Whole lot of little shops there that do well
when a masque's being planned. There's a fellow does trick
swords as slide into theirselves and make it look like they're
being swallowed, and . . .'

'Come,' said Brockley, 'don't give all the secrets away! It'll
spoil the fun to tell the audience how the trick's done. Sword-
swallowers want oohs and aahs and if a lady faints with alarm,
so much the better!'

His informant laughed and went on his way, and Brockley
followed the directions, which took him into a narrow, twisting
lane which, as promised, contained numerous interesting shops.
There was indeed one selling trick weapons – swords, daggers
and bows. The wigmaker's shop, however, was the next one
along. Brockley attached his horse to the hitching rail next to
the door and stepped in.

He expected the place to be dark, but it was actually well-lit
by virtue of a skylight. No doubt the work done here needed
a good light. The elderly proprietor was busy combing out a
flaxen wig which was positioned on a stand. Other stands,
with other wigs on them, were set in a row on one side of the
shop, and on the other, a young woman and a young man who
looked so alike that they were surely brother and sister were
sorting hanks of hair.

'Ah. Good afternoon.' The elderly man scanned Brockley
and assessed him. 'You're wanting a wig – helping with a
masque at the castle, are you?'

'Something like that,' said Brockley, 'but the wig is for me. I am taking part in the masque and supplying my own costume. I require a dark wig, shoulder-length.'

The proprietor left his combing and came to gaze at Brockley with interest. 'I think I can oblige. Aye. Dark, you say, and shoulder-length.'

'Sounds like that wicked king the third Richard,' remarked the young man at the counter. 'I saw a portrait of him once; I were delivering a couple of wigs to the Master of the Revels at the castle and they had the portrait there. It had been borrowed from somewhere because her majesty was to make a stay at the castle and they were doing a little play about the battle where her grandfather, the good seventh Henry, defeated Richard.'

'You talk too much, son,' said the elderly man, and then delved into a cupboard, emerging a moment later with a dark wig in his hands. He whisked the fair wig off the stand, put the dark one in its place and set about combing out tangles. 'This'll be the right length, I don't doubt it, and it's good quality, all real hair, human hair. Not cheap, mind you, but it'll last and last.'

'Let me see if it fits,' said Brockley.

It fitted very well, and the mirror which the young woman quickly brought, showed Brockley an unrecognizable version of himself. 'This will do,' he said.

He paid, allowed the wig to be placed in a leather drawstring bag, and rode off. He had another purchase to make, since his green hat was quite distinctive. He had better buy something that would look different. By the time this was done, the day was nearly gone. It was not a good time to start hunting for isolated houses. He went back to the inn.

In the morning, after asking the innkeeper for a noon-piece of bread and cheese and a flask of well water, he left early, still as himself, a commonplace figure in a buff doublet and hose and his old green hat, while his disguises stayed in the bag that hung from his saddle. But once out of sight of the town, he took off his hat, donned his new head of hair, put on the new brown cap that looked so different and pushed his green hat into the bag. He then shook up his horse and set out on his search. He was no longer Roger Brockley. During

his solitary night, he had chosen a new name, and taken some
care over it. It must have no echo of Hawkswood in it; must
not be any name that the players who held Harry might recognize. Sandley wouldn't do this time.

His new name must be commonplace but not to a suspicious
degree. He must not be called John Smith, for example. No.
He would be . . . he would be . . . he would be Robin Wilson.
And may God smile on my errand, he whispered as he rode
past the Ashley cottage (silent now, all doors and windows
fast shut though there was a thin trickle of smoke from
the kitchen chimney) and took the right-hand turn towards the
little village with the tiny church, and the open country beyond.
His anger was still with him, burning holes in him. It had
driven his cold away so thoroughly that he had almost forgotten
it. So far, he had been able to follow the route that Master
Ashley had taken when he set off to repair a roof damaged
by the gale. But from now on, he had no guidance. The countryside ahead was lonely and rolling. He decided to slant
towards the left, which was the south, and make for a hilltop
that would give him a good view all round. Then he would
work northwards, using hilltops when he could, tracing out a
kind of arc that would at all points be roughly an hour away
from the Ashley house.

It was going to be a long and tiresome ride. The day was
warm and the wig was hot. Also, the long dark hair that brushed
his shoulders felt strange. The first hilltop revealed nothing
helpful. Below, he could see a couple of thatched farmhouses,
with their fields around them, and a little hamlet just beyond,
but otherwise he saw only common land and woods. He rode
down the north side of the hill and set off for the next high
point.

From here, he could see a possibility. Yes, there was an
isolated house down there, maybe a mile from the foot of the
slope just before him. He rode hopefully down but on reaching
the place, realized that it couldn't possibly be the right one.
It was a big, cheerful-looking farmhouse, wide open to callers,
and as he rode into the yard, two small boys and a large
woman with a jolly expression came out of a back door to
meet him.

'I've just called to ask for directions. There's a house I am trying to find but I don't know its name, only its description . . .'

'Well, come you down, and my lads here will take your horse and you come inside to tell us all about it and take a bite. Ridden far, have you? I'm Emma Jones. My man's out in the fields, but my boys know how to take care of a horse . . . my, that's a fine one you have there . . .'

Jaunty was led away and Brockley was swept inside on a hospitable and garrulous tide, seated at a kitchen table, and plied with viands. He mentioned his bread and cheese but Emma Jones regarded them with disdain.

'Bless you, we can do better than that, sir. I've been making meat and pippin pasties this very morning; there's still a few pippins left over from last autumn. And there's our own cider and elderflower wine . . . where's Julie . . . ah, there you are, lass.' A girl of about twelve had come into the kitchen. 'Julie, you get out the pasties and the things to drink, and I'll talk to our guest here. He wants directions. Now, what be this house like, that you're looking for, sir?'

He described the house he wanted, as well as he could, realizing as he talked how little he really knew. 'I know it's built of grey stone, with a wall all round and it's lonely. Why I want to find it is a long story. Forgive me if I don't recite it to you. But it's important that I do find this house and my reason is honest. Do you know of such a place?'

Unfortunately, Emma Jones did not. Her husband came in while Brockley was still there and could not help either. 'It's nowhere near here, that's for sure, or I would know of it,' he said.

Brockley, at length, thanked them for the pasties and the cider, which he had preferred to elderflower wine and which proved to be excellent, and took his leave. He must ride on, northwards, and find another hilltop, not too close.

He was aware, as he rode, of feeling tired. As a rule, Brockley was as much at ease in a saddle as he was in his bed, but now, he thought ruefully, his years must be telling. There had been a time when one wetting would never have made him catch cold. He was better now, except for occasionally blowing his nose, but he had better bear it in mind. He was over sixty now and he had scarcely been out of the saddle since Harry's letter reached Hawkswood.

But at least Jaunty's sloping shoulders provided easy paces; the bay was a comfortable ride. Also, the meat and pippin pasties and the cider had been fortifying. Brockley pressed on.

An hour later, he had topped another hill and his hopes rose again. Below him was a valley with a village in it, and beyond that a hill much lower than the one where he had drawn rein, so he could see that on the far side of it there were fields and woods – and one lonely house, from which the village probably couldn't be seen.

He glimpsed a river that seemed to begin in the hills to his left and pass through one end of the village, and then wind on into the country west of the solitary house.

The house was too far away for details to be visible but he did have the impression of a grey surrounding wall. He thought he could also make out a farmhouse some way to the west, no doubt the place to which the fields belonged. The river seemed to flow towards it. Like the village, the farmhouse probably wasn't visible from the grey-walled house. There was a patch of woodland in between.

'Oh, let it be,' he said aloud, and urged Jaunty on.

His route took him through the village and there he found an alehouse whose proprietor was helpful. Yes, he knew of the place that Brockley described. Ivy House, it was called. Been taken over as a base by a group of actors, for working on a new play or something of the sort. Queer folk, keep theirselves to theirselves, but they pay their bills right enough. They send a cart into the village now and again for food and ale and whatnot. No, it's not far, not from here. An hour's ride, no more.

One more hour, and he was there. He drew up outside the gate, which was uncompromisingly shut. However, having settled his hat and wig more firmly on his head and run a caressing hand over his chin, which was now adorned with something more than mere stubble, he decided to take the risk and banged on the gate with the handle of his riding whip. Dogs at once began to bark and after a moment, there were sounds of bolts being drawn back and the gate was opened, though not very wide. Two big dogs immediately bounded forward, baying, but were ordered back by the man who had opened the gate, and who was now standing firmly in the entrance, blocking the way.

'I'm lost,' said Brockley resourcefully. 'I've come quite a distance.' The alehouse keeper had said that the village was called Timsford but he had better not say he was looking for that, as he might have been seen coming from that direction. 'I want to find the road to Warwick and I've gone hopelessly wrong. Can I come in for a moment? I'd be glad to get out of this saddle even for five minutes and my horse needs a drink of water.'

The man, who was clad in a sleeveless jerkin over a wool shirt, with breeches, leggings and boots on his lower half, looked uncertain but finally snapped an order at the dogs, who retreated and lay down. Then he stood aside so that Brockley could ride through the gate.

'Stable yard's through that arch on the right. Trough's there.'

'Many thanks.' Brockley dismounted and led Jaunty across the courtyard, trying as he did so to observe his surroundings. Grey walls. Ivy. Yes, this was assuredly the place. He led Jaunty through the arch to find himself in a small and untidy stable yard, where buckets and hay bales stood haphazardly about and wisps of straw were blowing over the cobbles. The trough was full and Jaunty really was thirsty, for when he scented the water, he pulled Brockley towards it, ears eagerly pricked.

The porter, or groom or whatever he was, had come with them and while Jaunty was drinking, began to give directions to Warwick. 'You're a long way off your course,' he said disapprovingly, clearly regarding Brockley as something of a fool.

'I'll find my way now. Many thanks,' Brockley said.

He was obviously not going to be asked into the house. Indeed, no one had appeared who was likely to have the authority to invite him. He must not arouse any suspicions. This was surely the place and for the moment, that was good enough. As he led Jaunty back through the courtyard, however, he glanced at the front of the house and saw a movement at an upstairs window. For a brief moment, a face appeared.

He could not be sure . . . but it looked remarkably like Harry's face.

He could not signal openly. He was in disguise and Harry had probably not recognized him – given that it really was Harry at that window.

Well, if this was the right house then it was likely enough! He compromised by smiling vaguely in the direction of the window. Then, at the gate, he mounted, repeated his thanks for the directions and Jaunty's drink, and rode away.

EIGHTEEN
Supper and Cards

While Brockley was searching for Harry's place of captivity, I remained in Sheffield, learning things about myself.

When Brockley had ridden away, I was once more forced into silent waiting, haunted by fears I could not discuss, did not want to discuss, even with Dale, who would be sympathetic, would be upset on my behalf, but couldn't help. In fact, she needed me to remain calm to make sure that she in turn remained calm and didn't talk carelessly.

It amazed me to discover just how desperate one could feel, without showing it. After championing Timmy, I found myself on quite amiable terms with Mary and now went through the unexciting days, smiling, pleasant, doing embroidery, sometimes playing cards with Bess or Mary, practising the lute and the spinet so that I could help to entertain them or take a turn at playing when we had dancing practice, consulting with Dale over which gown to put on each day, going out for rides on Jewel, usually as one of Mary's companions.

Yet all the time, inside myself, I wanted to scream, to throw myself onto the floor and pound it with my fists and cry out Harry's name. During that time, the only person to notice that anything was amiss with me was Russell Woodley, and his intervention was, as ever, embarrassing. He accosted me one morning as I was making my way to breakfast, and once again pressed me to tell him what was wrong.

'I *know* there is something on your mind, Mistress Stannard,' he said earnestly. 'I can see it. Please tell me. Perhaps I can help in some way.'

His eyes were kind and admiring as usual and should have been a comfort but were not. Instead, he was as ever an unwanted complication.

'There is nothing serious on my mind,' I said mendaciously. 'I am a little worried over things at my home. I am waiting for news. I have a stud of trotting horses, you know, and when I left, there were some problems to do with that.' Inspired, I added: 'I had just appointed a new stud groom but I am not sure about him yet.'

'You are much alone,' he said. I wanted to continue on to breakfast but the passage was narrow and he was standing in my way. 'Mistress Stannard,' he said, 'you are widowed and have the responsibility of two houses, with land attached, and you also have a stud to look after as well. All that is a heavy burden. Mistress Stannard . . .'

'No, please, Master Woodley, I wish you would not . . .'

'Please hear me out,' said this romantic nuisance, continuing to block my path. 'Please. I am not a fortune-hunter, I assure you . . .'

'Master Woodley, I have never supposed that you were and . . .'

'My father is in the drapery trade . . .'

'You told me that when we met at court and . . .'

'But did you really listen to me? Please let me explain myself again. It's true that I am a younger son but I shall still have a fair inheritance one day. As you know, my elder brother will have the business but I shall not go unprovided, for I have the inheritance in land through my mother, as I once told you. Meanwhile, I have a good post here. I am well paid and have been for some years. In fact, I have lately bought a smallholding which I rent out and from which I now receive a fair income. When I marry, I shall be well able to support a wife. You are a remarkable woman and I have admired you from the first moment I saw you and . . .'

'Master Woodley!' Three other people, also bound for breakfast, appeared from behind me and thrust their way past the two of us, one of them muttering crossly about the thoughtlessness of those who held council meetings in the middle of other people's rights of way. Even if I were in the least interested in Russell's proposal, a passage full of passers-by was hardly the place for it.

'I have no intention of marrying again,' I said firmly. 'I am well served and provided with advice, should I need it. I thank you for your compliment, but the answer is and always will be, that I don't wish for a new husband. Please, now, let me pass.'

'Mistress Stannard . . .'

'*Please!*' I said, and since others had already managed to get past him, I decided that I could do so too, and with determination, I thrust him aside. I made almost headlong haste to the dining chamber, afraid that he might pursue me. Fortunately, he did not.

After that, I avoided him, and on the whole, succeeded.

And then, I found that I had become a mystery to Mary.

'You are really a puzzle to me,' Mary Stuart, in her attractive voice with its French accent, said to me one morning, when I was with her and the two Maries. It was one of the times when I had been asked to play the spinet. They wanted to try out some new dance steps. But suddenly, Mary had stopped the dance, told Mary Seton and Mary Livingstone to take up the embroidery we were all sharing, the blue pattern on the silvery kirtle and the matching sleeves, and called me to sit by her in a window seat.

'A puzzle?' I said carefully.

'Yes. You are here as a guest of Lady Shrewsbury but she has made it clear that she wishes you to be in my company, and although I was much against that at first, I have come to see that the reason why you once failed me is also a reason to value you. You acted as you did because Elizabeth is your queen and your sister. I understand that. I wish I too could have your loyalty – such excellent loyalty! – instead. I find I do like to have you near me. But something about you puzzles me, as I said. Why does Bess want you, her guest, to behave as though you were mine? Why am I allowed to have a guest at all? Few people from outside are ever allowed to visit me. What are you doing here, Mistress Stannard?'

I opened my mouth and then shut it again. To say the least of it, this was a difficult question to answer.

I am here to convince a gang – yes, gang is the right

*word – of earnest patriots who want to rid England of the
danger that you represent, that I am preparing to assassinate
you! And if I don't make a move soon, they will begin to be
suspicious.*

*That is, if they have a means of knowing what goes on inside
this castle. I cannot know whether they have or not, but I fear
it and so does Walsingham.*

I could hardly say any of that to Mary. Instead, I said: 'I
am myself little more than a tool in the hands of my betters.
I was sent for by Lady Shrewsbury. Perhaps she had instructions from elsewhere. When I leave, I may perhaps be asked
to report on what I have seen and heard here. But I have had
no orders of any kind. I am as much in the dark as you are,
Your Grace.'

'I wonder,' said Mary, 'if you are telling the truth.'

To this, I returned no answer.

Mary sighed. And then gave the subject up. 'This evening,'
she said, 'I am proposing to have a little dissipation, with
a supper and card party, here in my parlour. The Talbots
have given permission. Bess will be with her lord, enter-
taining guests of their own, but I, my two Maries, and you,
could share a repast. My lord of Shrewsbury has kindly
provided some good wine – and we can have cold chicken
and a veal quiche with hot soup and saffron bread, and a
pudding of honey and raisins with rice flour, and with four
of us, there will be two pairs of card players, so we can
play piquet.

'I thought of inviting Lady Alice Hammond,' she added.
'She sometimes attends Bess when Bess visits me – well, you
have seen her here. She is one of the few allowed to visit me,
other than my Maries, my hosts and my servants, and she
amuses me. But this time Bess has said no, because Alice is
in disgrace again. She is sadly careless. I gather that poor
Alice has hopelessly spoiled a piece of embroidery by using
a completely wrong shade. It has all had to be unpicked. I am
sorry for the wench but Bess must run her own household as
she wishes. I am sorry that she can't be present. But you will
come?'

Of course I said yes. It did in fact sound like a very agreeable way to spend an evening. The sameness of Mary's days made them monotonous.

It was also, as I was keenly aware, an opportunity.

Back in my own rooms, and alone, I went to the drawer where I had hidden the phial of hemlock. I had emptied a small jewel box which had a lock, put the phial inside and put the key on my keyring. Then I had concealed the box in the drawer, under a layer of shifts.

I got it out, took its lid off, pulled out its stopper and smelt it, making a face. It was strong, and there was plenty there. It might well be quite easy, I thought, to put just a drop or two into Mary's glass of very good wine, just enough to make her somewhat ill.

If there should be someone in the castle watching for something to happen to Mary, they might well conclude that I had set to work, had perhaps misjudged the dose, or was planning a gradual process, so that her death would look like the result of a recurring illness. It would be a way to allay doubts and suspicions, to gain time, while – I hoped and prayed – Brockley found Harry's place of imprisonment.

That evening, when I changed my dress for one formal enough for an invitation to cards and supper with a queen (even one who no longer had a throne), I chose a gleaming green and pink damask one which as well as having a ridiculously wide farthingale and being designed for an open ruff which allowed for a fine display of a pearl and peridot necklace, also had a hidden pouch inside its open skirt. I slipped the phial inside.

As I was making my way to Mary's staircase, I encountered Russell, who had to press himself against the passage wall to make room for my spectacular farthingale, but nevertheless looked admiringly at my ensemble. 'Mistress Stannard, you are a joy to the eye. Bound for Her Grace's little party, I take it?'

'Yes. How did you know?'

'Oh, the kitchens have been bustling. Her Grace's chief cook is so particular. Well, away you go, and have a happy evening.'

When I reached it, I found the supper room most welcoming. The evenings were becoming long but candles had been lit nevertheless, shining from two branched candelabra and filling the room with the scent of sandalwood. It was the kind of thing that Mary liked. Elizabeth, by contrast, would have hated it. Elizabeth's nose was highly sensitive and the only perfumes she used for herself were light, flowery ones, and fugitive at that.

Two piquet tables were set out, with one of the Maries at each, and the cold chicken, a dish of salad and two flagons of wine had already been placed on a buffet table at one side. Mary, smiling and resplendent in a blue gown which, like mine, had an open ruff, came to meet me, hands outstretched.

'Here you are, Ursula! Well, you are welcome, and in your own right, *not* just as a replacement for Alice Hammond. Is that not so, my Maries?'

She shot a smiling glance over her shoulder to Mary Seton and Mary Livingstone. Mary Seton, who always looked a little stern, said: 'Indeed. Lady Alice is a sweet girl but a little talkative sometimes, though always very innocently.'

'From the way she chatters about the other women in Bess's household,' said Mary Livingstone, 'I'd say she is not only sweet and innocent but also mighty inquisitive! She notices things and I think she listens acutely as well as talking.'

'Now, Marie. She is just a young girl,' Mary said reprovingly. 'Don't imagine things. I *cannot* suppose that a lass like Alice is being employed to spy on me. I could believe it of Mistress Stannard here . . .'

'I hope you don't!' I said.

'But it doesn't matter,' said Mary cheerfully. 'For I have nothing to hide. How could I have? I am as enclosed in this castle as a Benedictine nun within her convent walls.'

Mary Livingstone said: 'I do sometimes wonder how much gossip Alice carries back to Bess's other women. But of course you are right, Your Grace. We are hardly a fruitful source of gossip.'

'I try never to gossip,' I said mildly, and suddenly wondered if Lady Alice was, after all, quite the simple young thing that she appeared to be. Could it be that the Lady Alice who listened acutely and noticed things was the real Alice, using naive chatter and inefficiency with embroidery and ruffs, as a disguise?

In fact, was it possible that Alice was the one who was here to keep watch on me? That Alice was the cat's paw of Harry's captors?

But for the moment, I had other things to think about. I was directed to sit down opposite to Mary Seton, while Mary partnered Lady Livingstone, and our card games began. 'The hot dishes will be brought in about an hour,' Mary said. 'We shall be ready for them by then, I dare say.'

I shifted in my seat and the hidden phial knocked against my left knee. I knew that it was securely stoppered, with its cap in place on top. It could stay like that if I chose. I didn't *have* to use it. Even if the opportunity arose, I need not take it.

If Alice Hammond were the spy, she would soon, no doubt, find out everything that happened at this party, even though she herself was not present. She would talk to the Maries and to me, and I would have to answer her artless questions. I certainly mustn't appear secretive. But if Mary were to be ill, Alice would hear of it. Bess would provide comforts, might even, since Mary liked Alice, tell Alice to deliver some of them. Oh yes, Alice would know all about Mary's sickness. She would be able to report back . . .

If she were the one, she would be able to tell her masters that Mistress Stannard was probably doing *something*. Was being careful, but had very likely made a start. Yes, it would gain time, time for Harry, time for Brockley. I gave a furtive glance towards the buffet table, trying to work out exactly how I might go about doctoring a wineglass and then direct it to Mary.

Mary had seen my glance. 'You are thirsty, Ursula? Well, we need not wait for the soup and the quiche. The flagons are full. Would you fetch us all a glass? Don't bring the flagons over – they'll be in the way, on these small card tables.'

I got up. My legs felt oddly stiff. I made my way over to the buffet table, took up the nearest flagon and began to fill glasses. Behind me, I could hear that Her Grace and the Maries had started an animated conversation about the progress of the blue and silver work we had all been doing. I did not turn my head. From the three at the card tables, my spreading farthingale completely hid any movement I might make in front of me. I could bring the phial out quite unseen.

It would be easy. Just a drop or two, a quarter of a thimble full. And then make sure that I handed *that* glass and no other, to Mary.

And then I knew.

I couldn't do it. I could not, literally could not, physically, reach into my split skirt and bring out the phial. My hands wouldn't do it. My head couldn't give them such a command. Still less could I make my fingers remove the phial's cap and stopper and use the cap to measure the dose, and drop it into a glass of wine.

Not even for Harry, even for my own dear son, could I do such a thing.

I wondered if he would blame me. If I were in his position, would I blame someone who could have saved me from slavery – and perhaps mutilation – by putting a drop or two of hemlock into a glass, without intending any serious harm, and yet couldn't bring themselves to it?

I didn't know. I only knew that I could not, *could not*, fetch out that phial and use its contents. I filled four glasses, all with harmless unadulterated wine, and brought them back to the tables. I handed them round and sat down again, smiling pleasantly. Mary Seton made a small, innocent joke (her jokes were never risqué), and I laughed and made a similar jest myself. I sipped my wine. So did she. At the other table, Mary Stuart and Mary Livingstone did the same thing. We went on playing.

Presently the soup and the quiche arrived, accompanied by saffron bread, still warm. When we had eaten the first course, the promised pudding of honey and raisins and rice flour was brought in and the maids topped up our glasses. It was a most enjoyable card and supper party, and afterwards, there were no ill effects for anyone.

Brockley. Where are you? What progress are you making? And Harry, my beloved boy! Where are you? Have I betrayed you? Have I done you terrible harm just by doing nothing? But I couldn't do what has been asked of me. Dear God, I couldn't! WHERE ARE YOU?

NINETEEN
Gathering Forces

The next day I rode out with Mary and the armed guard that always accompanied her when she rode, took dinner with the Shrewsburys, had supper and a game of back-gammon with Bess and then went to my room to talk to Dale about my choice of gown and jewellery for the next day. I was tired. That moment of revelation on the previous evening, when I knew that not even for Harry could I deliberately doctor Mary's wine, had left me shaken and exhausted and I was exhausted too by the constant effort of pretending, of appearing normal when inside myself I was roughly as normal as a blizzard in July. When someone tapped on the door, it was irritating.

'See who it is,' I said to Dale, and went on standing by my bed, looking at the three dresses spread out there for my inspection, and deciding that because I had been wearing pale green that day, I had better not pick a green gown for tomorrow, but neither the weather, which had turned wet, nor my unhappy mood suited the peach pink. It would have to be the dark blue velvet, not a favourite of mine and usually used for serious occasions. I could have a closed ruff for a change and wear a rope of pearls . . .

'Walter Meredith is here, ma'am,' said Dale, reappearing at my elbow, accompanied by the freckled page.

'Yes, Meredith. What is it?'

'Madam, there's a man asking admittance, to see you. He says he's Roger Brockley, but he doesn't look like him.'

I was instantly alert. 'Bring him! I can soon order him away if it isn't Brockley.'

Five minutes later, I was saying: 'How that beard changes you, Brockley. But Meredith really is a foolish lad. He saw you when you were stubbly and you don't look so very different from the way you did then.'

'I may look more dishevelled,' said Brockley ruefully. In fact, he didn't look like his usual self for reasons other than his scruffy beard. He was pale and rather grubby and his cloak and boots were mud-splashed.

But he smiled and his blue-grey eyes were as steady as ever, and bright with good news. He said: 'I think I have found Harry.'

'I was very careful,' he said, after he had finished describing his disguise, and the lonely house with the encircling wall, and the glimpse of the face that might have been Harry's. 'I didn't think they had any suspicion of me, but I took no chances. I'd asked them the way to Warwick and they told me, so I rode off in the direction they recommended. Until I was out of their sight. Then I sat down hard in the saddle and rode for Sheffield as though a fiend with horns and a tail was in pursuit! Thank you, Fran, love!' Dale, after giving her husband a welcoming hug, had hurried out of the room and now returned with a tray bearing a flagon of wine, glasses and a dish of cheesecakes.

'That will go down very well,' said Brockley with gratitude, seizing on a cheesecake while Dale poured the wine. 'There was a lot of cross-country riding. Fortunately,' said Brockley, gulping wine and engulfing cheesecake, 'Jaunty is a very good horse. So here I am, after two more days, and it's after dark, but I'm here. Eddie's looking after Jaunty now. I think we should keep that horse when we go home. He's an ornament to any stable.'

'Yes, we will. But Brockley, please go on!'

'There isn't much more to tell. If I'm right about the house I found and the face at the window, then Harry is safe for the present. What has been happening here?'

'I went to a card and supper party held by Mary, and I meant to slip her just a drop of hemlock in her wine, to give the impression to any prying spy that I was trying to do something but . . .'

Until then, I hadn't told Dale, who burst out in horror. 'Ma'am, you *couldn't*! You *didn't*!'

'No, Dale. I couldn't and I didn't. I couldn't bring myself to it.'

'You once smuggled poison to a man to save him from a worse death,' Brockley said, recalling an assignment I had had many years before.

'That was to *save* him, and he was glad to have it. He took it of his own choice. There's a difference.'

'Yes. Yes, I see that there is.' Brockley brushed crumbs off his beard and scratched his chin. 'Is there a barber in the castle? If so, I would welcome his services tomorrow.'

'I'm sure there is.' Most of Talbot's men were clean-shaven and short-haired and a resident barber would have plenty of work to do.

'And tomorrow,' said Brockley, 'we have to consider what to do next. We have to get Harry out of that house. Somehow.'

I said: 'I think . . . it may be time to talk to Sir George Talbot.'

'So that was it,' said Talbot. He had made no difficulty about seeing us, and Brockley and I were now in the study where we had first met him. Bess was also present. It was late on the same evening and there was a conspiratorial feeling about this gathering, lit by candles and with the window shutters closed. The Talbots had listened with increasing horror to the tale I had to tell. 'I take it,' said Talbot, 'that the queen and Sir Francis Walsingham know about all this?'

'Yes. But I dared not confide in you, not until now,' I said. 'My captors – who are also Harry's – threatened to sell him if there was any hue and cry after them, any public search. Until we knew where he was, we dared do nothing. Even now . . .' I looked at Brockley. 'You are sure?'

It was not the first time I had asked that question but more like the fourth. Brockley made the reply he had already repeated several times. 'The house matches the description that Harry gave us in his letter. He wrote that the place was built of grey stone with a slate roof and had ivy on the walls, a wall round the house and garden and a front courtyard. The house I found is also about an hour's ride away from the Ashley cottage. That matches with what his widow told me. And I *think* I saw Harry at a window.'

'It sounds as though it is enough,' said Talbot. 'Well, what do you want to do?'

Brockley, who had once been a soldier, promptly produced a soldier's solution. 'I think we need your help, Sir George. Help in the form of armed men. I think we should attack, preferably by night. It should be a secret business as far as possible – so as not to alert them if by any chance it's the wrong house. Though I don't think it is. We should burst in, in force, find Harry and grab him. And them!'

'You'll certainly need men for that,' said Bess. 'How many can we provide?'

'How many would be enough?' I saw with relief that Talbot was not shying away from the prospect of a violent assault on the lonely walled house. His hazel eyes were no longer grave but gleaming with enthusiasm. He was not noticeably like Brockley but in this, I could see that they were kindred spirits. They were both relishing the adventure. 'I can supply twenty,' Talbot said. 'Better too many than not enough. They can look on it as an exercise. They'll enjoy it.'

Bess was visibly thinking. She was a formidable woman with considerable intelligence. Now she said: 'If Brockley has it right, Harry is being held somewhere near Warwick. We can't take a force of twenty men from here to Warwick, a journey of two or three days, without being noticed. Especially if, as Mistress Stannard fears, there are people spying on her and events around her. Do you believe these conspirators really do have a spy here in Sheffield Castle, Mistress Stannard?'

'I can't be sure,' I said. 'It might be wise to assume so.'

Bess nodded. 'Then we need a good excuse for sending a squad of men galloping from here to Warwick – I take it we shall aim for Warwick first.'

'Best start by going to the castle,' said Talbot. 'I would like to consult with Sir Ambrose. If he's there.'

'He was expected when I left Warwick,' Brockley said.

'We are on friendly terms,' Talbot said. 'Yes, we should make for the castle first, so that I can talk with him, and we can establish a base, a secure place to bring Harry to, if we find him.'

Bess said: 'Last year, he and a number of his men visited us and we had some friendly competitions between his men and ours. Not a tournament, but competitions for marksman-ship, swordplay, races over obstacle courses and so on. Why should we not have a return match? That can be the excuse for taking twenty men to Warwick and we can make sure everyone we meet on the way knows about it.'

Talbot grinned. 'I can send a courier with a sealed letter for Sir Ambrose's eyes only, and have it on the way within half an hour.' He looked at me. 'Mistress Stannard, if there really is someone here, watching you, have you any suspicions about who it could be? Very few people have joined us recently, except for yourself. One of the cooks, I believe, and Lady Alice Hammond – that's all.'

'It could be a most unlikely person,' I said. 'And not neces-sarily someone who has recently joined your household.'

Brockley said: 'According to my wife, Master Russell Woodley has been paying you attention, madam. Have you considered that he might be the one?'

'Yes, I have,' I said. It had crossed my mind once or twice. 'But his symptoms,' I said dryly, 'began before Harry was taken, and in any case, they suggest a somewhat different disease!'

Talbot looked enquiring and Brockley looked startled. Bess laughed. 'I think he has proposed marriage to her,' she said. 'Someone overheard him – he chose to make his proposal in the middle of a passage when people were going to breakfast.'

'I declined,' I said.

The Talbots had, it appeared, often travelled to Warwick and had standing arrangements in place, at inns and private houses where accommodation was always kept in readiness, in exchange for payment. If haste were required – and we all felt a need for it – then everyone went on horseback, carrying basic necessities in saddlebags and shoulder-packs. Baggage wagons could follow.

Elaborate gowns couldn't easily be carried on horseback but Bess said that the Countess of Warwick would lend any ladies in the party fresh dresses until the baggage caught up.

'She has done so several times,' said Bess. She added that she would accompany us. 'And Mistress Stannard and I will take our maids. Our party will then look like a private excursion, for pleasure.'

'My wife is Mistress Stannard's maid,' said Brockley. 'But she is not able to ride hard, not as hard as we shall need to.'

'Then she can stay behind,' said Bess shortly. 'I will lend Mistress Stannard a younger woman. I will leave my usual maid behind and take Lady Alice as my attendant. It will keep her under our eye.'

'Once we get to the house,' I said, 'how do we get in? If there is a wall all round . . .'

Talbot smiled at me benignly. 'My dear lady, there are such things as ladders. We can collect those in Warwick. From what Master Brockley has said, the distance from there to the walled house is not too great.'

'Not much more than an hour, without ladders,' said Brockley. 'And with them, not that much longer. We can put them on a cart and drive it fairly fast.'

Talbot nodded, and went to his study door. He put his head out and shouted, which quickly produced a page. 'Everyone is to assemble in the great hall, forthwith,' he said. 'Find William Cropper and tell him I want him. Also, find Captain Grey and send him here. I shall order them to gather the household and the entire garrison. I want *everyone* there – cooks, scullions, ladies, my soldiers. As fast as possible!' Coming back, he said: 'I don't think I will be able to accompany you to the house itself, though I shall come as far as Warwick. The queen does not like her lords to be personally involved in – unorthodox actions. And you, Mistress Stannard, you will hardly want to be there with the raiding party, though I take it that you will wish to come to Warwick.'

'On the contrary,' I said, 'I shall accompany the raiding party. I shan't climb the ladders or go over the wall or wave a sword about, but when Harry is freed, I mean to be there for him. I'll use a pair of Brockley's old breeches and ride astride for the occasion. I won't look so out of place then and a cross-saddle probably is safer for hard riding in the dark.'

*   *   *

The next day dawned grey and cold, but with a promise of something better to come. The clouds were high and did not threaten rain. Fasts were broken in the chilly twilight of daybreak and full daylight found the raiding party assembled on horseback in the main courtyard: Sir George, Bess, myself, Brockley, Lady Alice, some grooms (though not Eddie, for I had left him to look after our coach horses) and a young waiting maid, Jenny, for me. Dale, tearfully, had had to agree to following with the baggage. In addition, there were the twenty armed men. No, twenty-one, for out of the crowd, Russell Woodley came spurring towards me.

'Mistress Stannard! Sir George has told me what is happening. I have had some training in arms and I am coming with you.' He smiled at me. 'You would not accept my hand but I beg you to accept my sword. I understand that your son was lost and needs rescuing. I will be so glad to serve you.'

This was no time to be coy. 'I accept your service,' I said gravely, hoping that it wouldn't lead to complications in the future. Russell Woodley looked pleased.

I shall long remember the journey to Warwick, which took two days and a couple of hours on the third. It will be with me always: the sense of urgency, the relentless hours on the road, the steady pounding of hooves and the tossing of manes and the creak of saddlery. And above all, the sense of taking action at last, of being on the way to Harry, to Harry, to Harry. His name rang in my head, in time to the rhythm of Jewel's hoofbeats.

In the inn where we stayed the first night, I went to the stable on the excuse of making sure that Jewel had been properly cared for, found Brockley tending her, and seized the chance of some private talk with him. From the moment of his arrival at Sheffield, my head had been so full of plans for Harry's rescue, that there were questions I had left unasked. I asked them now.

'When you left Hawkswood,' I said, 'what were things like there? Had you learned anything new?'

'No, madam.' Carefully, he brushed a tangle out of Jewel's dark mane, and ran a hand down her off foreleg to pick up the hoof and begin cleaning it. 'Before I left, as you know, I sent Philip to Guildford to trace Miller's movements there if he could. He returned just as I was setting off after Harry's letter reached me. He hadn't been able to find anything out at all. Meanwhile, madam, I had let Miller alone. There is no actual proof that he is involved in this business and I have to admit, he is very good with the horses. If we can once get Harry safely home, we can go into things further. If we take some prisoners,' he added, 'they may talk. If I get my hands on any of them, they *will* talk, I promise.' He looked up from his work with the hoof-pick and I saw how grim his face was.

My voice echoed that grimness, as I said: 'You would have my full support, believe me.' A thought crossed my mind. It had begun to niggle at me since Brockley recounted his search for the man Ashley, and the sad ending to that search. I said: 'Ashley. Do you think that he really died in an accident? Or did someone think that perhaps he knew too much, about the house, and so on?'

Brockley straightened up and looked at me. 'I think he was murdered, madam. There has been nothing I could do about it and when I got back from Warwick, there was something I didn't tell you. I didn't want to frighten you. But . . .'

I listened, horrified, as he told me how he had paused to look at a thatcher on the roof of a black-and-white house, and actually seen a man shift the position of a ladder, and only learned when he found himself at Ashley's funeral that Daniel worked alone, so that the man who moved the ladder was not his assistant, and therefore . . .

'If they suspect that Ashley helped Harry, they would be very worried about how much he knew and how much he might talk. And even if they didn't suspect Ashley of helping Harry, they might still have feared that he had noticed Harry and might talk *about* him,' Brockley said. 'We can't know what they thought or how much they suspected or how far they might go to stop his mouth or be revenged on the poor fellow.' He turned back to his work but said, very grimly indeed: 'But if they do suspect that Harry managed to get a message out, then I wonder how they found out.'

'You said you may have seen Harry at a window. If you did, he's still there. They haven't moved him.'

'I pray they still haven't,' said Brockley. 'Though I wonder why, if they had any inkling of the message that Harry managed to send.' He straightened up with a grunt. 'But I am as sure as I can be that Ashley was murdered. I think I saw it happen and didn't realize it.' His fists clenched. *'I saw it happen and could have stopped it if only I'd known! It sickens me to think of it.* I try to hope that what I saw wasn't sinister but I'm so sure in my heart that it was.'

'I wonder,' I said, 'if we'll ever know the full truth.'

TWENTY
Three Times Is Too Many

We reached Warwick Castle halfway through the morning of the third day. George Talbot's advance message had been received safely, so we were expected and were made welcome. Sir Ambrose Dudley, Earl of Warwick and his countess Lady Anne had indeed returned from their recent visit to court, and they greeted us in the great hall, amid a wealth of elaborately carved furniture and glittering silver plate and a wide paved floor in a red-and-white chequered pattern and wondrous wall-hangings.

These took the form of costly tapestries and Oriental carpets, alternated by weaponry arranged in patterns. There were two dozen spears arranged like a lethal fan, and four swords used as a frame surrounding a portrait of Sir Ambrose's father, John Dudley, Duke of Northumberland, beheaded long ago for treachery, but clearly still respected by his son. There were also numerous pairs of antlers, mostly red deer. One set, I noticed, had sixteen points, a rare achievement for an English stag, though I had seen such heads in France.

Ambrose was the brother of Robin Dudley, the Earl of Leicester, Elizabeth's beloved favourite (though not her lover, whatever rumour might say), and there was a resemblance. Sir Ambrose had the same height and the same long, dark face as his brother, though not the same presence. He was said to be a quiet, conventional man, which the flamboyant Robin certainly was not, and reputedly shared many of the views of the Puritans, who had lately become quite a force in the Anglican Church. His clothes were made of expensive cloth, but they were all brown and grey. He did not adorn himself with bright colours or jewellery, and he greeted us without effusiveness.

His lady was also quietly dressed and she was calm and smiling as she enquired about our journey and gave orders for wine to be served.

All the same, there was still a certain air of suppressed excitement about the two of them and my lord's dark eyes did have something of Leicester's adventurous sparkle. After his courteous speech of welcome and the distribution of refreshments, he drew me aside and said: 'I am fully apprised of your purpose here, Mistress Stannard. The message Sir George sent me was explicit. This is a terrible situation for you. To have a child in such peril . . . I can hardly imagine what it feels like!'

He had no living children, that I knew. There had been a daughter once, by a previous wife, but she had died young and there had never been any more. He said: 'I agree with Talbot that it would be best, for your boy's sake and indeed, politically, for this affair to be dealt with quietly and privately. I have agreed to lend another ten men for the purpose; that will give you a force of thirty, apart from any other companions you have brought. I think that like Sir George, I would do best not to come with you in person, much as I would like to.'

'I have my man Brockley, a former soldier,' I said, 'and a Master Woodley, of Sir George's household, is also with us.'

'Thirty-two, then. It should be enough to overwhelm one house and a handful of people! I will see that the men I send are trustworthy and well armed though it would be best to avoid bloodshed.'

That gleam of Dudley wickedness strengthened. 'Wounded men, let alone bodies, are so difficult to hide, or to account for if they can't be hidden, don't you think?'

'I would certainly prefer it that way,' I said. 'I shall be going with them!'

'Really?' Sir Ambrose was startled. 'I would hardly have expected . . .'

'Mistress Stannard is equal to anything.' Russell Woodley had come up to us unseen and now appeared at my elbow. 'I too would like to dissuade her but it is her son who is in danger and I can understand her wish to be there. We shan't let her climb any walls or run into any danger, I promise. I shall make a point of seeing that she doesn't!'

'The attack had best be by night,' said Sir Ambrose. 'Sir George agrees. He also agrees that it should be carried out as soon as possible, meaning tonight. I must speak with him again, if you will excuse me. Ah, here is my wife. She will look after you, Mistress Stannard, and show you your quarters.'

He led me away from Woodley and handed me over to the care of Lady Anne, who gathered up Bess and Lady Alice and Jenny as well, and showed us to the guest quarters. Bess and Alice were to share a room, and Jenny and I had one adjoining. Jenny was an amiable young woman, clever with her fingers and really gifted at dressing hair although in other ways not especially bright. I liked her, but I missed Dale and hoped the baggage wagons would not take too long to catch up, so that she could join us.

For the moment, we were all thankful to wash and change and take some rest before dinner, and after dinner, I think most of us rested, or amused themselves with quiet occupations, until the early evening, when we gathered again in the hall, where I was promptly drawn aside by Russell, who had evidently been waiting for me.

'I have been so anxious to speak with you, Mistress Stannard. There never seemed to be a chance before. On the road, we always seemed to be too close to other riders and the inns where we stayed were so crowded; there was no privacy. There's much more in this fine big hall. Come over to that window seat for a moment. Let us look out and seem to be admiring the view of the spring flowers in the knot garden. I believe my lady Anne is fond of flowers and positively harasses the gardeners to make sure that she has a colourful show at all seasons when flowers are possible.'

'My late husband, Hugh, was very attached to his roses and worked in his rose garden with his own hands,' I said, as he steered me across an acre or so of chequered paving to a seat below a tall, narrow window.

'Ah yes.' We sat down and gazed outwards. I was uneasy. I doubted if Russell really wanted to talk about gardening. 'Your late husband,' he said. 'But it was some years ago, was it not? Mistress Stannard, grief for a lost love is natural and admirable, but life goes on, and as I have said before, yours is full of responsibilities which surely you would like to share. I ask you again; will you not agree to share them with me? I will not be overbearing, I promise. I will not force ideas on you, or push you into the background . . .'

'Russell, please!'

'Nor,' said Russell, ploughing on like a team of oxen who are being beckoned with carrots, 'will I expect you to give me children. You may call it temerity and perhaps you are right but I have thought about your age. There are ways to enjoy married life without imperilling the health of a lady now in sight of . . . forgive me . . . the half-century. Perhaps I shouldn't speak of such things to you but when something as serious as matrimony is under discussion, it is best to be clear about these matters. I promise you . . .'

'*Russell!*'

'Yes, my dear?'

'I am very touched by your proposal, and very honoured, but when I say I don't want to marry again, I mean it. I really, truly, don't.'

I not only meant it; but the feeling had strengthened as time went on. It was, partly, that I was now accustomed to being the one in command. In that, I perhaps resembled my half-sister. I knew very well that Elizabeth, apart from fearing the physical side of marriage, also disliked the idea of sharing power. She preferred to be the queen, alone and in control, and by now I had learned, in my private life, that I too preferred to be the sole maker of decisions. Also, I had had three husbands and knew how much energy, how much sheer endeavour, went into creating the deep bond that marriage demanded. I didn't think I could summon up that energy again.

None of this was easy to explain and I didn't try. I looked at him, and met his uncomprehending eyes, and simply repeated myself. '*I do not wish to remarry. That is final. Please believe me.*'

'I see,' he said. It was as though a shutter had come down over his face. His eyes went blank. 'This is the third time you have refused me,' he said. 'Three times is too many. I could have given you so much, including love, a very real love, believe me. I would have worshipped you and cared for you all your life. Now, I must say farewell. I shall not trouble you again.'

He slipped from the window seat and left me. I watched him retreat across the hall and thought sadly that I had probably hurt his feelings badly; that it was no doubt a fault in me that I preferred autonomy to a good man's love, but I did not want to call him back. I had lost a friend and I was sorry, but no more than that.

Evening was setting in. Supper was to be served, we learned, not in the great hall but in a separate dining chamber and then there would be time to rest again before we must set out on our rescue mission. We were to leave at midnight.

I found myself keyed up, immensely nervous, anxious to be mounted and away and not hungry for my food, though the supper was excellent.

I didn't take much wine, fearing that it would make me sleepy. I was therefore very wide awake and noticing things, which included the fact that at supper there seemed to be an absentee. All members of the prospective rescue party were there, including the ten men that Sir Ambrose had already picked out, and the Talbot twenty, status was marked by the position of the salt. Near the salt, though not far above it, a place had been set that wasn't occupied. I was wondering who was missing when Bess, who was beside me, said: 'Where is Russell Woodley?' She turned towards her husband, who was on her other side. 'My lord, where is your clerk Woodley? His place is set but where is he?'

I looked again and realized that she was right. Russell was not there. But why not? Angry because I had refused him? Upset? Unwell? Brockley was just below the salt, some way off, but I caught his eye and beckoned. He rose at once and came to me. 'Madam?'

'Russell Woodley isn't here. Will you find out why?'

He nodded and was gone. Bess said: 'You are worried, Ursula?'

'Yes, I am. A little.' I turned my head to look at her. 'He has been courting me,' I said. 'As I suppose you know.'

'I've known since he began courting you at Richmond. But it was not my business,' said Bess.

'Or mine,' put in George Talbot, 'though I couldn't think him worthy of you, Mistress Stannard. However, I agree with my lady that it is for you to say, not us.'

'I have said,' I told them. 'I refused him when he first approached me, which was at the queen's court, and refused him at Sheffield and today I refused him yet again. He renewed his suit just now, when we arrived and were in the great hall, and once more, I said no. I wonder if I have made him angry, or unhappy.'

'He is entitled to be any of those things,' said Talbot, frowning, 'but not to indulge them when we have a serious venture before us, this very night. You have sent your man to find him?'

'Yes.'

'I hope he brings him here,' said Bess. 'He should certainly eat before he has to ride with the rescue party. Perhaps he asked for something in his room.'

Sir Ambrose, on my other side, had been listening. 'I can soon find that out.' He called to one of the serving men. 'See if a Master Woodley has asked for supper in his room. Quickly, if you please!'

The man disappeared on his errand and supper went on. I felt unreasonably worried. Dear heaven, even if I had hurt Russell's feelings, I surely hadn't done *that* much damage to him. After all, I had said no to him twice before and he had survived that without sinking into a fit of depression, or sulks.

The serving man reappeared in the hall just ahead of Brockley and came briskly to Sir Ambrose. 'No one has had supper in private this evening, my lord. Master Woodley's platter was set here in readiness for him and . . .'

Brockley did not arrive briskly. He arrived at a run, hurtling into the room, brushing aside the guard at the door, dashing across the floor to kneel before us. 'Madam! Woodley has gone! He took his horse from the stable a good hour ago! I hurried to his room and his things are gone as well. Everything. His sword too.'

Sir Ambrose and Sir George looked bewildered. 'But where can he have gone?' said Sir Ambrose.

'There has always been the possibility,' said Brockley, 'that someone in Sheffield Castle was keeping watch on Mistress Stannard on behalf of the enemy and the name of Russell Woodley has in fact been mentioned. Could it be that he is – or was – indeed the spy concerned?'

TWENTY-ONE
Manhunt

I shot to my feet. 'He left an hour ago?' I said. 'But . . . but . . .'

I couldn't think clearly. I lost my way mid-sentence and then said: 'Perhaps he has just gone home, back to Sheffield, upset by my hard-heartedness and . . .'

'Perhaps he has. But perhaps he hasn't. We can't afford to ignore the possibility that he's made for Ivy House to warn them about our plans, that he is part of this horrible conspiracy!' Sir George was emphatic.

'But he . . .' Again I lost my way. Could Russell, could anyone, have sworn so much love and yet still go off to betray not just me but my son as well? Had he been all the time involved in this ugly plot? Had all his expressions of passion been pretence? Or was he hopefully pursuing both purposes? I sat down again, my head spinning.

Other heads were steadier. 'If he's going to Ivy House, he's two-thirds of the way there by now!' Brockley said. 'We'll never catch him in time!'

It was Sir Ambrose who said decisively: 'Well, we have to get after him. Whether or not he has actually gone that way. And we must do it quickly!' and he too rose, throwing down his napkin and heading out of the room all in one swift, complicated movement. In that moment, I suddenly saw that there really was a decided resemblance between him and his colourful brother Robin. When it came to the point, the quiet Earl of Warwick could turn in an instant into a soldier and a general. As he reached the door, he shouted: 'Men! Follow me!' over his shoulder and from below the salt, the thirty men who were our picked force sprang up and went after him. So did Brockley.

I got up again, taking command of myself, aware that I was

not only bewildered and hurt but also very angry. If Russell had really gone to Ivy House then . . . then the sooner he went to the block, the better. 'I must go too,' I said, and began to push my way out between my seat and that of Bess. She caught at my sleeve.

'Ursula, you can't, you mustn't. It was all very well when it was the raid to rescue your son; I could understand that. But a lady can't go on a manhunt . . .'

'This *is* the rescue raid! We'll end up at Ivy House for sure and then we'll rescue Harry, if we can. Let me go!' She had no choice for I had already wrenched my arm away from her. 'I must make ready!'

I ran, headlong past the lower table, where I scooped up Jenny, and swept her, bewildered and expostulating, out of the dining hall, through the castle and up the stairs, into my chamber.

'I had some old breeches in my baggage!' I gasped, looking round. 'Where are they? Have you put them away? We're leaving now – I mean the raiding party is leaving – something's happened – Russell Woodley has absconded, an hour since . . . *Where are those breeches?*'

'Ma'am, surely you can't . . .'

'Yes, I can! Don't argue! Find them, there's no time to waste, the rest will be mounted and away in next to no time and I must be with them. This is *it*!'

'But . . . what . . .?'

'Find them!' I shouted, wishing with all my heart that Dale were here. Dale would probably be flustered too but at least she wouldn't gape at me as though she couldn't understand English.

Jenny looked at me wildly for a few seconds more, obviously overset by my loud orders and air of frantic haste, but at last pulled herself together, scrabbled in a chest and produced the breeches, along with a shirt and an old doublet. I had used the outfit before, now and then. I always had it with me. She came to help me, undoing laces, pulling my sleeves off, half-lifting me out of my kirtle. I scrambled into the male clothing, rushed to the press where a dress hung that had my hidden pouch and its usual contents in it, grabbed the said contents, bundled them into a drawstring bag and hung it on my breeches belt. Then I pulled on a pair of boots, kissed Jenny and fled.

I reached the stable yard just in time. Twilight was near and the yard was shadowed by the castle's bulk, so that a couple of men were holding up lanterns to make fiddling with straps easier while the horses were being saddled. It takes a little while to get saddles on to over thirty horses, which had given me time to change and catch up. The quiet-spoken Captain John Grey, leader of Talbot's men, was shouting orders and when I caught sight of Brockley, I shouted orders too.

'Saddle Jewel for me! Cross-saddle!' He stared at me and began to shake his head but I shouted: 'Do it! Oh, all right, I will! This *is* the raid, taking place early, that's all! Where's the bloody tack-room?'

'*All right!*' Brockley spluttered, recognizing that I wasn't going to be gainsaid. He led the way and we did the job together; with Brockley seeing to the bridle while I flung a saddle over Jewel's back and dealt with the girths. I led her out of the stable and mounted in haste. A horseman moved alongside me and to my surprise I saw that it was Sir George Talbot. He caught my eye. 'The queen might not approve, but a man in my employment, Russell Woodley my trusted second secretary, may have betrayed us. I feel responsible. I am coming with you after all.'

'And so am I.' Sir Ambrose was there as well, kneeing his horse to my other side. 'If Sir George is riding with you, I'm damned if I'll be left behind!' And in the lantern light I saw him grin and saw the spark in his dark eyes, once again saw his flamboyant brother the Earl of Leicester look out of them.

Brockley came out of the stable last, at a run, to where someone was holding Jaunty for him, and fairly threw himself aboard. And then we were off.

Oddly enough, that furious ride through the gathering darkness is a good memory. Despite my fears for Harry and for myself, and my longing for him, there was a kind of joy in this crazy expedition, as there had been on the ride from Sheffield. Only this time it was more intense, for now I was going direct to Harry; God willing I might see him within the hour; the rescue party was on its way; and we were riding

fast, fast, as swiftly as we could while there was any light
at all. It had been a clear day and in any case, a full moon
was already rising. The fierce hammering of the hooves all
around me was in time with the pounding of my heart, and
we were *on our way* and nothing was hindering us and if
we did catch Russell Woodley, if he really had betrayed us,
then heaven have mercy on him, for I would not and nor
would Brockley.

We had brought no ladders. If Russell Woodley had indeed
made for Ivy House, then he would assuredly get there first,
so stealth was pointless; the enemy would be warned. At the
moment of starting off, Sir Ambrose had said: 'We'll trust to
superior numbers, demand entrance and break the gate open
if we have to, and go straight in.'

The wall and the gate, a massive, two-leaved affair, loomed
up on us suddenly, lit by the moon and the very last gleam of
the dusk. Sir Ambrose signalled to one of his men, who drew
his sword and hammered on the gate with the hilt, shouting:
'Open up! *Open up* in the name of the queen!' in a most
commanding fashion.

The first response was an outburst of baying from what
sounded like some very large dogs, but the man who was
pounding on the gate persisted and eventually, one leaf was
drawn back and a defensive figure, a man with a cloak
wrapped over a nightshirt, appeared in the aperture. 'What
is all this? What's this about, all this shouting about the name
of the queen? Who are you, making this racket? And how
many are you . . .?'

The indignant voice faded as its owner stepped forward and
peered at us, and then rose again, in new outrage. 'You look
like an army! What's the meaning of this?'

'We're coming in,' snapped Sir Ambrose, 'and if you don't
want those dogs spitted on our swords then get them under
control!' Grumbling, the man in the cloak and nightshirt called
his hounds to order, and with that, we entered. The porter, if
that was what he was, stood aside, scowling. The house was
in front of us, across a cobbled courtyard. There was candle-
light in several windows, and a lantern over the front door,
which had a short flight of steps leading up to it.

We clattered across the cobbles and then the front door was flung open and another man came out to the top of the steps, holding up a lantern, by which we could see that he was dressed, though probably in haste for he had an open shirt under an unfastened doublet and with his spare hand was still pulling at his hose. 'What's the matter? Why this incursion?'

George Talbot was swinging out of his saddle. 'Is this Ivy House?'

'Yes, it is, and I would like to know . . .'

'Who are you, sir?'

'Who am I? I'm the master of the house, William Corby! And here is my wife, Frances, and this . . .' he pointed to the man who had opened the gate '. . . is Thomas, my brother.' A woman, enswathed in a mantle, had appeared behind him. 'We live here with our servants. What *is* all this?'

Talbot said to me: 'Do you recognize him, Mistress Stannard?'

'No,' I said. I had been staring at him but as far as I could make out, he was unknown to me. The lantern showed a very ordinary looking man with a pale, indoor face and short, mousey hair, and as the other two moved into the light, I could see that they too were nondescript; and that none of them looked at all like any of the players who had come to Hawkswood and later, kidnapped me.

'We are here,' said Sir Ambrose, also dismounting, 'to search these premises for a missing boy and a man called Russell Woodley and we don't intend to ask permission.' He looked over his shoulder. 'Cullings, Miller, Watts, stay to look after the horses! The rest of you, dismount and forward!'

Other figures had now come into view in the entrance hall behind the Corby family and they were gaping and exclaiming, but we were a crowd against a handful and we surged into the house like a giant wave overwhelming a sea wall. Inside, more orders were barked and the house was suddenly filled by the sound of striding feet, up and down flights of stairs and across floors, of room doors and cupboard doors being flung open and heavy furniture being yanked aside.

There were shouts. *There's an attic up here! Look out for a priest's hole! Don't miss the cellars; Hayley and Banks go*

*down and don't be fooled by any walled-off bits; look for
hidden doors! Nothing up here, sir! Make sure – don't miss
any cupboards! Nothing in the cellars, sir, though the wine
barrels look fair tempting!*

Brockley had gone with the searchers but Sir Ambrose, Sir
George and I found our way through an open door into what
proved to be a well-lit kitchen where someone had evidently
been having a late supper, as the fire was still burning. The
light came from numerous candles, benches were drawn close
to a pinewood table and on the table were some wooden platters with crumbs and chicken bones on them.

The three Corbys came with us, glowering. All six of us
were still just standing there when the others began to return,
including Brockley, looking crestfallen.

'This is the house I found, madam, but there's no sign of Harry;
or Master Woodley, not a trace and now I'm wondering . . .'

'You may well wonder!' said William Corby furiously.
'What all this is about I have no idea, but I can only say that
for a gentleman's house to be attacked like this, after dark and
without warning, or any explanation, is outrageous. In the
name of the queen, indeed! Taking her majesty's name in vain,
that's what that is. I demand an explanation!'

He thumped a furious fist on the pinewood table, making
the platters jump. One of them sent a chicken wishbone onto
William Corby's wrist. He flicked it off with a fastidious
movement.

And then I knew. I had last seen him with black hair to his
shoulders and a bronzed face but I knew those unnaturally
long fingers. I had seen them flicking through a pack of cards
as though the cards were made of water; and I had seen them
twisting nervously together as he talked to me of the dreadful
choice that lay before me.

'That's him!' I shouted, pointing at him. 'That's their
ringleader! He looks different but I know that's him, the
leader of the players who seized me, the one who does card
tricks with those queer, long fingers! He was in disguise
but I know him. It's *him*! We are in the right place, we are!
And . . .'

The search party were still coming in, in twos and threes.

Now came a pair of them, two men that I recognized as part of the Talbot garrison, excitedly brandishing trophies.

'We found these! Outside in a barn where fodder is stored, in a sack, tossed in among some other sacks with oats in!'

'The sack looked funny. Knobbly, like. Not like oats. So we had a look! And there they were. Do they mean anything?'

'They look like disguises!'

They were. The trophies the two delighted Talbot men were flourishing included half a dozen wigs of long dark hair and one wig of red hair, several motley coloured tunics, a bright green gown sewn with crystal beads and a glass bottle full of some dark liquid. One of the Talbot men saw me looking at it and said: 'Walnut juice. Could be used to make faces brown.'

All three Corbys had gone pale. Brockley, stepping forward almost as though he, and not Sir Ambrose or Sir George, were in charge, addressed William Corby. 'Where is Harry? Where is Russell Woodley? You'd better tell us.'

'I've never heard of this Harry, or this Russell Wood! What are you talking about?' But William Corby was blustering. There was sweat on his pale forehead. Brockley turned to me: 'Madam, this will not be pretty. Leave us.'

Sir Ambrose suddenly emitted a sound like *Humph* and Brockley glanced at him and bent an apologetic head. 'Your pardon, sir, and Sir George. But Harry is the son of Mistress Stannard, whose servant I am, and in himself is dear to me. Please forgive me, sir, for usurping your authority. Madam . . .'

I opened my mouth to protest at being shooed away, but Brockley, now usurping my authority as well, caught hold of my arm and actually pushed me out of the door. '*No*, madam! You must not witness this! We're going to make him talk.'

He went back into the kitchen and shut the door and I heard a bolt crash home. For a moment I stood irresolutely in the entrance hall, which was dimly lit, since William Corby had dumped his lantern on a small table. Then I took the lantern up and found my way through another door which seemed to divide the kitchen quarters from the rest of the house. I tried a further door and arrived in a room which looked like a parlour. I had left both doors open behind me and from the kitchen, faintly, I could hear sounds: a man crying out, a woman weeping. I sank down on a stool.

This was the right house and therefore Harry had been here lately: surely he had. I could almost sense him here. But he hadn't been found. Oh, dear God, did Russell get here in time for them to spirit him away and if so where had he been spirited to? Harry. Oh, *Harry*!

Then Brockley was calling me and I rose and ran back to the kitchen. This door too was now open. The Corbys, all three of them white-faced and trembling, were seated, under guard. The woman was in tears, the so-called Thomas Corby looked as though he had been stunned and William Corby's mouth was shaking.

Most of the searchers had gone, and sounds in the house suggested that they were searching again. But the ones who had found the disguises, along with Sir Ambrose and Sir George, were present and looking happy. Brockley met me with a grin. 'We haven't hurt him, madam. We didn't have to. Just threats were enough. Certain threats.' Corby tightened his mouth but his eyes were terrified.

'Russell did come here,' Brockley said. 'We guessed right. He has warned them and Harry has been got away. It seems that these people have no safe houses other than here and Heath House at Epsom, but they've whisked Harry off to an abandoned and very lonely shepherd's cot, some miles to the south. Russell and the man called Lucas took him. We're going there now.'

'And Master Corby here is going to show us the way,' said Sir Ambrose. 'Aren't you, my friend?'

'I . . . I don't know the way. I've never been there myself! I . . .'

'Then perhaps your . . . er . . . brother knows, or your wife, if she is your wife, or one of the others – your servants? Where *are* your servants, by the way? We've seen no sign of them. Have they melted into the air?'

'They were all inside the stable, sir.' One of Sir Ambrose's men had come into the kitchen behind me. 'We found them saddling up in frantic haste. We've got them.'

'*Someone* in this household must know where this shepherd's cot is,' said Talbot. 'Bring them all here and let's find out! I do hope, Master Corby, that you haven't been telling us any naughty lies? I take it that there really is a ruined shepherd's cot and that it really does lie to the south? Because if you have lied . . .'

'No, it's to the north!' Corby had evidently tried to the last to mislead us but something in Talbot's voice and in the implacable faces around him, had broken the last of his nerve. The sweat was now streaming down his temples. 'Yes, yes, it's real enough and yes, that's where Harry has been taken, but it's north, not south. I do know where it is! I can show you.'

'You'd better,' said Brockley, in a voice that was positively silky.

'The horses must be tired,' I said to Brockley, as we thundered northwards, in force except for six men who had been left in charge of Ivy House, where the occupants had been made prisoners, under lock and key. This time, the only light was moonlight, in which trees and grass were an otherworldly silver and shadows were impenetrable.

'They will hold up,' Brockley said. 'This is the last journey. At the end of it, madam, we will find Harry. His ordeal is nearly over. We gathered that he was taken off only a short time before we arrived, and it would take about an hour to get to this ruinous place they've taken him to. We'll be hard behind them.'

'I hate to think of Harry being with that man Lucas. I remember Lucas. I know which one he was. He looked – he sounded – cruel.'

'We'll rescue him soon. Very soon, madam. Take heart. You're tired yourself, you know.'

'No, I'm not, Brockley. I'm too angry, too desperate, to be tired. I want to find Harry safe and unharmed. He must be so frightened. I could kill that man Corby. Why didn't you want me to be there when you . . . persuaded him? I would have been glad to be there; I would have liked to see him break!'

We were riding side by side, just behind Corby and his

escort. In the uncertain moonlight, wise riders watched the track. But now I saw Brockley's face turn towards me.

'You are a gallant lady, and I value you for it, even though at times I have wished that you would lead a less dangerous, more womanly life. You have seen and done much that no woman should have to see or do, in my opinion. But there are still things that you have *not* seen or done, and I pray that you never do. I want you to remain, always, my gallant, honest lady. Madam, I pushed you out of that kitchen in case we had to proceed to extremes. I don't want you . . . please, madam, I wouldn't want you to become corrupted.'

'*Brockley! I . . .*'

I could say no more. I didn't know what to say. Brockley turned away from me again and once more gave his attention to the track. And then, in front of us, I saw the group round Corby slowing down, and one of them threw up an arm and shouted: 'Easy, easy! There's something ahead . . .!'

There was. A horse and rider had just emerged, at a gallop, from a copse of trees a furlong or so in front. They tore straight towards us and then the horse half-reared as the rider tried to pull up, just as Corby's escort moved to surround them. One of the escort dragged the rider from his saddle and another grabbed the horse's reins, and then the man who had seized the rider had turned his own mount and was coming towards the rest of us. They came into a patch of full moonlight and, pressing forward with Brockley, I saw the face of the person who was now perched before his captor. Who was laughing as he said: 'Madam, is this who we're looking for?'

'*Harry!*' I gasped.

His young face peered at me wildly from his captor's arms. Then the man came close beside me and I realized that he was Captain Grey. Very carefully, he shifted his burden from the withers of his horse to Jewel's withers instead. My arms closed thankfully round him. 'Oh, Harry!'

'Mother!' said Harry. 'I killed him. That man Lucas. I killed him, Mother.'

It came out as a whimper and then I saw that he was crying, and that he was clutching a dagger and that although the stains on it looked black in the moonlight, I knew very well that in moonlight so does the colour red.

Brockley was beside me. 'Take heart, young man,' he said. 'If you killed Lucas, I'm overjoyed to hear it!'

'But I'm being chased!' Harry was twisting round, trying to look over his own shoulder and past that of his rescuer. 'I'm . . . here he is!'

And so he was. Another rider now came flying out of the copse, riding far faster than was safe in tree shadow, leaning forward on the neck of his horse, encouraging it to greater speed.

He rode straight into our arms.

Russell Woodley.

TWENTY-TWO
My Son, My Son

We were too far from Warwick Castle and most of us were too tired anyway to go back to it that night. We returned instead to Ivy House, where the men who had been left on guard – the ones called Hayley and Banks were in charge of them – told us that the prisoners were still safely secured, up in the attic.

'The woman won't stop crying and the men won't stop cursing,' Hayley informed us. He was the taller and better-looking of the two, with very blue eyes, a small beard and broad shoulders. Banks was younger, pink-complexioned, a little plump, with bright, pale and very intelligent eyes. He looked as though he was enjoying the adventure. 'We let them have some wine,' he said. 'The cellars are full of it and if they get drunk they'll maybe fall asleep and stop making such a racket.'

Many of us laughed, and we took ourselves into the kitchen, where candles were still burning. The night had turned cold but Hayley and Banks had kept the fire going. The room was overcrowded for a moment, but Sir Ambrose gave orders and three men marched William Corby off to join his fellow conspirators in the attic. Most of the rest were sent to investigate the cellar and a hopeful-looking door from the kitchen. They shortly reappeared with ale, bread and cheese and slices of cold lamb. A couple of men had been despatched to find bedding so that everyone could have somewhere to sleep. Harry, who at first had been distressed and tearful, had now become calmer and was able to tell them where to find a supply of blankets. Then Sir George and Sir Ambrose, Captain Grey, Hayley and Banks, Brockley, Harry and I all seated ourselves in the kitchen and for the moment we kept Russell with us. It was at my request. 'There are things I want to ask him,' I said.

I looked at Harry with concern, for although he was now quiet, he was still drawn and white with exhaustion, and his dark eyes seemed enormous. He needed rest. But I also knew that he was strung as tightly as a lute string and that he would not sleep yet. For the moment, he was better where he was, in the lit, warm kitchen, among friends.

I turned my attention to Russell, who had been thrust into a seat, with Hayley and Banks on either side of him. 'Why do you want him here, Mistress Stannard? Shouldn't he be with the other prisoners in the attic?' said Sir Ambrose, picking up a couple of spare candles and starting to light them from the ones already there. Brockley quietly took them from him and finished the task.

'I need a few explanations from him,' I said. 'We can lock him up later. Russell, how could you? After all you have said to me! You swore you loved me!'

He glared at me.

'Well, why?' I said. 'I really want to know. It is a dreadful thing that you have done to me – and nearly done to Harry. What made you do it?'

'From the moment I first saw you,' said Russell, 'when we were all at Richmond, I wanted, I longed . . . for you! I am, and I was then, already part of the Players – that's what we call ourselves. We are the Players, honest patriots, who only want to protect our country! But I would have abandoned them on the instant if only you had said yes! Only you kept saying no. You were so remote, so withdrawn, so indifferent! Yes, I loved you! I think I still do but if you won't love me . . . then I remain a Player, in a game that is no game, but a true attempt to protect our queen, our realm. If only you had said that you would marry me!'

'I see. So it was all my fault!'

'Don't talk to my mother like that!' Harry shouted.

'If I'd caught up with you in time,' said Russell malevolently, now glowering at Harry, 'if only I'd got hold of you before you met your saviours, I'd have had you safe in hiding by now. Not in the ruined cottage; we knew you would be sure to find out about that. We were aiming for an old charcoal-burner's hut instead, two miles further on. We'd have taken you there, and then I'd have made you wish you'd never been born. But when you attacked Lucas and broke away, my damned horse was upset and threw me. I got back on but you'd had too long a start . . . God wasn't with me! Oh, dear God, why not, why weren't you?'

'Oh, take him to the attic!' said Talbot. He stared at Russell. 'I trusted you. I thought you were a good, reliable clerk, an aide to my chief secretary and of value to my household. Instead, I find you are a conspirator, an abductor of children and in league with slavers. You are dismissed from my service and under arrest.' He looked at the guards. 'Just get him out of my sight!'

Hayley and Banks took him away. He did not resist but he gave me a parting look over his shoulder. It was a look of mingled anger and grief. I turned away. Brockley was telling Harry who everyone was. Having done so, he said: 'Now, Harry, can you tell us your story? Just what happened tonight? How did you get away from Russell and Lucas?'

Harry shivered. 'It was all such a muddle.' His eyes looked more enormous than ever.

I said: 'One moment. If there's wine in the cellars, could someone fetch some and mull it? We could all do with it and Harry can have a little, too. He needs something.'

Captain Grey went with Brockley to fetch the wine and together they set about mulling it. I looked for some glasses and at the same time watched Harry, knowing that he was trying to gather his narrative together. When the wine was ready and I had found the glasses I wanted, in a small cupboard, I poured for us all, with a small measure for Harry, and handed everything round. Smiling at Harry I said: 'Tell us, then. What happened?'

'Someone arrived,' Harry said. 'I was in bed. There was a great to-do. He banged on the gate and was let in and I got up and looked out. My window faces the front. I saw him dismount . . . he almost fell off his horse, he was in such haste! . . . and then people were running about and shouting and then he – this man who'd arrived in such a hurry – and that man Lucas came running into my room, pulled me out of bed, told me to dress, fast, fast, and then they rushed me downstairs. That's when I heard Master Woodley's name; Lucas called him by it. Two saddled horses were ready in the courtyard and Lucas mounted and Master Woodley grabbed me and threw me up to him. Lucas sat me in front of his saddle, and said if I gave him any trouble, I'd be dead!'

His voice shook at that point and I urged him to sip his wine. He did so and seemed to take heart. 'He showed me his dagger and said if I didn't want it stuck into me, I'd better behave, and then we were off, galloping out of the gate and away. He sheathed his dagger because he needed one arm and hand for holding me and the other for the reins. I did ask where we were going and Master Woodley . . .'

'You can drop the respectful *Master*,' remarked Brockley. 'He isn't worth it.'

'Well, neither of them answered at first, but they started to talk about an abandoned cottage. They sounded as if they'd talked of it before, as if it was a plan they already had. Only, Woodley said, since you were certainly going to attack, you'd probably find out about it; you'd frighten someone into talking. Then Lucas said he knew of a deserted charcoal-burner's hut. No one would find us there. It was all by itself in a wood, well beyond the cottage. I was so frightened, and angry. I'd realized that rescue must be on its way but I wouldn't be there to *be* rescued and I wanted to be sick . . .'

He stopped, and drank a little more. Then he said: 'I felt frantic. It seemed someone was coming to rescue me but they wouldn't be able to find me! I was terrified. We seemed to be riding for ever, galloping when the light and the ground allowed it, and Lucas was gripping me so hard, so hard and I hated him, hated him . . . and then I heard Woodley say we're getting on, we're near the abandoned cottage and the charcoal-burner's hut isn't so very much further, and suddenly it seemed to be now or never. Lucas had sheathed his dagger, the way I said. His arm was round both of mine at first but I'd managed to wriggle a little bit loose. Somehow I jerked my right hand free, snatched at the dagger hilt, got it out and just . . . just thrust it into him. Into his body. All very quickly.'

He had begun to shake. 'Steady,' said Brockley.

'He just fell,' said Harry. 'Lucas just fell, toppled out of the saddle. I somehow got myself into it, heaved myself backwards over the pommel.' He looked at Brockley and for the first time managed a faint smile. 'Like the horseback games you've taught me. You always say they'll help me to feel at home on a horse. I knew how to get myself back over the pommel and properly into the saddle. I turned the horse and started back, flat out. I thought I'd better come here; I didn't know where else to go, and if rescue had been coming, I thought well, it's surely there by now. I couldn't think what else to do. As I started off, I saw Woodley's horse bucking.'

'It would have sensed violence. Horses do,' said Brockley.

'Well, I rode like fury. Clinging on. I couldn't get my feet into the stirrups, the leathers were too long for my legs. I just gripped!'

'I've not only taught him horseback games, I've also made him practise riding bareback,' remarked Brockley. 'It's a good way to make sure a boy has a strong seat.'

'I heard hoofbeats behind me,' said Harry. 'I thought – that man Woodley! But then I found you.' A great weariness settled over him. 'Mother . . . I want to sleep.'

'We'll find your room,' I said. 'You can go back to bed. I will find another bed and bring it in, and stay with you tonight.'

On the way up the stairs, Harry said: 'Mother, when I'm in bed, will you fetch Brockley? There's something I have to tell you, and him.'

I did as he asked. When he was settled, and Brockley had searched for and found a truckle bed that I could use, Harry said wanly: 'Please close the door. No one else must hear.'

'Now, what's all this?' Brockley sat down on the window seat and I sank onto my truckle.

'It's something I couldn't tell anyone . . . not Sir Ambrose or Sir George Talbot. Not until I'd told you. So that you could decide.'

His voice was low, but calm. My son, I thought, my dear, dear son. You look so like your father Matthew but you will be a finer man than he was. You are already brave and resourceful beyond your years.

'Tell us, Harry,' I said.

'They – the Players as they call themselves – already knew that rescue might be coming for me, before Woodley got here. They knew I'd got a message out. One wet day when I was reading in my room – they let me have books – I heard a messenger arrive. I looked out of the window and saw him being let in. Lucas went out to meet him and he gave Lucas a letter. They came inside with it and then uproar broke out. I went to my door and looked down the stairwell and saw Lucas running across the vestibule and heard him shouting that the brat – that was me!' said Harry, with sudden resentment, 'that the brat had somehow got a message to Hawkswood, and thank God someone had been there to let us know, only he didn't actually say *someone*. He said a name. He shouted it!'

'Foolish of him,' observed Brockley.

'Lucas was nasty,' said Harry. 'But not very clever, I think.'

'Well, what was the name?' I asked. 'Was it Miller?'

'Miller? No.' Harry's face was unhappy, almost gaunt. He looked far older than nine.

He dropped his voice. That what he said sounded like a thunderclap has nothing to do with the level of sound.

'He shouted, *Thank God Sandley was there!*' said Harry.

We stared at him, shocked into silence. Harry said: 'The day I was seized, it was Master Sandley who told me which way to ride – he said where a path crosses the one towards White Towers, go to the left because it leads out of the wood on to that sunny heath where I can have a gallop if I like. I think he must have helped to plan it all. There was a terrible fuss when they found out about my message and I was beaten again.' He shuddered. 'I know they talked of moving me but they had nowhere safe to move me to – at least nowhere where I could be kept for long. It seemed that they only had Ivy House and the place where I was taken when I was first seized. But someone thought of the ruin, which would do for a while if necessary. They were all ready to whisk me off to it, anyway.'

I said: 'Philip Sandley told us he had recommended you to take the path to the right. He led me that way when I was taken.'

Harry blinked. 'When *you* were . . . Mother?'

'There is much we have to say to each other,' I said. 'But after you have slept.'

Brockley was staring into space, his face blank with shock. 'My son,' said Brockley blankly. 'He told them about Harry's letter. Because of him, that poor fellow Daniel Ashley was killed, his children left without a father, his wife a widow. My son is responsible. *My son!*'

TWENTY-THREE
Face to Face

S ir Ambrose and Sir George took charge of the situation. We returned to Warwick Castle the next day, and it was there that Harry told us the earlier part of his story, of his capture and of his short stay in what must have been Heath House, before the decision was taken to capture me as well, and Harry was taken away to Ivy House, so that he would not be at hand when I was brought in.

For the time being, most of us stayed on at Warwick Castle. Dale duly arrived with the baggage waggons, and I sent word back to Sheffield that Eddie was to collect our horses and our coach and join us. Meanwhile, Sir Ambrose and Sir George had exchanges with Sir Francis Walsingham at court and from him, they received instructions. So did I.

There was an inquest into the death of the man Lucas, whose full name, apparently, was Lucas Dean, but it was brief, simple and discreet. Harry Stannard, a young boy, had been abducted for the purposes of ransom, with the threat of selling him into slavery if the law was put on their trail. His family had sought to find him, trying to keep their efforts secret, and had virtually succeeded when his captors tried to get him away. He struggled and managed to escape and had stabbed Lucas in the process. No one blamed him. It was self-defence and justifiable.

He was indeed commended for his bravery (remarkable in one so young, said the coroner), and for his cleverness in getting a message to us. No mention was made of the fact that someone at Hawkswood had told Harry's captors about the said message.

It was over. The prisoners we had taken at Ivy House had been induced – I preferred not to ask how – to name the rest of the conspirators, who had also been arrested. They were a small group; only a dozen all told.

They claimed, as I already knew, to be a group of honest patriots who wanted the best for England and the queen and felt that the demise of Mary Stuart would be the best. They were warned not to make that claim when they were tried. They would be charged with abduction with intent to extort a ransom. No mention would be made of the queen or the Duke of Alençon and Anjou or Mary Stuart, and if the conspirators were foolish enough to do so, they would make their fate harder than it would be anyway.

At both the inquest and the trial, I gave evidence which had been carefully edited by Walsingham. Many people knew of my abduction; that could not well be concealed. But Walsingham's instructions to me told me to state that I had been seized only for purposes of negotiating the ransom. *There is no need to be explicit about the currency in which you were to pay it*, said Walsingham's letter to me dryly. It also said *under no circumstances must the names of the queen or the Duke of Alençon be mentioned.*

It was left up to me to decide on the size of the ransom that I should say had been demanded. I was to say that I had been released to raise it, but had also set about trying to find Harry and rescue him. Harry, after he too had been instructed to pretend that he had only been taken for ransom, told his amended story at both the inquest and the trial very convincingly. I was proud of him.

The trial was finally held at Warwick, in the second week of June. The ringleader, who was not called William Corby but was in private life a Sheffield innkeeper called Simeon Wilmot, was executed and so was Russell Woodley, whose guilt was compounded by his final betrayal of the woman he had professed to love, and of his employer, Sir George Talbot. I tried to plead for him – since his proposal to me had apparently been sincere if horribly muddleheaded – but failed. I was congratulated on my womanly goodheartedness, but told that the processes of the law could not be altered by such a thing.

The others – except of course for Lucas, who was dead – were imprisoned at the queen's pleasure and heavily fined. That probably bore harder on some than on others, for the Players were a mixed set of people. The seven principals, the ones who had actually seen to the capture of Harry and me, were the innkeeper Wilmot, his wife Eva, a gamekeeper (Lucas Dean), a real-life tumbler and three people who had held good positions in big houses.

The others had been peripheral players, who had provided money and advice and aid of various kinds. They included Russell Woodley and a prosperous cloth merchant from London, a pickpocket from Stratford (for whom the authorities had been looking for a long time) and a tailor, a very dull sort of man, who gave the impression, at the trial, of having been treated as negligible all his life, and having longed for adventure and to have all eyes upon him. He had got what he wanted, and lost his business, since it must now be sold to raise the money for his fine. He and the pickpocket were the two men who took Harry to Ivy House and guarded him while the seven players stayed near Hawkswood to kidnap me.

The peripheral players also, of course, included Philip Sandley but he was not mentioned at the trial. I think Brockley had something to do with that. I know he managed to have speech with the prisoners before they were taken away from Ivy House and I suspect he offered inducements of some kind, perhaps assistance with fines, if they would keep silent about Philip. Brockley was a provident man and no doubt had savings. I had never enquired and now, I asked no questions. Brockley asked me and Harry not to mention Philip, and we did as he wished.

So it was over. It had been a curious, ramshackle conspiracy and yet it might have worked, if I had been a different kind of woman. In the darkness, night after night, I wondered what I would have done if I had really been forced to the wall, if it had been a straight choice between betraying Harry or committing murder. I didn't know the answer and felt guilty about it, as though I *should* have known. Only years later did I find an answer of a sort and that was because I had told Harry, who was a grown man by then, and he looked at me in amazement and said: 'But Mother, of course you couldn't assassinate anyone! I'm glad you couldn't! Brockley once told me how he sent you out of the Ivy House kitchen in case he had to use force to make my captors say where I had been taken; he didn't want you to be corrupted, as he put it. I wouldn't want it, either, even if I had ended up as a slave in Turkey. After all, there was always the chance that I would escape!'

My guilt died then, but it was a death long in coming.

As it was, the conspiracy was over and when the trial finally finished, we could go home. Before we went, though, I found a silk merchant in Warwick, bought a charming shawl of blue silk, embroidered with silver stars, and sent it to Lady Alice Hammond as a farewell present. I hoped she would like it and she need not know that it was in truth an apology for the unfounded suspicions I had had of her.

I asked Sir George Talbot to make my farewells to Mary Stuart. I couldn't ask Bess because she didn't intend to return to Sheffield, but to her beloved other home, Chatsworth, in Derbyshire. She had had it built for her and said it was a much pleasanter place than Sheffield Castle.

'I have no wish to see *Her Grace* again,' she said to me, though privately, for it wasn't the kind of thing she would have said in public.

'I always thought you didn't like her very much,' I said.

'Like her? She's easily the silliest woman I've ever met,' said Bess with vigour. 'She has an ambition to die as a Catholic martyr – did you know?'

'I know she admires them.'

'She probably will die on the block,' Bess said coolly (and prophetically, as it turned out), 'and she'll try to pretend she's dying for her faith, when really it will just mean that the queen is tired of being plotted against by Catholics and has given way to Sir Francis Walsingham, who has been longing for years to chop Mary's head off. Mary encourages plots, you know. Every chance she can manage.'

'I know,' I said, thinking that Bess, like the queen, wouldn't have felt too upset if I had forced myself to lace Mary's wine with hemlock. I did not pursue the conversation.

Brockley meanwhile was being rueful about Laurence Miller, just as I was about Alice Hammond. 'I shall have to apologize to Miller,' he said. 'For the unfounded suspicions I have had of him!'

We set off for home at last. It was well into June by then and sunny and we rode through a world where the trees were laden with leaf and the roadsides with cow parsley and mead-owsweet, dog-roses and clover, tall feathery grasses and golden dandelions and we did most of our travelling in the morning and evening, because the middle of the day was hot and fly-ridden. Our arrival was expected; we had written ahead to Adam Wilder to let him know that we were on our way, and someone had been watching for us. Freya and Prince came bouncing vociferously out to greet us, which almost brought tears to my eyes as I remembered Goldie and Remus and how much I had missed their noisy canine welcomes. Home felt and sounded normal once again. Indeed nearly all the human members of the household were out in the yard to meet us when we rode in.

Sybil and Gladys were both tearful with relief at the sight of Harry. Others present were Laurence Miller, and Philip Sandley, who beamed as broadly as though the sight of Harry were truly welcome to him and hurried forward to hug the lad as he dismounted. Harry would have resisted, I think, but I caught his eye and he accepted the embrace, coolly, but it seemed no more than a matter of a boy on his dignity. I had of course written to Sybil about the progress of the inquest and the trial and Philip must have feared for himself but then become easy in his mind as no one arrived to arrest him. As yet, he did not know he had been identified.

It was dinner time and food was ready. John Hawthorn had been making preparations all morning. We changed out of our travelling clothes, and dined. I shared the table with Dale and Brockley, Sybil, Gladys and Philip and, of course, Harry. Brockley had little to say to Philip and Harry had nothing at all but I had foreseen this and made sure it wasn't too notice-able, by seating them well apart from him. Harry was between me and Brockley at the far end of the table, and we talked animatedly together all through the meal.

When it was over, Dale and Sybil went upstairs, saying that they would look through my luggage and see how much damage had come to my dresses after so much travelling. Brockley looked at me and said: 'Madam, it is time,' and I nodded.

'What first?' I asked.

'First, let's get the business of Laurence Miller out of the way.'

Brockley fetched him from his quarters at the stud and brought him to the big east parlour, which clearly surprised him. He had probably expected us, if we wished to talk to him, to see him in the hall or the study. His air was as dour as it usually was as he enquired if we wanted a report on the work of the stud.

'Things have gone well,' he said. 'All the mares have foaled now; we lost only one foal. The others seem to be thriving. But I have doubts about the stallion. He is too temperamental and temperament can be inherited as well as long legs or a deep chest. I think . . .'

'We'll discuss all that later,' I said. 'Brockley has something to say to you.'

'I wish to apologize for unworthy suspicions,' said Brockley. 'We had wondered if you were in some way connected with the abductions. When Harry got his message to Hawkswood, someone here let his captors know. They were ready with their plans when we found out where they were and took a rescue party there. We feared that you were their informant . . .'

'*Me?*' Miller actually gaped, in an astonishment that could not possibly be faked.

'You went to Guildford and didn't come back when you were expected, and although Brockley and then Philip Sandley both tried to discover where you had been, they couldn't. You told us you had visited your mother but that turned out to be not true, and there was mention of some mysterious woman but we couldn't trace her, either.'

'She exists, though,' said Laurence, and for the first time ever, I saw him look amused. 'Though if any of you had found her, you might have been surprised.'

'We know now,' said Brockley, 'that Philip's reports of

failure were probably lies, aimed at keeping you under suspicion.'

'Philip's . . . Master Brockley, do you mean that Sandley, your son . . .?'

'We fear so,' I said. 'And we apologize for suspecting you. And your private affairs are, of course, no business of ours. As long as the stud is well run . . .'

'My private affairs are your business up to a point,' said Miller surprisingly. 'You may as well know. I had a preference for keeping my own counsel; I thought my task would be easier. But I believe you knew, when Dr Fletcher was the vicar at your parish church, St Mary's, he reported to Sir William Cecil, Lord Burghley on events concerning you. It was for your safety, in view of the work you do for the queen, and your relationship with her. You might as well know who Dr Fletcher's successor is. It isn't the new vicar, Dr Joynings. It's me. The woman I visited in Guildford is my contact. She sends my messages on to Sir William Cecil.'

'*Well!*' I was thoroughly taken aback.

Laurence was now smiling broadly. 'She is an elderly but active lady who could well be my aunt though she isn't. The day when I went to order harness, I also went to visit her but she was not at home. However, her maid knows me and let me wait there for her. She was late returning. The maid gave me dinner, and when her mistress eventually came home, *she* urged me to stay for an early supper. By the time we'd eaten it, the sky was darkening. I was invited to stay the night rather than ride home through a storm and I was glad enough to accept.'

'I see.' I was still almost lost for words.

Miller regarded me calmly. 'It's for your protection, Mistress Stannard. Though this time, I agree, it didn't protect you at all. You were vulnerable through Harry. If I may advise, care should be taken from now on to safeguard him.'

'It will be,' I said in heartfelt tones.

'So now,' said Miller, 'I take it that you will deal with Sandley.' The amusement had gone and he had suddenly acquired an air of authority. He was no longer simply the Hawkswood stud groom, subordinate and respectful in the presence of his employer, but a skilled and responsible set of eyes and ears in the service of Lord Burghley.

He said: 'I have no desire to witness that, though I shall have to report on it. May I be informed of the outcome?'

'Yes,' I said. There was no point in saying that I detested being watched and having reports made about me, even with friendly intentions. Miller would obey his august employer and earn his pay. I turned to Brockley. 'Now?' I said.

Laurence Miller left us. I went to the door and called. Phoebe came in answer and I sent her to tell Philip he was wanted. He came in looking grave. 'You wished to see me, Mistress Stannard? And Father? I'm glad to have a few words with you, for Harry has now shut himself in his room and won't talk to me. What is the matter with him? Is he just exhausted? I can understand that, but he seemed all right when you all first arrived and . . .'

'Be quiet,' said Brockley. 'We know. We know that you informed Harry's captors of the message he got to us, which enabled them to have plans in place for getting him away if the hunt came close to them, as it did. Because of what you did, a harmless thatcher was murdered – the man Harry gave his message to. They feared that Harry may have told him things – which Harry actually did not – and that he might be a danger to them. To you, for you are one of them. You advised Harry to ride on a path where they would be waiting in ambush and you lied to us about that, hoping that we would search for him in the wrong direction.'

'And when I went out with you, the day I was seized,' I said, 'it was you who chose the way that we should go. I rode into a trap. And, yes, you warned your fellow conspirators that Harry had got a message out.'

He stood still, looking from me to Brockley. For a moment he was silent and then he said: 'Yes. It is true. I am one of the party . . .'

'One of the conspirators,' said Brockley.

'If you wish to call us so,' said Philip. 'I was one of the group who decided that England must be rid of Mary Stuart, so that we can all be safe from her ambitions, and the Duke of Alençon no longer afraid to marry the queen. It could bring such benefits, that marriage. It is England we care for! I know that both of you think of yourselves as true servants of the queen but so am I and so are the friends I have been working with. We want . . .'

'It isn't what you want that matters,' said Brockley. 'It's what the queen wants and as it happens, neither she, nor a great many of her council and indeed, the people of England, are happy about the French marriage. It isn't for you and your little pack of so-called patriots to make the final decision. And to kidnap Harry! A young boy, and your pupil as well, and threaten him as you did! I can't believe that any son of mine could do such a thing.'

'But I *am* your son, just the same.'

'Yes, I can see that you are! Unfortunately,' said Brockley bitterly. 'I wish you were not. At this moment, I would willingly kill you. I take it that when you were found dazed in the woods, and complained afterwards of a blow on the head, that it was all pretence.'

'They scraped my scalp a little so that there would be some blood. There was quite a lot. It looked convincing,' said Philip. 'And it was sore enough, God knows.'

'My poor boy,' said Brockley savagely. 'My heart truly aches for you!'

There was a silence. I had never seen Brockley look so wretched. 'How did you get involved with your . . . friends?' I said, turning to Philip.

'Lucas Dean. He's my foster brother.'

'Your . . . but you were reared by the Sandley family,' I said.

'Lucas was a few years older than I am. Mistress Sandley had a previous husband, a Master Dean. He died shortly after Lucas was born, and then after another year or so, she married Master Sandley. We were always friends, Lucas and me.'

'You choose your friends badly. Ask Harry,' said Brockley.

'I'd rather not. I have learned now that it was Harry who . . . who . . .'

'Put a dagger into him in self-defence,' I said. 'Tell me, did you come here, and apply to be Harry's tutor, as part of the conspiracy? To help them get hold of Harry?'

'Yes. But I was so glad to find my father too. I knew he was my father and thought that that would help me to get the tutor's post here. But it was a splendid thing, to find you, sir!' He looked at Brockley with something like appeal.

But the silence that followed was frigid. Eventually, Philip said: 'What now?'

'Your name has not been mentioned,' Brockley said. 'Neither I nor Mistress Stannard have told what we know and your fellow conspirators have not spoken of you, either. I persuaded them not to. You are safe from the law. But things can't . . . I can't bear the sight of you!'

His voice faded. I stepped in again. 'You cannot remain here as Harry's tutor. I would hardly suppose you want to, considering what happened to Lucas who you say was your friend. In any case, Harry would not accept you and nor can I. After what he and I have been through, there can be no question of such a thing. You must leave this house. You will be paid for your services; you won't be cast into the world penniless. I will even give you a testimonial as a tutor, for I think you are a good teacher. A pity you didn't keep to your real business in life instead of haring off after political schemes, tangling with matters you don't understand! But I want you gone by tomorrow. That is, if your father agrees and does not have any other suggestion.'

'Some people might have a number of other suggestions,' said Brockley grimly. He stared at Philip and then, to my distress, I saw his features pucker, and there was a glint in his eyes which suggested tears.

'That a son of mine could . . . could ever . . . conspire to throw a young lad, one in his care! – to the corsairs of Algiers . . .! And that poor thatcher. Poor Daniel Ashley. Be gone from this house tomorrow morning, Philip. Never return. And leave early, so that I need not see you.'

'Will that be the end, then?' Philip had paled, realizing, I thought, that having found his father, he had now lost him again, and that he minded.

So did Brockley. 'When you are settled again,' he said,

'you may send word to tell me where you are. In time, perhaps we may . . . be now and then in touch. Perhaps. But I promise nothing.'

I said: 'Your money and your testimonial will be made ready and sent to your room tonight.'

'Thank you, Mistress Stannard.' He did not ask permission to leave us, but simply did so. Brockley watched him go and without turning to look at me, muttered: 'How can I disown him? When I've only just found him. But . . .'

He couldn't go on talking. With his face averted from me, he followed Philip out. But as he went, I glimpsed his expression and it tore my heart. But I could not help him. I had no right. Only one person was entitled to do that.

I followed him out and hastened upstairs to find Dale. As I expected, she was still with Sybil, sorting through my baggage in search of garments with stains and rents.

'Dale,' I said, 'Brockley is upset. We have just ordered Philip to leave the house tomorrow.'

'Ordered *Philip* to . . .?'

I realized that in our determination to keep Philip's name out of the business, Brockley and I had not even told his wife.

'Brockley will explain,' I said. 'He is unhappy. He needs your help.'

'Was Master Sandley somehow . . . involved? One of the plotters?' Dale asked acutely.

'I'm afraid so. Yes.'

'I'm not surprised.' Dale sounded quite venomous. 'I never liked him.'

'But it is hard for Brockley,' I said. 'Go to him now. He needs your comfort.'

'So, Mary Stuart still lives,' said Queen Elizabeth grimly.

'She lives,' I agreed.

It was a mournful apology for a June day. The heatwave had gone. Beyond the latticed window, the gardens of Hampton Court, the trees and the grass, dripped greyly under a steady drizzle and the sky was leaden. It was cold, as cold as Elizabeth's pale, shield-shaped face.

Quietly, I said: 'There are things I can't do.'

'Even for Harry? Even for your son?'

'Even for him. It isn't a matter of choice; it isn't a matter of taking a decision. I couldn't do it. I tried to make a pretence . . . give her something to make her a little unwell, so as to give the impression that I was trying, in case someone was on the watch. Which someone was – the man Russell Woodley. I couldn't even bring myself to do that much. My fingers would not unstopper the phial of potion.'

Elizabeth nodded. 'Oddly enough, I understand. Because there are things that I can't do. I – know what you mean.'

'Do you, ma'am?'

'Yes, Ursula, my sister, I do! These conspirators,' said Elizabeth, 'they wanted Mary out of the way so that Duke Francis would feel safe in coming to England to marry me. I wanted her out of the way because she's a danger to me and to England and would be, even if Francis had never been born. He is a different, separate matter. I must deal with him myself.'

'How, madam?'

'I can't marry him,' said Elizabeth. 'Like you, I find there are things that I can't do. You couldn't assassinate anyone or even pretend to try; I can't marry anyone. It's as simple as that. I *can't*! I can't give myself away to anyone; I can't share the rule of England with anyone; I can't share the privacy of my body. Or risk childbirth, improbable though that now is. It is just, barely, possible. It isn't my duty to England to risk death, it's my duty to live and reign and keep my people safe and just because that's what I *want* to do, doesn't make it wrong. It's right. Though I have some very wearisome explaining to do.'

'Majesty, I should make someone else do it for you,' I said. I smiled. 'The Earl of Sussex, perhaps?'

'Thomas Radcliffe?' Elizabeth snorted. 'He has always earnestly wanted me to marry. He wants it so much that he closes his eyes to the dangers.'

'He is also one of your most diplomatic councillors and one of your most loyal servants. He would do it better than anyone, once he understood that you meant it.'

My sister sighed. 'You may well be right. Dear Ursula. I was angry at first, when I realized that you were not going to carry out my wishes, but of course, private coteries of mis-guided patriots can't be allowed to roam my kingdom, abducting young lads and threatening to sell them to corsairs. I realized that quite quickly. Have you found a new tutor for Harry, by the way?'

'Not yet but . . . how did you know . . .?'

'I haven't known for long that Brockley's newly discovered son was one of the conspirators. I have been told now, however. I have done nothing about it; Sir William Cecil advised against it. He said it was not what you or Brockley would wish. His informant, of course, was the individual who has taken over from Dr Fletcher, keeping Sir William informed of affairs at Hawkswood.'

'Oh yes,' I said. 'Laurence Miller. Of course.'